FORBIDDEN PLEASURES

Janet Lambert's respectable parents and even more respectable husband-to-be would have blanched if they had peeked into the world that Janet had entered in sophisticated London.

It was a world ruled over by the scandalous Lady Ralston, whose liberal ideas were as shocking as her cutting wit.

It was a world filled with such bizarre figures as poets, painters, artists and others of the type who actually preferred trading *bon mots* to hunting foxes, and who valued beauty above bloodlines.

And even more dangerous to Janet's good name and peace of heart, it was a world in which she was wooed by Anthony Northbridge, Duke of Stour, the most infamous rake in London—and the most irresistible man Janet had ever met. . . .

The Disobedient Daughter

The Disobedient Daughter

Barbara Hazard

A SIGNET BOOK
NEW AMERICAN LIBRARY
TIMES MIRROR

NAL BOOKS ARE AVAILABLE AT QUANTITY DISCOUNTS WHEN USED TO PROMOTE PRODUCTS OR SERVICES. FOR INFORMATION PLEASE WRITE TO PREMIUM MARKETING DIVISION, THE NEW AMERICAN LIBRARY, INC., 1633 BROADWAY, NEW YORK, NEW YORK 10019.

SIGNET TRADEMARK REG. U.S. PAT. OFF. AND FOREIGN COUNTRIES
REGISTERED TRADEMARK—MARCA REGISTRADA
HECHO EN CHICAGO, U.S.A.

SIGNET, SIGNET CLASSICS, MENTOR, PLUME, MERIDIAN AND NAL BOOKS are published by The New American Library, Inc., 1633 Broadway, New York, New York 10019

First Printing, June, 1982

1 2 3 4 5 6 7 8 9

PRINTED IN THE UNITED STATES OF AMERICA

*For Jack . . . in fond memory,
and for his gallant lady*

I

Prelude

⫷ 1 ⫸

It was impossible to imagine Berks County without the Lamberts of Aylesford Grange, for they had been landed gentry there forever. They were as conventional a family as you might find anywhere in England in the year 1809, hardworking and plain-living even though their title went back so many generations that they might have cut a dash in town anytime they liked. In addition to farming, they had on many occasions over the years been of such service to the crown that it had increased their consequence enormously, as well as adding to their ever-expanding acreage and wealth. For as long as anyone could remember, there had always been a Lambert at the Grange, trying new methods of farming and increasing the herds through cross-breeding, while others distinguished themselves in the army, the church, or as courtiers.

They were Englishmen first, last, and always. Indeed, if you had seen any one of them in the farthest corner of the earth, you would have known his nationality immediately. Not that the Lamberts were at all given to foreign travel, except in the course of their military duty, for they considered it a frivolous waste of time which might be more profitably spent at home. They were healthy and robust, honest, dependable, trustworthy, upright, respectable, serious, determined, opinionated, and self-righteously convinced that *their* way of life was the only conceivably proper way to live; in short, they were dull.

They were so dull, in fact, that they would have been amazed to learn that others in the world considered them afflicted with this unattractive trait.

The Lamberts prided themselves that their family had never harboured a poet or an artist, that there were no scholars or philosophers, no one who excelled as a musician or as a wit with his pen, and they would have stared if any member of the family so forgot himself as to choose any such trivial, disgraceful occupation. They were supremely unaware—and to be fair would not have cared a jot if they had known—that people with the merest affinity for the arts shunned them and considered them bores. They did not wish their children to be clever or talented, for they thought such characteristics to be extremely suspect; instead they required their sons and daughters to uphold the Lambert traditions by following closely in their elders' footsteps.

How very unfortunate that to this illustrious and praiseworthy line had been born in 1794 a daughter so unworthy of the name; to wit, Miss Janet Rose Lambert.

The present Lord Lambert was no exception to tradition. Predictably, he had inherited the Grange on the death of his father. His younger brothers had long since left to seek their predictable Lambert fortunes; one to the Life Guards, one to the church, and the last—rather daringly—to the navy. Lord Lambert's eldest sister had married a duke, his younger one a wealthy gentleman of equally impeccable lineage. These ladies were often held up to Lord Lambert's daughters as the epitome of successful womanhood. Truly, the Almighty had smiled upon the Lamberts, and the current lord was confident that He would continue to do so, for virtue should ever be rewarded.

Lady Lambert, a lady originally from Sussex, hid an iron will and just as rigid a sense of duty as her husband possessed under a deceivingly gentle voice and soft, pleasant manner. She was a tall woman who even as a girl could not have been called willowy, for she had a large bone structure and broad hands and shoulders. She had produced six Lambert children without a bit of fuss, and in spite of gaining a great deal of weight in the process, carried herself well, for of course a Lambert never slouches. At the present time, she was an imposing matron with her ash-brown hair severely arranged, and she was always neatly if somewhat plainly dressed, for she considered the fripperies of fashion to be both decadent and unnecessary. Her third daughter, Janet, thought her like a well-upholstered armchair—the kind that looked comfortable, but never gave an inch when you sat upon it—but this comparison she was careful never to voice.

Of her six children, the firstborn had been a son. Naturally. All the children were given traditional Lambert names; good English names such as their ancestors had used: Horace Junior, Agatha, Wilbert, Elizabeth, the aforementioned Janet, and Henry. Not for the Lamberts a Clorinda or Glorianna, a Ronaldo, Adolphus, or Ferdinand!

Lady Lambert hid the daily problems of raising such a large family from her husband very well, for even though eventually they would grow up to emulate their parents, as children they were often in the scrapes that youth is prone to. Lady Lambert dealt firmly with these problems, whether it be bad reports from the boys' tutors, broken bones, contagious diseases, sibling rivalry, or childhood arguments. Lord Lambert hardly saw his children except when they were washed, combed, and dressed for the occasion, so it is perhaps no wonder he proclaimed them paragons. Lady Lambert could have disabused him of his folly, but since she considered it her exclusive duty to raise the children and care for the household, her husband was spared many of the aggravations other fathers had to face over and over again. In the Lambert household there were no masculine thunderings from the dining room to set the servants quaking—no *"He did what?"* or "Is it possible that a daughter of *mine* . . . ?" Surely Lady Lambert was the most excellent of women!

If punishment was required, as it regrettably often was, Lady Lambert never shrank from her duty, and that included the use of a switch, and later, a leather belt. If none of her children could be said to love her, at least they all had the greatest respect for her, for she never varied in her treatment of them, nor was she ever moved to forgiveness by childish tears or womanly softness. The boys admired their father, since he was held up as a model of the best a man could be, but the girls were more than a little afraid of him. The worst punishment Lady Lambert could threaten them with was that she would tell their father of their misbehaviour. She never did so, of course, but the possibility that she might, never lost its power to bring them swiftly into line. She raised her daughters a good deal more strictly than she did her sons, and they were not very old before they realized that their primary mission in life was to marry well into one of the families acceptable to the Lamberts—and that as soon as they could contrive it.

All the Lamberts were blessed with rosy complexions, a robust build that fell just short of plumpness, and masses of light brown curly hair; all of them, that is, but one. The next-to-last Lambert child, Janet, was completely different.

She was slender and pale, and her enormous blue eyes seemed too large for her little pointed face. Her nose was straight, not tip-tilted like her sisters', and she had a generous mouth that was quite unlike their tiny rosebud lips. Instead of the charming brown curls of the others, she was cursed with midnight-black hair that refused to curl no matter how many papers or irons were applied to it, and arching black eyebrows to match. Her looks were not that unusual, but among her large, hearty family she managed to appear strangely exotic.

Lord Lambert had never noticed the difference, being more than slightly imperceptive, until one Christmas Eve two years past when he chanced to see his children all together and was struck by Janet's foreign appearance. The others were excited by the occasion, and the food and festivities to come, and as much as they dared were behaving in the typical fashion of the young when an unusual treat was in store, but Janet sat alone and somehow aloof, her head bent as she listened to a music box. It had always been a favorite of the children, since their visits to the drawing room were few, but tonight, only Janet was engrossed in the tinkling tune.

Lord Lambert stirred uneasily and looked at his wife. Her ash-brown head was bent over her youngest son, Henry, whom she kept close to her side with a firm hand on his arm, just in case he should misbehave and give his father a dislike of him, and Lord Lambert could not help but compare his boyish sturdiness and rosy cheeks with this . . . this waif by the music box. Suddenly Janet looked up and saw him watching her, and she returned a long, level stare, which was most unusual for a young miss of only thirteen. Lord Lambert looked away first, much discomforted. He had it in his mind to reprimand her, but he had not the slightest idea for what. She had only been looking at him after all!

Later that evening when he was alone with his wife, he could not help remarking the unusual looks of his fifth child, and Lady Lambert sighed in her gentle way.

"Indeed, m'lord, I do not know where she got her looks! There is no one like that in *my* family! Can you remember anyone of the Lamberts who might have passed his dark hair down to Janet?"

Lord Lambert was about to declare he had no recollection of any Lambert so ill-endowed when he remembered a distant cousin with black hair, and confessed the matter to his wife.

"Of course, m'dear, he is not in the *direct* line, and the reason I did not immediately recall him is that no one in the family has spoken of him for years! He is a disgrace to our name!"

Lord Lambert's face had turned an angry red, and his wife, although curious as to what the gentleman's faults had been to cause such banishment, wisely decided not to question her husband further.

Lord Lambert would have changed the subject, for remembering Janet's resemblance to Black Jack Lambert made him uncomfortable, but his wife sighed again and

7

said, "If it were only her looks, Horace! But I fear she is a very naughty girl as well!"

This was so unusual that Lord Lambert could only stare.

"She is most willful, and what is worse, an air-dreamer!" her fond mother continued. "It is not that she runs away from her chores, but she does them so carelessly! Her needlepoint is a disgrace and her darning worse! And what is even more distressing, no amount of punishment or lecturing seems to move her to improvement!"

"I say!" said Lord Lambert, much astounded that his wife should speak at such length. He shifted his considerable bulk as if he was going to rise, but for once Lady Lambert was not to be deterred.

"In fact, my lord," she added, "her most distressing fault is that although she does not outwardly rebel—and I can assure you I would know how to handle *that*!—she appears to be far, far away, somehow above the work that she is given. And she has a way of looking at us . . . I do not know how to describe it! Almost as if she watched the rest of her family from a great distance, trying to discover who these strange creatures might be!"

This was quite possibly the most fanciful statement Lady Lambert had made in years, but her husband, remembering Janet's long stare in the drawing room that evening, did not attempt to argue the point.

"You shall have to be more strict with her, Ada!" he finally replied. "I know how excellent a mother you are, how firm yet fair. The other children do you such credit, I cannot believe you will fail with this one!"

Lady Lambert shook her head. "She has another fault, Horace! She refuses to ride, saying that horses upset her, and you know how we Lamberts pride ourselves on our horsemanship!"

"Is there nothing she does well?" Lord Lambert asked, desperately trying to find some virtue in this most wayward daughter.

"She plays the piano very well," Lady Lambert admitted, "and she dances beautifully, if sometimes with an abandon I cannot like!"

It was true that although the Lamberts disdained practitioners of the arts, each daughter was taught to sing, play the pianoforte or harp, and to dance, for these were considered social accomplishments. Lady Lambert was shrewd enough to know that the sight of a pretty girl accompanying herself while singing a gentle ballad had more than once brought a gentleman to the point of proposing. But as soon as the girls learned to perform a few songs creditably, their lessons stopped. The elderly music master she engaged for each of her daughters had despaired of the Lamberts, knowing that as soon as Agatha and Elizabeth had painfully conquered the fingering of *"Für Elise"* and could perform it almost up to tempo, he would be dismissed until the next Lambert girl was old enough to sit at the piano and span an octave without unduly stretching her hands. He had certainly never expected that Miss Janet Rose Lambert would be any exception, but when he was summoned again to begin her lessons, he was amazed that at the very first session she not only played her scales without mistake but also gave an accurate rendition of the Beethoven piece as well, and with a great deal more expression than her sisters had certainly ever shown. Lady Lambert did not require interpretation; it was enough if none of her daughters ever struck a wrong note.

When he questioned her, Janet admitted she had often hidden behind the sofa while her sisters had their lessons, and afterward had spent hours at the piano teaching herself the music they played so poorly. Mr. Booth, the piano master, was astounded and delighted at her talent. For so many years he had had to listen to the poundings of children who had no feeling for music, who were poorly prepared and who would not practice, and to have such a natural talent combined with the desire for hard work almost brought tears to his eyes. When he would have rushed to tell Lady Lambert of her unusual prodigy, Janet begged him to remain silent.

"If Mama knows that I can already play, I will not

have any more lessons!" she said woefully. "And I do so want to learn how to play something else! Something harder!"

Mr. Booth could only beam at her industry and promise to keep the secret, especially since Miss Janet smiled at him so winsomely, a deep dimple in her cheek coming into play as she added demurely, "And I am so very tired of *'Für Elise,'* aren't you?"

Mr. Booth thought her a very taking child, once you removed her from the overlarge bosom of her family, and agreed wholeheartedly.

Of course they were discovered when Janet was fifteen, for Lady Lambert considered it her duty to hear her daughter's progress at regular intervals, and Janet could not resist showing off her talent. Later, when Lady Lambert announced she would let Mr. Booth go, she begged her mother to allow him to remain as long as he had for the instruction of her sisters.

"Please, Mama!" she pleaded, "I will be so good, I promise! I will even begin my needlepoint again! I do so long to play the piano well!"

"But you have already outstripped your sisters, Janet," her mother said. "Of what possible use can any further training be? You hardly think to set yourself up as a musician, do you?" She spoke in such a gentle yet sarcastic way that both Agatha and Elizabeth tittered over their sewing, and Janet subsided. She knew what was expected of Lambert daughters, and she hung her head.

Lady Lambert felt she had won that particular battle, and bade her daughter to apply herself to her sewing and household chores with the same kind of fervor she had brought to her music, for that would surely be of more benefit in the long run.

"I myself was thought to have a pretty touch on the harp," she continued, "but of course, after I married, there was never any occasion for me to play. Such things are trifles—bagatelles! A truly worthy woman puts more stock in the condition of her stillroom, the neatness of her linens, and her well-stocked larder. You will thank me someday, daughters, when you are married and have the ordering of your own households, the instructing of your own servants. Janet, I shall require you to help me with the jam all day tomorrow, and let us hear no more of music! I am pleased, to be sure, with your accomplishment, but the level of proficiency that you have reached is ample for our purposes. Besides, I could not like the way you *bent* over the keys and even *swayed* to the music as you played. Most unseemly!"

She waited until Janet curtsied and whispered, "Yes, Mama," before she swept from the room.

As soon as the door to the salon closed, Agatha put down her needlepoint, and unmindful of her mother's domestic lecture, drew a small silver mirror from the pocket of her dress and began to admire herself. "What a silly child you are, Janet!" she said, with all the superiority of the twenty-year-old over the fifteen. "If only you had stumbled over the notes, or played the wrong chords, you might have continued to have your lessons! But no, you had to prove you were better than your sisters!"

"It serves you right!" Elizabeth agreed. "But who would want to have more lessons anyway? Not I! How strange you are!"

She left her seat and went to beg her sister for the use of the mirror. At seventeen, she was fighting a double battle with baby fat and spots, and she searched her face carefully several times a day to see if the new lotion her mother had given her was beginning to work.

The two girls made a pretty picture even so. Agatha, seated on a deep blue velvet chair with the sunlight glancing through her brown curls, was most attractive, and Elizabeth showed promise of becoming just as lovely. Their rosy cheeks and the wealth of their curls, and the modest expanse of bosom that they were allowed to display in their muslin morning gowns, was sure to attract a bevy of suitors. Agatha was still getting over a bitter disappointment, for a Mr. Wilkinson had not come up to scratch the past summer, although he had paid her many distinguished attentions that had quite turned her head. He was a distant relation of the Lamberts and worth 15,-000 pounds as well, but alas, he had been snared by Ce-

11

cily Natterby, at whose home he was visiting, and Agatha had had to swallow her chagrin and suffer as well her mother's air of disapproval, as if she had let the Lamberts down most lamentably by allowing Cecily to nip in before her with such an eligible *parti*.

There had been a tearful session with Elizabeth and Janet, recently admitted to the young ladies' parlour, when she learned the news of his betrothal to her rival. Elizabeth petted and soothed her and said it was just that Mr. Wilkinson had been forced by politeness to ask his hostess for her daughter's hand, and Agatha was on the way to believing that it had been only a matter of proximity and courtesy when Janet asked, "But why would you want to marry him, Aggie? He is fat and ugly and shorter than you are!"

At that, she was pummeled by both her sisters and banished from the room as being too young and ignorant to understand. As the door was slammed behind her, Janet thought to herself that fifteen thousand pounds seemed to magically erase any amount of physical repulsiveness, but she held her tongue.

Now she held her tongue as well, for she had a scheme in her mind that she was thinking about seriously, so she did not hear her sisters' belittling her musical talent.

When they saw she had disappeared into her usual reverie and did not rise to their baiting, they began to talk with excitement about Lady Lambert's declaration only that morning that she meant to take Agatha to London for the Season, and that possibly Elizabeth might be allowed to join them as well.

"Oh, I pray I can come!" Elizabeth wailed, clasping her hands and rolling her eyes heavenward.

"But you will not be allowed to attend dances, Lizzie! You are only seventeen and not out!" her older sister reminded her. "Or go to Almack's or to routs, or . . . or anything! Why, I daresay you will be bored in a week!"

"Bored? In *London?* When I can ride in the park, and accompany you and Mama to tea parties and all those exciting shops, and perhaps be allowed to go on picnics or riding expeditions with Mama's friends? I shall not be in the least bored! Besides, I will be eighteen before very long; you know my birthday is the first of June!"

Elizabeth hugged herself with delight, and then added rather unfortunately, "I am so glad you did not snare Mr. Wilkinson, Aggie, for then we would never get this chance to go to town!"

Her sister frowned. "Do not mention his name to me, sister! To think I was so taken in! I do hope that Cecily is happy, but I feel for her to be married to one who showed such wavering of purpose, such indelicacy of mind—why, he is probably setting up a mistress even now!"

"Ssh!" Elizabeth said, glancing quickly in Janet's direction. "Remember the *child*."

"I know all about mistresses, Lizzie," Janet said calmly.

Her sisters looked astounded, and Agatha was quick to ask, "And how is that, miss? It is most forward of you to pretend anything of the sort! Where would *you* find out about things like that?"

"It is often written of in books," Janet replied, calmly threading her needle with deep green thread. "I have read all about it."

At this her sisters burst into laughter, but when they heard their mother's voice in the hall, they were quick to stifle their merriment and pick up their sewing once again, and Lady Lambert was rewarded with a cozy domestic scene when she opened the door. Nothing more was said of mistresses, or errant suitors, or the excitement of visiting town, for Lady Lambert undertook to read to them all from a book of sermons she had by her, so that as they stitched, the tones of their minds might be improved by some excellent moral precepts. It seemed a very long morning to Miss Janet Rose Lambert.

And it seemed a very long month to her older sisters before Lady Lambert felt satisfied that she had done all she could to ensure the smooth running of her household while she was away. First, she had to instruct her housekeeper, Mrs. Peevey, in the way she wished the domestic life at the Grange to continue in her absence. Then the boys had to be settled. Of course, Horace Junior, at twenty-one, and Wilbert, at eighteen, were old enough to be trusted to their own devices, at least most of the time, but Lady Lambert felt uneasy about Henry. He had more often than the others shown a lack of judgement that she deplored and although he was only thirteen and sure to grow out of it, she was careful to engage a new and even stricter tutor, a Mr. Jackson, with whom she spent a great deal of time explaining his duties. Janet was to be allowed, as a special treat and when all her household chores were complete, to join her brother for some of his lessons—"such as might be suitable for a young lady," Lady Lambert said in her soft voice, fixing Mr. Jackson with a steely blue eye. He nodded in complete understanding.

The children's old nanny assured Lady Lambert that she would keep an eye on Janet, and at last the lady was satisfied, and positive that when she returned home she would find everything just as she had left it. She told her husband that she hoped to have Agatha settled quickly, and that it was by no means impossible that Elizabeth might also become engaged before they returned.

She was careful to stress—more than once, to be sure he remembered—that he was to keep his sons in line. Rumours had recently come to her concerning Wilbert and a certain barmaid in the village taproom, and when she told Lord Lambert of this, he promised to watch Wilbert carefully. Lady Lambert sighed, for she knew men often took a different view of barmaids than ladies did, and she could only hope that her second son's breeding and the inherent Lambert steadiness would guide his steps.

The Lambert ladies had been invited to stay with Lord Lambert's younger sister, Mrs. Meccleston. Lady Lambert had hoped her older sister-in-law, the Duchess of Meresly, would invite them to come to her, but although the duchess answered her letter promptly and kindly asked them to call when they were in town, she declared that her health at the present time was such that she did not feel able to withstand the racketing about or the noise and confusion that having two young nieces in the house for an extended visit would entail. Lady Lambert was indignant.

"You would think that they were children, hardly out of leading reins!" she exclaimed to her husband. "Racketing about, indeed! Well, I shall say no more! I am sure we will enjoy Jane's hospitality, and she is, after all, as much of the *haut ton* as the duchess. It will give me a great deal of pleasure to call on *her* with the girls and show her how well-behaved they are. Confusion? Noise? In a Lambert? I never!"

All the time the preparations for the trip to London were taking place, Janet Lambert had remained silent and withdrawn, and one morning her mother took her to task for sulking and set her a punishment of polishing all the brass in the drawing room. Janet was quick to tell her she had not been sulking at all, she had just been thinking, and at that statement, Lady Lambert added all the silver in the salon as well, and Janet subsided.

"I am not pleased with you, Janet, no, not at all! To answer me back in that pert way! I sincerely hope that while I am away you will ponder your attitude and employ your time well. I shall count on seeing at least four chair covers completed in needlepoint, and I shall expect good reports from Mrs. Peevey and Nanny about your industry around the house as well. You are to forget this silliness about music! If you have time after your work, you may of course practice your pieces, but I shall be most displeased if I hear that you are spending an inordinate amount of time at the instrument. Do I make myself clear, miss?"

"Yes, Mama," Janet replied, her eyes lowered demurely, for she knew that if she looked up and her mother saw her expression of rebellion and resentment, she would probably have to scrub the entire two miles of the drive on her hands and knees! If Agatha and Elizabeth could hardly wait to leave, Janet was even more anxious for the day of departure. It is true that she had been sad and depressed when Mr. Booth had been dismissed, although he left her with several difficult pieces to learn on her own, and some fingering exercises that she knew would improve her skill as soon as she could master them. She had thought originally of asking her father if she might have Mr. Booth return as her teacher, as soon as Lady Lambert drove away, but she had come to see that her father would never do anything so against his wife's wishes. And he knew what Lady Lambert thought, for he had teased Janet one evening about her skill. Since Janet had never dared to ask him a favor, she shrank from attempting to gain such a major concession, and besides, when her mother learned what she had done, the punishment was sure to be terrible and lengthy.

She had thought that when her mother left, she would be able to spend as much time as she liked in the big drawing room at the piano, but now it appeared that both Mrs. Peevey and Nanny were to be set to watch her. A tide of resentment rose in her breast, and she clenched her hands together tightly, under her apron. It was not fair: no, not in the least little bit!

When her brother Henry came into the sewing room a few days later to grumble to Janet about the morning he had had to spend with Mr. Jackson conjugating Latin verbs, she looked up from her sewing and fixed him with sad eyes.

"I know, Henry! It seems we are to be hedged about most strictly while Mama is gone. I had hoped it would be different, too!"

"Silly goose!" he answered idly, his good-looking Lambert face frowning in discontent as he arranged the spools in her workbasket in a more pleasing color design. "To have any such hopes! To be sure, I did think myself that Papa would mostly ignore us as he always has, but I have heard Mama telling him over and over how he is to keep an eye on us." He spilled the threads with a careless hand and sighed.

Janet removed the workbasket from his reach and then she asked in a small voice, "Do you love Mama and Papa, Henry?"

He stared at her in amazement. "Love them? I don't

know, I guess so! We're supposed to love our parents, ain't we?"

"That is what we have been *taught*," Janet said, stressing the last word. "But I can feel only dislike, especially for Mama! Father does not seem to care a jot for any of us, except for Horace Junior, and that only because he is the heir, but Mama goes out of her way to be hard and unfeeling. Why should we always have to do things *her* way? It is not as if we were so bad, after all!"

Her brother was shocked, for this was going beyond anything he had ever allowed himself to think, and certainly never to voice, and he was quick to break in on the treasonous thoughts his older sister was expounding.

"Why, Janet! What a thing to say, when Mama is only concerned with our well-being! You know how she always says she is only punishing us for our own good, and that we will thank her for it someday when we are grown. I will not listen to you anymore!" He went to the door, turning as he was leaving to add, "You must remember that we are Lamberts. Mama is only anxious that we have the best upbringing, the kind that will ensure our happiness as grown-ups."

"But what of our happiness now while we are growing up? Are we never to know any at all? And why is present happiness such a wicked thing?"

But she spoke only to the closed door, for Henry had left in a hurry, disturbed by his sister's remarks and determined not to listen anymore.

Finally, one fine day in April, Lady Lambert and her two eldest daughters drove away to London in the Lambert carriage while the rest of the family stood on the front steps waving their handkerchiefs in farewell. In spite of the fact that Mrs. Peevey, Nanny, and Mr. Jackson had been set to watch her, Janet felt as if a great weight had been lifted from her, and for the first week or so she hugged herself with joy whenever she thought of her freedom from it. Never to be surprised by Mama coming into a room to see how she was getting on, and then unmercifully criticizing her work, never to be told to finish quickly because there were several more tasks to be done, never to have to answer questions about what she had been doing, what she was thinking about, what she intended by *that* remark!

Lord Lambert tried briefly to remember all his wife had instructed him to do, but since the household seemed to be running smoothly, he forgot and left his progeny very much to their own devices. Nanny, who had the best of intentions as regards Janet, suddenly fell ill with a serious case of fever and influenza, and was confined to her bed. As she tossed and turned, she reminded herself that even if she had to keep all contact between herself and the rest of the family at a minimum, there was still the excellent Mrs. Peevey.

Mrs. Peevey took one look at Janet's brass and silver polishing and resolved never to ask the young lady to help again. She had very little sympathy for Lady Lambert down deep inside, for she felt it ridiculous to insist on young ladies of quality wielding a duster or a needle when there were so many maids with little enough to do, and the work was, after all, their job. If she had had the good fortune to be born to wealth, she told herself, she would never lift a finger again! Janet suddenly found herself with more hours of freedom than she had ever enjoyed before, and although she was still expected to report to Nanny—through her closed bedroom door—every afternoon, and ask Mrs. Peevey if she had any commissions for her every morning, she was able to read and amuse herself a good deal more than she had ever been able to in the past.

The only time she saw her father and older brothers was at the dinner table, and since Lord Lambert and his heir monopolized the conversation by endlessly discussing the Grange and its agricultural problems, to the exclusion of all else, Janet was able to make a good dinner although she was heartily bored. She suspected that Wilbert and Henry were too, but Lord Lambert never inquired after their interests. Janet told herself that dinnertime was an excellent exercise in patience.

Her mother had decreed a daily ride for her, in an attempt to instill a more Lambert-like regard for horsemanship, and dutifully Janet went every morning to the stables, where her mare was waiting. She was glad she was still too young to need a groom in attendance, even though she had passed her sixteenth birthday just before her mother left, for she only rode slowly out of sight of the Hall before she swung down from her horse, and tying the reins loosely to a branch, settled down against a tree to read. The mare certainly didn't mind, and browsed happily in the new green grass, and she was never caught in her deception, for she could always tell where her father and Horace Junior were apt to be from their conversation the evening before, and accordingly she went in the opposite direction.

But pleasant as these interludes were, she was still frustrated by the lack of time she was allowed to spend at the pianoforte. The half-hour that Nanny considered ample was soon up; indeed she could barely warm up her fingers and play a few scales before a maid would come to tell her she was wanted in the stillroom, or the dairy, or the sewing room, doing those horrible needlepoint seat covers. Mama had told her they were part of her trousseau and that someday she would be glad of her industry when she saw all twelve of them adorning the chairs in her very own dining room. Janet often stared at the murky colors Mama had chosen, and the insipid design of birds and flowers and leaves, and thought that the first thing she would do when she was married was throw them away! But she had to finish four of them, and she was getting behind already.

The reason for this was that she had discovered that if she rose very, very early, long before the maid came to light her fire and bring her hot water and morning chocolate, she could creep down to the drawing room and practice the piano for well over an hour. There was never anyone about in this part of the house then, for the maids were all busy upstairs or in the kitchen, and no one came to dust or clean the drawing room until later. Even Thomas, the butler, was absent from the front hall.

She was always careful to close the doors tightly, and she never played very loudly for fear of disturbing her father, fast asleep in the master bedroom above her head.

19

Fortunately the Grange was old and very solidly built, so no sounds wafted upward to disturb his slumbers.

Now that summer was approaching, it grew brighter much earlier, and she did not have to light candles to see the music. She tried hard to keep track of the time, but once she had forgotten, and it had been a very near thing. She heard Thomas' voice as he came to the front of the house, and was only just behind the draperies at the window before he threw open the doors, saying over his shoulder, "You will 'ave the goodness, Pickles, to be more prompt to your dooties! I 'ave waited about for you ten extra minutes this morning; see that it doesn't 'appen again!"

When he had left with the young footman, Janet was able to slip out the French doors to the terrace, and a few minutes later appear at the front door as if she had been out for an early-morning stroll. She thought Thomas looked at her suspiciously, and told herself she must be more careful.

But with the extra time, she was making great progress with her playing and soon came to the end of the pieces Mr. Booth had left for her. Sadly she began to perfect this last sonata, wondering what she was to do after she had it mastered. As her fingers touched the keys and she began to play, she put it out of her mind, immediately lost as she always was in her music.

The early-morning rising at five, however, was making her sleepy by midafternoon, and several times she fell alseep over her needlepoint. When she finally awoke, it was to discover that an hour or so had passed, and not a stitch had she taken. She told herself she had to do better!

Lady Lambert wrote faithfully, and her husband read her weekly letters to the family in the drawing room after dinner. Janet often wondered if he were leaving something out. Surely Mama must say something personal, just for him, but it appeared that that was not the case. The letters were only descriptions of the events of their lives—and who was presently paying court to Agatha. Lady Lambert allowed a small amount of pique to show through when she reported that this was all taking much longer than she had thought it would, and that Agatha did not seem to grasp the fact that she was not there just to amuse herself! Elizabeth had displeased her Mama as well, but what her crime was, was not reported. Janet silently cheered Agatha's indecision, and prayed she would not fall madly in love with a suitable gentleman too soon. It did not really matter what Lizzie was doing, for Janet knew that traditionally the eldest Lambert daughter always married first, and until that event was a foregone conclusion, she was safe from her Mama's presence.

Lady Lambert also sent instructions to her children, instructions they had heard many times before. Horace Junior was to emulate his father in every way, Wilbert was ordered to cultivate sober habits and an upright character, Henry was to attend diligently to his studies, as was Janet to her household duties.

Although Janet waited breathlessly through each letter, Lady Lambert never told her husband what she required of him; perhaps after all these years, he was expected to have it by heart!

❧ 2 ❧

As late May gave way to early June, Lord Lambert announced one evening that his old friend Lord Baggeston was to come and stay with them for a week or so, bringing another gentleman with him. Lord Baggeston was anxious to inspect the Grange's new stallion, and the Hampshire sow's latest litter, and Lord Lambert wrote that he and his family would be delighted to welcome them both. To his children he confided that Lord Baggeston was an excellent man, thought just as he ought, and was one of his oldest and dearest friends. Janet decided she was not looking forward to meeting him at all.

On the afternoon the guests arrived, she was busy helping Mrs. Peevey plan some menus, and so she missed welcoming them in her mother's place, and only saw them for the first time at dinner.

Lord Baggeston was elderly, and heavy and hearty, and so very much like her father that Janet smiled a little as she curtsied. She was rewarded by a large smile and a hearty kiss.

"So this is your little daughter, Horace!" he said.

It is plain to see that I am not his son, Janet thought. She was wearing her best gown of pink muslin, and her hair had been braided and tied with matching pink ribbons. Mama did not believe in young ladies putting up their hair too soon. She felt gauche and young and shy, especially when she was introduced to Lord Baggeston's protégé.

"Allow me to present Anthony Northridge, the Marquess of Hallowsfield, Miss Janet!" Lord Baggeston exclaimed in his overloud voice, and Janet looked up to see a very elegant young man in his early twenties. He was impeccably dressed, and his swarthy complexion and dark hair looked most unusual among all the Lambert fairness. He bowed, one eyebrow quirked.

"But you must all call him Tony, you know, no formality here, nor does he wish it," Lord Baggeston continued. "He is a distant nephew of mine, come to see how we old men farm, Horace! At least that is what his mother, the duchess, wrote in her letter. I myself don't think him at all interested, and I tax him with it, you may be sure! He has lately returned from the Grand Tour, y'know! Fascinatin'! Fascinatin'!"

Janet stole another glance at the marquess, and wished Lord Baggeston would stop talking, for she would have liked to ask the marquess of his travels. When he was finally allowed to edge in a word, she thought he had a very pleasant voice, deep and resonant, and with never a hint of hauteur as he answered her father's questions easily. At dinner, he was seated to Lord Lambert's right, with Lord Baggeston to the left, and they were flanked by the elder Lambert sons. Janet and Henry found themselves relegated to the foot of the table as usual.

"Pity my wife and elder daughters are not at home, Lord Northbridge," Lord Lambert said formally, for he was a great stickler for ceremony, and would have been amazed if the son of a duke allowed himself to be addressed informally by his first name on such early acquaintance. "Lovely girls, and exceedingly well-brought up, if I do say so myself! They would be sure to entertain you well, but alas! They are in town for the Season!"

Janet thought the marquess looked as if he would be able to stand the disappointment of not having Miss Lambert's and Miss Elizabeth's acquaintance very well, and when he looked down the table at her, she ducked her head over her soup, afraid from the twinkle in his eye as it met hers, that he had read her mind. She concentrated on her dinner after that, and although Lord Baggeston kindly asked her a few questions, they were mostly about the Grange and her duties there.

She was delighted to leave the gentlemen to their port and withdraw with Henry to the drawing room. She knew she could not be excused until the tea tray was brought in, for her mother considered it excellent training for her, to have to pour out each evening, so she took a seat disconsolately near the fire, wondering if it were worthwhile to fetch a book. If Papa and Lord Baggeston had a great deal to reminisce about, there might be time to finish her chapter, but she did not dare to leave the room, for if Papa were to come in and find her gone, he would be very vexed.

Henry, who had had the forethought to bring a book with him, was deep in its pages, so she looked around the old-fashioned room idly. The heavy hangings at the windows seemed oppressive to Janet, but then, crimson velvet, much decorated with gold braid and tassels, was not to her taste. The sofas and tables and chairs had all been in the family for years, for the Lamberts considered their ancestors' tastes to be perfect, and saw no need to follow the whims of fashion by redecorating every time a new style came in. She wondered what the marquess thought of it all, sure he was used to much grander surroundings than this. She was still daydreaming a little when Thomas entered the room, trailing a footman behind him whom he instructed to open the piano and place a branch of candles to one side.

"Your father wishes you to play for his guests, Miss Janet," the butler said, bowing before her.

Janet started up. She had been far, far away, sitting in a palace in Venice and staring down at the brilliant scene of the canal beneath her balcony, and it seemed a very long way back to the stodgy drawing room.

"Play? Papa?" she asked in a bewildered voice.

Henry laughed. "Come, now, Janet! Finally someone is

asking you to play, and you can only stare! Up with you and get ready!"

He strolled over to her and drew her to her feet, and walked with her to the instrument. "It is probably that the marquess is bored, or maybe that Papa and Lord Baggeston are having a heavy time of it entertaining him!" he said. "I do not think he looked at all interested in the poundage of Princess Patty!"

Janet had to laugh as she opened her music with trembling hands. Princess Patty was the Hampshire sow, and although she had a long and illustrious title, as befitted her lineage, she was always known as Patty. She had a few moments to warm up her fingers before the men joined them in the drawing room, but she immediately stopped playing as the doors opened, not at all sure she could have understood the butler correctly. Papa wished her to play? *Papa*?

"No, no, do not stop, young lady!" Lord Baggeston said as he bustled in. "Just the thing to settle that excellent dinner, eh, Tony?" The marquess was not allowed to voice an opinion, for Lord Baggeston led him to a chair near the piano before he turned away and went at once to Lord Lambert's side, where they soon had their heads together deep in conversation. Horace Junior and Wilbert looked pained as they took their seats, Henry winked at her, and the marquess folded his arms and stared into the fire with a resigned expression. At that, a small spark of anger rose in Janet's breast. No doubt he expected to be forced to listen to a childish rendition of "The Dance of the Fairies," she thought as she composed herself.

She began simply with *"Für Elise,"* partly out of spite, and partly to calm her nerves, for she had never played for anyone before, but when she was finished, she barely waited a moment before she began a Mozart piano concerto. As usual, she forgot the guests, her family, the Grange, and the rest of the world as she played the hauntingly beautiful melodies. When the last chord sounded, she looked up, her eyes still far away, to the sound of applause. Of course, only the marquess was applauding; her brothers looked as if they were half-asleep, and her father and Lord Baggeston had not stopped talking for a moment.

When Lord Lambert heard his guest clapping, he rose to his feet and came quickly to the piano. "That was very nice, my dear, but we have had enough music for this evening. We don't wish to bore Lord Northbridge, now, do we?"

He held out his hand and Janet rose obediently. As she did so, the marquess came up to them, saying, "But it was hardly boring to be entertained by such a talented musician!"

Lord Lambert clapped him on the shoulder and smiled weakly. "Say you so, m'lord?" he asked. "We think Janet quite the tinkler ourselves! It is so very Italian of her; no one else in the family has half her skill!"

He spoke as if this were no such great matter, and when he turned back to the others, Lord Northbridge leaned closer to Janet and smiled down at her.

"How old are you, Miss Janet?" he asked, and when she replied in a shy voice that she had just had her sixteenth birthday, he took her hand and shook it. "It is most impressive to hear such a performance from one of your age! The Mozart 'Concerto in D,' was it not? I first heard it played in Vienna last year, and I do not mean to flatter you when I tell you that your performance was excellent, and most faithful in interpretation!"

Janet paled with pleasure, for outside of Mr. Booth she had not had any praise before, nor had she ever met another who knew anything about music. "Really, m'lord?" she asked in disbelief. "Thank you so much! Oh, how I would love to listen to a real *artiste* play it, for I have only heard it performed by my music teacher, and that was several months ago!"

"Are you not still having lessons, then?" he asked in some surprise. "But you must! It would be a crime to let a talent like yours wither for lack of training! I can see you are most diligent in your practice, but even the most talented musician needs instruction!"

Janet wished she might ask him to hush, but a scared glance over her shoulder told her that her father was talking to Lord Baggeston once again. She allowed the marquess to lead her to a sofa and take a seat beside her, and she wished, rather obscurely, that she was not only sixteen and a child in his eyes. For an enjoyable half-hour she was allowed to converse with him about music and art and his travels before the tea tray arrived. It was the most pleasant evening Janet had ever spent in her mother's drawing room and she went to bed reluctantly, remembering his compliments with pride.

For his part, the marquess was only too happy to indulge the child in conversation, for he had been quick to see that there was no one in residence of any interest to him at all, and he had already been heartily bored by Lord Lambert and his own elderly uncle. The Lambert sons he stigmatized as clods.

The next morning Janet woke early, and a little smile curled her lips as she remembered his words again. Then she threw on an old morning dress and some worn slippers, and hastily washing, and brushing her long black hair and fastening it back carelessly with a ribbon, she made her way to the drawing room. For a moment she hesitated, but then she remembered that Mrs. Peevey had put the guests in the west wing, so there was no chance they would overhear her, and she knew Papa had had a great deal of port last night to celebrate his old friend's arrival, for she had smelled it on his breath when he came up to the piano.

She began slowly with her scales and chord exercises, and then could not refrain from playing the Mozart concerto again, to relive her triumph of the evening before. When she had finished, she took up the hardest piece of music she had, the very difficult fugue by Bach, and began to practice it. One whole set of measures troubled her, and she played them over and over until she had the notes perfectly, although she was still not sure she was interpreting it correctly. Should she play the music faster or slower? And was the emphasis to be on the chords or the secondary melody that threaded through the composition?

Completely unaware, she had not heard the drawing-room door open, or the marquess come in and quietly take a seat. He was dressed in country clothes, as if he had been out for a walk, and he settled down and crossed his legs and prepared to listen.

"No! That's not right, idiot!" she exclaimed out loud to herself. "Play it correctly!" and then she swung around on the piano seat, startled, as the marquess said from across the room behind her, "The melody should always be the major theme, Miss Janet. Do not be so taken with the fingering of the left hand that you forget."

Her hands went to her throat, and when he saw that she was trembling, he came to apologize for frightening her.

"I was just about to go for a stroll," he explained. "I am often an early riser. It seems the best part of the day to me, when everyone else is still sleeping and there is time for solitary contemplation. And I see that you agree with me, to be up so early. Unless, of course, you are so busy the rest of the day that this is the only time to practice, and that I find hard to believe."

Janet swallowed and put away her music, suddenly realizing that it was much later than she had supposed and that she would be discovered if she remained in the drawing room any longer.

"You must excuse me, m'lord" she said hurriedly. "I must leave—I should not be here! Oh, do not think me rude, but if I am discovered, it will ruin everything!"

Lord Northbridge bowed. "I shall let you run away, then, but I shall demand an explanation from you another time."

Before he could continue, she was gone, running swiftly to the drawing-room doors and peering around them as if she did indeed fear to be discovered. He shrugged. He thought her a strange child, and if he had not been so indifferent to his companions and his situation here, probably he would not have given her another thought. Since he was as little interested as Janet was in farming, however, he wondered about her actions all day as he trailed around the estate behind his host and Lord Baggeston.

He made a point of coming up to her that evening before dinner and inquiring how she had spent her day. Janet blushed and answered in a monotone. She could not tell him, but she had spent the day in dread, afraid that he would mention her early-morning sessions at the piano. She felt tongue-tied and awkward, for she had no idea how to ask him to remain silent, and if her father knew, her mother would be sure to find out very shortly as well. Fortunately the marquess did not refer to it before the gong sounded for dinner, and Janet was able to relax and enjoy the soup, the pigeon pie, and the roast beef, as well as the delicious trifle that followed.

The conversation centered around the Grange again, with Lord Northbridge making few comments, and then only when he was directly addressed. Janet thought he must be disgusted to be forced to discuss pigs, even such an excellent pig as Patty, at the dinner table, and if that did not sufficiently weary him, he had only to look up to see her brother Wilbert, his eyes glued to m'lord's cravat as he chewed large mouthfuls of his dinner, for he was trying to memorize how it was tied so he might attempt a like fall of glistening white linen. The Lamberts prided themselves that they were hearty trenchermen. Horace Junior, although closer in age to the marquess, had decided he was an out-and-outer from divers things he had said, even if he was the heir to a dukedom, and ignored him as much as possible. He was unable to see that Lord Northbridge had been teasing him gently, hoping to find some topic of mutual interest.

When Lord Lambert caught Janet's eye, she rose obediently at the end of the meal, and then she heard Lord Northbridge say, "I hope your daughter will honor us with more of her excellent piano playing this evening, m'lord!"

She stopped, her face turning whiter than her second-best gown as her father frowned and said, "If you wish it, m'lord! But, Janet"—shaking a finger in her direction—"let us have something more tuneful, more sprightly tonight! A reel, or a jig, or a good old country tune. I could not like that music you chose last evening, so solemn and so long."

Janet curtsied, her eyes lowered demurely, and she was careful not to look toward the marquess when she left. Whatever would he think? A reel or a jig? She knew if she saw his expression she would giggle, and that would never do!

She played very simple tunes that evening, and since she did not have to concentrate on the music, she was able to wonder about the marquess. She had never met anyone like him before, and she thought him very handsome, and so much more sophisticated and worldly than her father and her brothers. He had traveled, he had an informed mind; he was not smug and self-satisfied, content to spend his life on his own acres, as they were. She was sure he must despise all the Lamberts, even though he had such excellent manners this was never apparent.

He sat in the same chair as last evening, his chin propped up on one long white hand, adorned with a beautiful sapphire ring. His evening dress fit his masculine form without a single crease, and although he looked slight next to her hearty relatives with their broad chests and powerful thick legs, she somehow knew he was no weakling. He gave the feeling of power like a coiled spring, she thought, watching from the corner of her eye as one elegant leg crossed over the other and beat time gently to the music.

She longed to play something she knew he would enjoy, but she did not dare disobey her father, even though he was deep in conversation with Lord Baggeston again. At last she stopped when that gentleman rose, taking pity on her brothers.

"Very fine, most pleasant, Miss Janet!" he said as he bustled forward. "What an excellent thing for young gels to have such accomplishments to keep them busy, eh, Horace? But now, what say you to a game of whist? I think Tony would enjoy that, would you not, my boy, even if we do not play for such stakes as you are used to! We must not continue to be selfish and lost in our conversation, agreeable as it is, my old friend! We must remember the younger generation!"

Although he had never considered the likes or dislikes of his children to be at all important compared to his own desires, Lord Lambert nodded stiffly. He did not like gaming, and even though they only played for penny points, he was sure Lady Lambert would hardly approve, especially since two of her sons were starting up eagerly. He turned and beckoned to his heir, and Wilbert and Henry subsided in disappointment.

Thomas was called to bring some cards and set up the table, and Janet went to the fireplace and took a seat. She had brought her needlepoint with her this evening, but although she made great strides on the chair cover, her eyes wandered often to the marquess. He had not thanked her for her playing this evening, and he had gone to join the others at the card table without a word, as if he often sat down to such a game, which Janet was sure was not the case. Lord Lambert and Lord Baggerston were competent if indifferent players, but Horace Junior had never had much experience and played a woefully sad game.

She was disappointed when she bade the guests good night that Lord Northbridge barely looked up from his cards, and with such a black look on his face that she could hardly smile as she curtsied.

The next morning, he did not come to the drawing room, although she found herself listening for his footsteps, for the first time finding it hard to concentrate on her practicing. And why are you so disappointed? she asked herself as she put her music away. What are you but a mere child to someone as grand as Lord Northbridge? He was just being kind, to show such an interest in your playing, and now he has forgotten all about it. Well, she told herself stoutly, I most certainly shall not repine about it! But she wondered why she felt so sad, not having the slightest idea that she had, for the first time in her life, fallen in love. And in love with someone who would never have looked her way twice were he to meet her anywhere but here at the Grange.

Later that morning, when she went to the stables for her daily ride, she looked around eagerly, but Lord Northbridge was nowhere in sight. She turned her mare toward the home woods, for she knew her father intended to show Lord Baggeston some stock that were grazing in the Furlong Field. She did not want to be interrupted.

But her book was not nearly as interesting as it had seemed before, and she was not sorry when she heard the sounds of hooves coming toward her. She rose hastily, brushing off her habit as she went hurriedly to her mare. If it were Horace Junior, he would be sure to tell her father that she had not been practicing her horsemanship, and that would never do! But around the bend in the ride cantered the marquess, astride a large black gelding. He halted his horse and raised his hat, and Janet blushed, frozen to the spot.

At that, he quirked one black eyebrow at her, and swinging down from his horse, came toward her, smiling easily.

"Miss Janet, servant! Now, what have you been up to that you look so conscious, I wonder?" He spoke in a bantering way, for all the world, she thought, as if she were Henry's age.

"I . . . I just dismounted for a short rest, m'lord!" she managed to stammer. He looked down at the book she was holding, and then at her mare, happily munching the grass that grew along the verge of the ride.

"And why should you not, if you want to?" he asked in surprise.

Janet was stung to answer him, and before she thought, she said, "I am not allowed! I mean, I am supposed to be practicing my riding. I have no skill, you see, not like the rest of my family, and my mother has ordered me to ride for an hour every morning. I do so dislike it!"

She stopped aghast at what she had revealed, but the marquess did not seem to be offended by her frank speech.

"And so, instead, you ride out of sight, and then dismount to read a book?" he asked, tying his horse to a convenient branch. "Come, sit down and tell me about it, it seems very intriguing. Why don't you like to ride? And why *must* you do so, if that is the case?"

Janet reluctantly joined him on the flat rock he had chosen as a seat. "I do not care to be bounced and jounced about for pleasure, but since all the Lamberts are excellent horsemen and pride themselves on their ability, I must try to conform," she answered him.

"But why is it necessary?" he asked in bewilderment. "You have other talents—your music, for example."

"But that is not admired or encouraged," Janet replied with downcast eyes.

"Is that why you play so early in the morning, when you can be sure to be alone?" His voice was very gentle, and when she looked up and saw how kind and sympathetic his eyes were as he observed her, somehow she could not lie to him.

"Yes!" she whispered. "You see, Mama feels I have more than enough skill as it is, and should now devote myself to the household tasks she considers such important training for a young lady of quality. But since she has been in London, I have been playing every morning. I cannot give it up, no matter what she says!"

"Indeed, why should you? You have a vast amount of talent! I am surprised, for I would think they would all be proud of you!"

Janet shook her head. "No, it is not like that at all, m'lord. You do not understand the Lamberts. What is most admirable is to be like all the rest of them, interested only in the estate and living a sober, industrious, and upright life. Music, art, literature—none of these is at all important!"

She missed the shudder he gave before he spoke. "I see! But how boring, don't you agree?" When she would have replied, he added quickly, "But I should not say that! It is only that I am in such sympathy with you. My mother insisted that I come with Lord Baggeston; she feels it is time for me to learn to be a landowner, and since my father—the duke, y'know—has as little interest

33

in the estates as I have myself, she has sent me along with my prosy old uncle to be initiated into the mysteries of cocks and cows and crops!"

He sighed, for although he seemed very old to her, he was only twenty-four.

"And pigs?" she couldn't resist asking. "How did you find Princess Patty, m'lord?"

"Bah!" he said, with such a look of disgust on his face that she laughed out loud, a silvery cascade of complete enjoyment. The marquess studied her more closely. Once Miss Janet was away from her stodgy family, she was a different girl—gay and alive and with an intriguing face that lit up in innocent amusement. Her dimple deepened as she threw back her head and laughed again, exposing a long, slender neck.

"If I may say so, Miss Janet, the Lamberts' Princess Patty, while being a very model of superior pigginess, a mountain of pedigree, and a most prolific breeder, is the most boring animal I have ever laid eyes on!" he said frankly.

"And she smells so!" she couldn't help adding, "Even though she is cosseted as much as any baby!"

"Exactly! It is true that there are bad smells in London, indeed in every large city, but you can escape them, and there are so many interesting things to do there—concerts and operas and art galleries, libraries and exhibitions, to say nothing of balls and parties and brilliant company. And since we are wealthy, why should we not enjoy them? That is why we have estate managers, and cowmen and herders and pigmen. My father and I are in complete agreement there."

Janet nodded eagerly. "How I would love to attend just one fine concert!"

The marquess rose and held out his hand to help her up. "When you are the right age, I am sure you will be brought to town for the Season," he said kindly, "and then you can explore all its wonders!"

Janet sighed. "Mama has no interest in the arts. Her only purpose in taking my sisters to town was to find a husband for Agatha. As soon as that is accomplished, she will return here. Then there is Elizabeth to settle as well, and if she can find me a suitable husband here in Berks, I shall not get to go at all!"

She blushed as she realized she had spoken much too frankly, but Lord Northbridge pretended to ignore her embarrassment as he held out his arms so he could help her to mount the mare.

"Then if you wish it, you must refuse each and every offer, no matter how flattering!" he said lightly.

"You do not understand!" Janet found herself saying again. "I shall not be allowed to refuse. Mama and Papa choose our husbands for us, it has always been so. That way they can be sure we will marry someone worthy of a Lambert. And if Mama especially feels that an excellent man has offered for me, there would be no way that I could refuse him!"

As he mounted his horse and the two of them began to return to the Hall, Lord Northbridge made a mental note never to spend a moment in Lady Lambert's company if he could help it, and to invent urgent business in town if she should suddenly appear at the Grange with the two older Lambert daughters in tow.

Changing the subject, he asked about her music again, and Janet was soon pouring out her heart. When he learned that she had mastered all the pieces that Mr. Booth had left for her, he promised to send her some new compositions as soon as he returned to town. Janet shook her head and told him that she would not be allowed to accept them, but he said that he would speak to Lord Lambert in such a way that he could have no objection to the gift.

Janet's eyes glowed with happiness, and when he lifted her off the mare in the stable yard, he realized that although he had thought her a well-enough-looking youngster, it was apparent now that someday she would be a beauty, and not one in the usual peaches-and-cream style, either. Her glossy black hair shone in the sunlight, and her dark blue eyes sparkled, and the faint color that had come to her cheeks from the fresh air and the feeling that she had found a friend at last, made her uncommonly handsome. He hoped her mother would not insist on marrying her to some hearty farmer, for it would be such a waste!

≫ 3 ≪

To Janet Lambert, it seemed a very short time that Lord Northbridge remained at Aylesford Grange. She wished he might stay with them all summer, but of course she knew he was anxious to be away, and since Lord Baggeston had to return to his own properties, it was not more than a few days later that they were gone. Although the marquess did not often single her out, Janet was always conscious of him, and occasionally they would exchange glances at the table or in the drawing room and smile at each other.

The marquess made good his promise to speak to her father about her music, and when Lord Lambert said he was too good and that he must not go to any trouble, for the little puss was much too busy to learn any new pieces, Lord Northbridge firmly insisted. Since this conversation took place in the drawing room after dinner one evening when everyone was present, Lord Lambert could only thank him, especially since the younger man pointed out that her parents were indeed fortunate to have a daughter blessed with such an unusual degree of talent, and he was sure they would want to do their utmost to encourage her. This made Lord Lambert stare, but he held his tongue out of deference to his guest. Encourage her to waste her time over such foolishness? Never!

Janet sent the marquess a look of profound gratitude, and he winked at her when her father turned his back.

She was very sad when the two guests drove away. How was she ever to bear Aylesford Grange without Lord Northbridge? He was so handsome, so understanding, so superior to anyone she had ever met, and the first friend she had ever had. She sighed and told herself she would never forget him, even if she never saw him again. And indeed she did think of him often throughout the following days, and sigh, for first love can be so very consuming, even when the young lover is not aware of the cause of her malady. Lord Northbridge, although he promptly put every other Lambert from his mind as soon as he left the Grange, had every good intention as regards the scores he had promised to send that funny, musical child, but when he arrived at his town house in London, he discovered an urgent express awaiting him from his mother the duchess. His father had had a heart attack and was very ill, and she implored her son to come to him at once.

Not even waiting to change his clothes, he posted back into the country again, but when he came to Stour, it was to find black crepe already adorning the huge wrought-iron gates and the front door, for his father was dead from a second attack, and his mother was prostrate.

In the grief and turmoil that followed, and with the responsibility of becoming the sixth duke and the head of the household in such a sad and unexpected way, it was no wonder that the new Duke of Stour completely forgot Miss Janet Rose Lambert. He forgot her; she could not forget him. She went to bed thinking of him, she woke remembering his face and the deep tones of his voice, and even at the piano she sometimes daydreamed of the things he had said, and the twinkle in his dark eyes.

Janet was not allowed to brood over his departure for long, however. Nanny summoned her to her room after her recovery from the influenza, and questioned her severely about how she had been spending her time. For once, Janet was able to stand up to her, saying that she had been helping to entertain her father's guests, and although she had not had time to finish the third chair cover, she intended to do so without delay. Nanny looked after her in consternation as she left with her head high. Lady Lambert was not going to like such assurance and pertness! But Janet's newfound confidence and defiance were not to last long, for only a few days later, Lady Lambert and her daughters returned. The new Duke of Stour would never know how close an escape he had had.

With the ladies came a gentleman who was introduced as Lord Farquhar, Viscount Craffordshire. Lady Lambert was all smiles as she ushered him into the hall. She had not informed her family of their arrival, so she found only Janet in the drawing room, fortunately diligent over her needlepoint.

Her daughter dutifully kissed the cool cheek her mama extended, and hugged her two sisters, her heart sinking at this sudden return to her mother's domination and her loss of freedom. She made her curtsy to Lord Farquhar, whom she thought a most singular-looking young man. He was extremely tall and reed-thin, with blond hair that was rapidly balding, although he appeared to be only in his early twenties. His two most arresting features were a huge beak of a nose and a receding chin. Janet thought he looked very like a stork, and he looked inquiringly to the others, wondering why he was there. When she saw Agatha go up and take his arm, blushing prettily as she did so, she understood the situation even before Elizabeth pointed and nodded and grimaced behind his back.

"And where is your father, Janet?" her mother asked, handing her travelling cloak and bonnet to the butler.

"I believe he and Horace Junior are gone to the market town today, Mama, for they did not expect you. What a surprise! Not that they—we all—are not delighted to see you, of course!" she added hastily at her mother's severe look.

Lady Lambert turned and smiled at the young viscount, and directed Thomas to show him to his rooms, and to make sure that he and his valet had everything they required. The gentleman had not spoken a word, but now he endeavoured to do so. He had such a pronounced stammer that it was almost impossible for him to get out, "I th-th-thank you, L-L-L-Lady Lambert! Mo-mo-most kind!"

Janet did not feel the least desire to laugh at him, for he must be pitied such an affliction, poor man. After Thomas had ushered him away, Lady Lambert allowed her daughters only a few moments of excited chatter before she quelled them all with her quiet but firm voice, telling them that if they all insisted on speaking at once, no one could possibly be understood. She had summoned Mrs. Peevey, and when the housekeeper came in, told her that they were to have Lord Farquhar as a guest for some weeks, and she would expect a special attention to meals, and excellent service for the young man, for he was a most important visitor. Mrs. Peevey curtsied and left.

"But who is Lord Farquhar?" Janet asked, looking from one to the other.

"A most excellent young man!" Lady Lambert said, "and he has asked if he might pay his addresses to your sister. It is for that reason that we have returned so precipitately, so that he might speak to Lord Lambert without delay!"

Janet wondered a little cynically if her mama was afraid the young man might change his mind if he were allowed to consider the situation by himself and had bustled him down to Berks to forestall any such occurrence. She also wondered how m'lord would ever be able to p-p-p-pop the question!

Several times that evening at dinner, Janet wished Lord Northbridge was still in residence, for the questions her father asked the young viscount, and his agonized answers, would surely have brought tears of laughter to her friend's eyes. Janet was careful to keep her own eyes on her plate, even when Henry kicked her under the table.

By the time the ladies withdrew and left Lord Farquhar to the mercies of Lord Lambert and his two older sons, Janet had learned that the viscount was heir to considerable estates near Melton Mowbray, that he was the eldest of four children, that he admired all things rural and her sister Agatha in particular, and that he had merely been passing through town when he made Miss Lambert's acquaintance at a small dance, and if he was not immediately smitten, had been intrigued enough to remain in town long enough to fix his attentions. Lady Lambert disclosed that he was distantly related to Miss Plumber, Lord Lambert's cousin twice removed, which was surely the final seal of his eligibility.

Janet thought her eldest sister looked smug, but not at all in love. In the drawing room, Elizabeth whispered that besides being everything that Mama most admired in a man, the viscount was as rich as Golden Ball as well, and wasn't Aggie lucky? Janet reserved judgment. Perhaps there was more to him than his peculiar looks and awkward stutter, but for herself, she would have shuddered at the thought of spending the rest of her life waiting with bated breath for him to finish a word, let alone a sentence. She could not help but compare him with Anthony Northbridge, to Lord Farquhar's detriment.

Lady Lambert inquired most particularly of her third daughter's activities in her absence, so Janet was not allowed to continue to daydream of the marquess, but she was quick to mention his visit, and Lord Baggeston's.

"Northbridge? Anthony Northbridge?" Lady Lambert asked slowly, eyes intent in thought. "I do not know him, or his family, and yet . . . there is something. I am sure I have heard of him. Now, where was that?"

Janet wished she might strangle her sister Aggie when she said brightly, "But isn't that the young man Aunt Meccleston told us about, Mama? Always gambling and travelling abroad, and such a flirt with the ladies that mamas hurry their daughters from his very vicinity. She said he was on the way to becoming a premier rake, and at the age of only twenty-four too!"

Lady Lambert nodded. "Of course! I remember now. It was when we were driving by his town house that she thought to mention him. And to think he stayed here, at the Grange! Whatever was Lord Lambert thinking of? Thank heavens that neither of you two girls was here!"

Elizabeth sighed, as if she could not agree with her mother's revulsion, for at her sister's description of the

41

marquess, her eyes lit up, and she sat with her little mouth ajar, drinking in every word.

"But it cannot be the same man!" Janet could not help exclaiming. "Lord Northbridge was a gentleman, and so kind! Aunt Meccleston must have mistaken him for someone else!"

Lady Lambert fixed her daughter with a steely eye and frowned her to silence. "He is the Marquess of Hallowsfield, I believe?" At Janet's miserable nod, she continued, "There can be no doubt in that case of his identity, and I am most displeased to hear you contradict me, Janet. I see that in my absence you have become even more difficult than before. I shall be forced to speak to your father if you do not mend your ways."

Janet swallowed and subsided, and then Horace Junior and Wilbert came in to join them, and she was forgotten.

"Where are your father and Viscount Craffordshire?" Lady Lambert asked them.

"They have gone to Papa's study," the heir announced, and then in what he considered a playful tone, he said, "A little bird tells me that we shall soon be wishing you happy, Aggie! Unless it is Elizabeth m'lord fancies?"

"You forget yourself, Horace!" Lady Lambert said. "Unfortunately, Elizabeth has shown herself completely unworthy to be married to such a paragon as the viscount. But no more of that now!"

Janet stole a glance from her needlepoint to see Lizzie turning pale and hanging her head, and wondered what on earth she could have done to incur such displeasure from her mother.

It seemed a very long time before Lord Lambert appeared and beckoned Agatha from the room. In a few moments he came back alone, and he did not keep his family in suspense, telling them at once that the young man had indeed asked for his daughter's hand and was even now proposing. "I can only assume that he has met with your approval, my love," he said to his wife, "since you brought him here to the Grange."

"A most excellent alliance, Horace," Lady Lambert replied. "I knew you would be pleased. He is most definitely 'our sort.'"

"And what of this young gel, eh?" Lord Lambert asked, tipping up Lizzie's chin in one large red hand. "Was there no one in town for her?"

"We will not speak of it!" Lady Lambert said in an awful voice. "I shall tell you all when we are private, sir."

"Hmm!" Lord Lambert replied, dropping Lizzie's chin abruptly.

Since all eyes were on Miss Elizabeth Lambert, Henry whispered to Janet, "Now she's in for it! I wonder what she did? Tell me when you find out, all right, Janet?"

She nodded as Lady Lambert spoke again. "Janet has informed me, m'lord, that you had guests while we were away. I am sorry to hear of it, for I understand that Lord Northbridge is a most undesirable young man. I wonder that Lord Baggeston dared to bring him here, knowing our rigid standards."

"How can you say so?" Lord Lambert asked, his eyes popping out in confusion. "He is heir to a dukedom, and Baggeston's nephew as well, and although I found him difficult to entertain, for he was not at all interested in the important things of life, I saw nothing to take objection to."

Lady Lambert tightened her lips. "I have it on good authority that he is a rake, sir, a ne'er-do-well, and a here-and-thereian as well. I am sorry that Lord Baggeston is related to him, for even though he will eventually be a duke, that does not excuse the stigma of his indecent loose living."

Janet sat quietly, although it took a great effort not to come to her friend's defense.

"Say you so indeed?" Lord Lambert commented. "I am sorry to hear it. He was quite taken with Janet," he continued. "Asked to hear her play the piano every night. And he actually told me that she had great talent and should be encouraged to pursue her music, if you can imagine. Promised to send her some pieces from town."

"Is that so?" Lady Lambert bridled, but what she would have said about the matter further was lost, for just

43

then a beaming and triumphant Agatha came back to the drawing room on the arm of her new fiancé, ostentatiously displaying a large diamond-and-ruby ring on her left hand. In the general congratulations and well-wishing, and welcomes to the bosom of the Lambert family, Lord Northbridge was allowed to fade into the background. Janet was miserably aware that her mother would not forget him, however, and would question her most particularly as soon as they were alone.

The festive evening closed with Agatha, at her mama's request, playing *"Für Elise"* on the piano for her husband-to-be. Janet thought he must be madly in love or tone deaf to be able to sit through her bad performance with such a delighted smile on his face. Unfortunately for Beethoven, Agatha could not resist waving her engagement ring about between the measures, and this added nothing to the music.

It was not long before all the Lamberts knew what Elizabeth's sin had been, for Lady Lambert told her husband that very evening in the privacy of their bedroom; Agatha told Horace Junior, who passed it on to Wilbert, and Janet learned of it from the culprit herself and told Henry the next day. Lizzie had come to her bedroom and curled up on the end of the four-poster to pour it all out.

"It was not *so* bad, Janet!" she said, tossing her head in its linen nightcap. "And I did give up Mr. Cantrell when Mama said I must! But how was I to know she would not approve of Mr. Damon and Lord Fitch? They are both members of the *haut ton*; why, you may meet them anywhere, and both quite unexceptional. And they were *both* after me—la, Janet, it was so diverting! Although Mama never learned of it, thank heavens, they almost had a duel over me!" This last statement was delivered in an awed whisper.

"Was that all?" Janet could not resist asking. Somehow it did not seem enough to warrant the severe disapproval of Mrs. Lambert, even with her rigid notions of propriety. After all, she had disposed of the inappropriate Mr. Cantrell without any trouble; why had she not just forbidden Lizzie to receive the young men, or to dance with them?

"Well, no," her sister admitted, pleating the quilt in suddenly nervous fingers, her eyes downcast. "I did do something worse." There was a moment's silence, and then she added, "But nothing at all came of it, and for Mama to declare that I had ruined myself and brought shame to the Lambert name—why, it was no such thing!"

"But what did you do, Lizzie?" Janet asked impatiently.

"I met Lord Fitch alone in the park one afternoon by arrangement," Lizzie said. "And worse than that, I dismissed my maid. But he only kissed my hand, Janet— good heavens it was broad daylight, and it was only for a few minutes. And if horrible old Mrs. Quarrent had not seen us and run to report it to Mama, she would never have known anything about it. But you see, she declares I have put myself quite beyond the pale, and that was one of the reasons we returned home so soon. She said she could not hold up her head in society anymore, for such wanton behaviour from a *Lambert* was worse than from anyone else."

"Well, she will forget it soon, especially since Aggie has made such a good catch," Janet tried to soothe her sister, although she did not believe it for a minute.

"But that is not the worst!" Lizzie exclaimed. "I am not to be permitted to go to town, ever again! I am to remain here at Berks! And, oh Janet, there is no one *in* Berks. How shall I live? After London it will be too terribly flat."

Janet wisely did not try to bring Lizzie to her senses by any such nonsense as a recital of the population of the county, for she knew exactly what her sister meant. There were no *beaus* in the neighbourhood worthy of her attention, not now after she had been pursued by the likes of a Lord Fitch and a Mr. Damon. She felt vaguely sorry for Lizzie, although she thought she had been very foolish to get in her mama's bad graces. Lizzie took herself off to bed, disconsolate, and left her sister not much happier, for now that Lady Lambert was again in residence, there could be no thought of any more early-morning sessions at the piano. Lady Lambert did not indulge in port, and she was known to be a light sleeper.

In the days that followed, Lizzie was indeed treated like a pariah. It was fortunate for her that the viscount was in residence, or her punishment would have been much more severe. Obviously the viscount had not heard of Lizzie's indiscretions, and Lady Lambert had whisked him away from town before he should do so and have second thoughts about the wisdom of marrying into such a family.

He and Agatha were often together, strolling in the gardens, riding about the estate, and paying calls on such of the neighbours as Lady Lambert considered worthy. The wedding date was set for early October, and Agatha and her mother were to travel to Melton Mowbray early in August so that Agatha might visit her new home and become acquainted with her in-laws. Until that time, the viscount remained at Aylesford Grange, to Lizzie's relief, although she was set to sewing and mending and polishing all through July.

Lady Lambert never mentioned Lord Northbridge again, to Janet's surprise, although she waited breathlessly for some days after the travellers returned from town. But Lady Lambert, having dismissed the young marquess as unworthy of any Lambert's attention, was busy planning her daughter's wedding. At least there was *one* Lambert daughter who did just as she ought, she told her husband, and preparations were being made for a series of small dinner parties and a gala ball to introduce the happy couple and announce their betrothal. Aunt Meccleston and her children were to come for a week preceding the ball, and there was much to do to prepare. In the hustle and confusion, Lord Northbridge was allowed to sink out of everyone's mind—everyone's but Janet's of course.

The long-awaited, promised music never arrived, although Janet always tried to be the first member of the family in the hall when the post was delivered. She could not believe her friend had forgotten, and wondered anxiously if he had fallen ill, or been called away on im-

46

portant family business, but she did not have much time to brood about it, for she was very busy helping her mother with the wedding preparations.

Agatha was to be married from the village church, and Lizzie and Janet were to be her attendants. This had been decided only after many discussions, for Lady Lambert was of the opinion that Elizabeth should be denied the honor in punishment for her behaviour. It was only when Lord Lambert pointed out how unusual it would look if she were not amongst the wedding party that Lady Lambert relented. To think that others would talk and wonder and gossip—and about a Lambert! It was not to be thought of!

The village seamstress was engaged to make over some of the London gowns for the occasion, and Janet was to have a new dress for the ball as well.

This largesse was announced by her mama after a dinner party to which Janet had worn her pink muslin. It had been so difficult to hook that she wondered if she were succumbing to the Lambert plumpness, but Lady Lambert was quick to see that her third daughter, now turned sixteen, definitely had been growing up while she was away, and had developed what Lady Lambert called "a shape." The pink muslin, new only that year, pulled across her young breasts and forced them upward out of the bodice in a most immodest way that Lady Lambert could only deplore. It was especially noticeable since Janet's waist was as slim as ever.

Elizabeth did not dare to protest when the new gown was taken from her wardrobe. It had been made in London, and Janet thought it vastly pretty. Of pale blue silk, it was trimmed with lace flounces and had tiny puffed sleeves and a narrow skirt. She hoped Miss Jerdon, the seamstress, could make it fit, for when she tried it on, it hung about her in folds and was much too long, Lizzie being so much taller and more robust. Lady Lambert left careful instructions with Miss Jerdon, who nodded even as she frowned. When the dress was completed, Janet was disappointed, for it still fit her loosely, and there was an added flounce of lace above the low neckline. She told herself it was only Mama's economy after all, so that she might get more than a year's wear from it.

As she was dressing for the ball, assisted by one of the youngest maids, Janet wished Lord Northbridge was going to be present. She thought she looked very grown-up in her new ball gown, and wondered what he would think of it. She had spent the day in seclusion in her room, wearing curl papers, for her mama had insisted her hair be dressed in long curls such as her sisters wore. She could see as the maid tried to arrange them that the experiment had not been a success, and that before long they would be drooping and coming uncurled, but she had no idea what to do about them. Neither had the maid, so she was forced to go down to the others dissatisfied with her appearance. Perhaps it was just as well the marquess could not see her! She wondered again where he was, and if he ever thought of her.

Unbeknownst to her, the new Duke of Stour was in London for the first time since his father's death. His mother had left Stour to visit friends, and after the initial work of picking up the reins had been accomplished, Anthony Northbridge was delighted to leave estate matters in the hands of his capable staff and take himself back to town. He was still saddened by his father's sudden demise, but he knew that remaining at Stour and brooding over it would not help.

He was engaged that evening to escort his Aunt Ralston to a concert that her husband, the earl, had not wanted to attend. Of all his relatives, Tony admired this aunt the most, for she was a great wit and enjoyed music and the arts as much as he did himself. Equally important, she never took him to task for his profligate ways, for she agreed with him completely that if you had money, what was there to do but spend it and enjoy it after all? She had lived by this philosophy all her life, and since she had had the good fortune to marry a very wealthy peer, she had been able to indulge herself royally.

As he settled her into her seat in the concert hall later, she smiled up at him and promised to tell him all the latest *on dits* and *crim. cons.* which he had missed during his stay at Stour.

"I shall cheer you up, Tony dear boy, never fear! And do not be thinking your father would not applaud my efforts if he were here. He was a great gun; never a mealy word in his mouth, and he would have been glad to see you here in town again!"

Tony, remembering his father, knew she was right, and the two of them were *tête-à-tête* until the pianist appeared and took his place at the piano. As the strains of the Mozart "Concerto in D" sounded through the hall, Tony felt a vague uneasiness but he could not understand why that should be so. He certainly did not associate the music with his father, for the late duke had cared nothing for music. Was it anything to do with his trip to Vienna? Surely he could not be repining over the Italian princess he had dallied with so delightfully there, and so cheerfully left when his stay was over. It was a puzzle, but he put it from his mind and sat back to enjoy the music.

The ball at Aylesford Grange was a great success, although Lizzie whispered to Janet that it was a poor affair compared to some she had attended in town. "If only Mama was not such a squeeze-penny!" she said, waving her fan, for the evening was warm and she had been dancing almost continually. "No lobster patties nor cakes from Gunter's, the tiniest orchestra, and only garden flowers from the estate to decorate the hall! And no abundance of champagne—just a single glass for a toast when the engagement is announced. It is not at all the thing!"

She smiled up at the eager young man who was just then bowing and reminding her that she had promised him this dance, and she rose to take her place in the set. Lady Lambert had watched her carefully all evening, and no matter how warm it became, she had ordered her not to leave the ballroom for any reason whatsoever, and most especially not to stroll in the garden!

Janet had danced with her brothers and the few young men that they brought up and introduced her to, for this was her first ball, and she had been honoured by her brother-in-law-to-be as well, so she did not feel like a complete wallflower. But she had no enjoyment in her partners, for none of them was remotely like Anthony Northbridge.

Lady Lambert looked around the drawing room and was satisfied that everything was just as it ought to be. In between greeting her guests and keeping an eye on Lizzie, she had taken a moment to speak to Wilbert, who seemed determined never to leave the punch bowl; had instructed Janet to retire so she might fasten up her drooping curls; and had had a word with Henry as well, which, although it was delivered with a gentle smile and in the softest of tones, had him making his exit in a matter of moments.

Shortly after the ball, the viscount and his betrothed, along with her mama, went to Melton Mowbray, and there was a period of calm at Aylesford Grange. Janet was quick to start serious practice again, although she continually regretted the lack of new music that the marquess had promised her. Lizzie was not much of a companion, for she had been confined to the Hall unless she was accompanied by an elderly footman who had been carefully instructed by Lady Lambert. Her conversations with Janet were full of the unfairness of it all, and stories of her past triumphs, interspersed with cries of boredom. It was not especially amusing to her sister. If Nanny had not been still convalescent, she might have wondered at Lizzie's sudden interest in matters religious, but even when she insisted on attending both morning and evening services every Sunday, and was always making up bouquets for the altar, or talking about taking a Sunday-school class for the village children, Nanny remained unsuspicious. Janet was very worried, for she had seen Mr. Bates, the new curate, as well as her sister had, and although he was young and shy, she could not deny that he looked very handsome in the pulpit with his blond hair touched by a wandering sunbeam streaming through the stained-glass window, and his clerical robes to lend him dignity. She told herself she was being foolish, for certainly Lizzie was safe with a member of the clergy!

In due course, the Lambert ladies returned to the

Grange, and as September drew to a close, wedding presents began to arrive, and guests to assemble, and one fine morning in early October, attended by her two sisters, Miss Agatha Ann Lambert became the bride of Percival Farquhar, Viscount Craffordshire.

Agatha looked very lovely in her wedding gown of white silk and the Lambert lace veil, with her rosy cheeks and brown curls. Janet, who with Lizzie was wearing pale lemon yellow trimmed with white flowers, stood quietly to one side of the altar and watched her sister pledge her vows. She could not help noticing Lizzie smiling openly at the curate who was helping the rector perform the service, and was glad that her mama, from her seat in the front pew, could not see. Lizzie looked just like a smug little kitten who had tipped over the cream bottle! Janet shook herself mentally, and tried to appear suitably solemn while her new brother, Percival, stammered his replies.

In spite of a growing fondness for the viscount, she did not envy Agatha one little bit. No, that was not quite true, she thought, as she knelt to help adjust the bride's train at the end of the service. There was one thing that she did envy her—Agatha was now a married woman, and as such, was free of the Lambert prosiness, their strict notions of propriety, and their pompous self-consequence as well. As she walked back down the aisle behind the happy couple, she tried not to add that as Viscountess Craffordshire, Agatha was also free of Lady Lambert's domination forever.

II

Intermezzo

II

Intermezzo

❧ 4 ❧

After the triumph of Agatha's wedding, Lord and Lady Lambert settled down to their usual pursuits for the winter season, happy that all the fuss and excitement were over and that a period of peace and quiet could ensue. Alas, it was not to be, which came as a nasty shock to everyone but Janet.

As Christmastime approached, Lady Lambert made the fatal mistake of lessening her surveillance over her second daughter, and Elizabeth was not slow to take advantage of her lenience. If her mother thought that the slow pace of life at the Grange and the severe punishment she had been forced to endure had brought Lizzie to a more decorous frame of mind, she was to be vastly disappointed, for Lizzie lost no time in pursuing the helpless curate, Mr. Bates, with all the single-mindedness of a tigress stalking her prey.

Janet tried to make her see reason, pointing out the dire consequences that would ensue if Lizzie were not careful, but that young lady, denied the excitement of another London Season, was feeling very rebellious. Janet realized that for Lizzie, there had to be a man in attendance—any man—tall, short, ugly, handsome, rich or poor, as long as he was male and adored her, she was

55

content. When Janet asked her if she meant to marry Mr. Bates, Lizzie laughed.

"How silly you are, Janet! And you are sixteen now, too! Of course I have no intention of marrying into the clergy, for I cannot conceive a more boring existence than always having to be saintly, and pleasant to everyone who comes to church, and constantly concerned with good works about the village. Then, too, there could be no pretty clothes and trips to town, or balls and parties or travelling! I have asked Whitney—Mr. Bates, I mean—and he has painted such a gloomy picture, quite without meaning to, of course, that I am determined to avoid it. But there is no harm in a flirtation, no matter what Mama says! And you must admit that Mr. Bates is a very handsome man; indeed, I cannot resist him even though I have no intention of marrying him! And if Mama should hear of his growing attraction for me, she may very well decide I would be safer in town. The Bates family is not to be compared to the Lamberts!"

She laughed gaily as she left the room, and Janet shook her head over her sewing. The whole thing seemed most unfair to the young curate, and she did not think her mama would be at all apt to give Lizzie another Season just to separate her from a man who was not worthy of her.

The Lamberts managed to survive the harvesting, All Hallows, and the first gentle snowfalls of December before catastrophe struck.

The gentry of the county were beginning to give parties to mark the advent of the Christmas season, and of course all the Lamberts were invited. Elizabeth was a favorite with all the young bucks, and even though Janet had at first been indifferent to the parties, she had acquired a few gentlemen admirers of her own. Lady Lambert, finally realizing that this daughter's hair would never curl, no matter what stringent measures were taken, had given her permission to wear it brushed back severely and then wound into a large chignon at the back. This was softened on formal occasions by ribbons or ornaments, and Janet was delighted to be free of curling papers forever. She had no idea how flattering the hairdo was to her oval face, for it brought into prominence her large deep blue eyes and dark brows and lashes. She still looked like a changeling next to her brothers and sisters, but at least, as Lady Lambert pointed out to her husband, she was becoming a less unattractive one.

Shortly before Christmas, the Lamberts were invited to attend a ball at Chestnut Court, the main estate of Lord and Lady Justin. Even though the Justins resided most of the year in town, they never failed to come and spend a few of the winter months at this, their principal seat. Lord Lambert did not approve of them, but there was no way he could refuse to attend their parties without being rude, and since Lord Justin had a much more exalted title than he did, being the Earl of Walloston, he was forced to show him every courtesy and attention.

Lady Lambert, after inspecting both her daughters before they all went out to the carriage that fateful night, resolved to keep a very close eye on Lizzie. She was sparkling in anticipation of the evening, and looked very lovely in her silk gown of deep rose, and Lady Lambert was sure the Justins, as was their custom, had invited several guests for Christmas. Even though they themselves were middle-aged, there was every chance of some sprigs of fashion or daredevil young Corinthians on the strut being present, and she was not entirely convinced even now that Elizabeth had learned her lesson. Janet she dismissed with a nod, although she looked quite as lovely as Lizzie, dressed in white silk trimmed with dark green ribbons, and with a matching bow in her hair, for Janet was still very young in her eyes, and showed no signs of flirting. Horace Junior and Wilbert helped the ladies to their seats in the carriage, and Lord Lambert gave the order to the coachman to let 'em go!

Janet had never been old enough to attend a party at the Court before, and she was dumfounded when she saw how beautiful and elegant it was. There were footmen in livery standing at attention along the entrance-hall wall, and maids to take the ladies' wraps. The main hall with its polished marble floor was decorated with Christmas greens and exotic flowers, and she could hear an orchestra playing in the ballroom. Beside her, Lady Lambert sniffed at what she considered a most ostentatious display. She had spent the ten-mile drive to the Court in cautioning her children about their behaviour, most especially Elizabeth and Wilbert, neither of whom listened to more than a word of the familiar homilies. As soon as they had greeted m'lord and lady, Lord Lambert led them to the ballroom, brilliantly lit with many chandeliers and wall sconces. Several of the guests were already dancing, and Janet's eyes widened. Surely even a London ball could not be so elegant! The Lamberts moved about the room, greeting their friends, and both girls were often begged for a dance. Wilbert and Lord Lambert disappeared into the supper room, where the punch bowl was located; Horace Junior was soon deep in conversation with one of his friends; and Lady Lambert took a seat near an elderly lady of her acquaintance whom she had not seen for some time, due to that lady's indifferent health.

"What a marvelous evening this is going to be!" Lizzie whispered to her sister as she smiled up at a young gentleman approaching her. "Oh, see, Mr. Bates has been invited! I did not know he knew the Justins. I wonder if he will ask me to dance."

Janet's heart sank a little, but before she could caution her sister about her behaviour, Lizzie went off to dance, and it was not a moment later that Janet was also asked to join the set that was forming.

She thought Mr. Dabney very funny, for though he was trying very hard to appear blasé and grown-up, she knew he was attending a ball for the first time. She soon forgot her sister in her enjoyment of the evening.

From her seat against the wall, Lady Lambert watched her daughters dancing, and nodded to herself in satisfaction.

It was much later, after supper had been served, that she broke off a confidence and looked around the room again. There were Janet and Horace Junior talking to an elderly neighbor, and there was Wilbert—tch! with another glass of champagne!—but where was Lizzie? Excusing herself from the group of ladies she had been sitting with, she made her way from the ballroom.

Lizzie was not in the ladies' withdrawing room, nor was she in the main hall, nor strolling about the Justin portrait gallery as some of the other guests were doing. Lady Lambert's lips tightened as she went through all the ground-floor apartments. There was a room set aside for cards for such guests who did not care to dance, and there were several salons where an occasional couple could be found *tête-à-tête*, as well as the supper room, where Lady Lambert surprised some of the servants busy clearing the tables. Lizzie was not to be found anywhere.

It was not until Lady Lambert reached the conservatory that she came upon her second daughter, and in such a position that she was forced to hold on to a chair back tightly, she felt so faint.

There, among the gardenias and exotic plants, was Elizabeth, being passionately kissed by the curate. His arms were tightly around her, his hands caressing her back, and it was plain to see that Lizzie was no reluctant participant in the embrace, for she held him to her closely while one hand played with the blond hair at the back of his neck. It was a very long kiss, and might have been even longer if Lady Lambert had not recovered herself and surged forward, her usually soft voice slightly raised.

"What is the meaning of this? Elizabeth? What *are* you doing?"

Since it was perfectly obvious what they were doing, the couple broke apart guiltily. Mr. Bates's face was very flushed, and his breathing was as hurried as if he had been running, and Lizzie, with her hair falling down and her soft lips parted, looked very wanton to her mother. "I never!" that lady exclaimed. "I never thought to see the day when a daughter of mine—a *Lambert*, mind you!—would so forget herself! How could you, you bad girl? And as for *you*, sir"—here she turned, her bosom swelling, and withered the young curate with a look of loathing—"I wonder that a man in holy orders could so behave! Lewdness, immorality, looseness of character,

59

and in a man of the cloth, too! It is a disgrace to your calling. *Disgusting!*"

Having run down temporarily, she stopped to take a deep breath, and Mr. Bates hastened forward, dragging a reluctant Lizzie with him.

"Your pardon, m'lady!" he said, the blush on his face going right up to the roots of his blond hair. "I know what it must seem, but I am in love with Miss Elizabeth, and she with me. I apologize for my unseemly behaviour, but I do not intend to be loose . . . or, ahem, lewd! Of course I intend to make Elizabeth my wife!"

"Your *wife?*" Lady Lambert asked, as if she had never heard of such a thing. "And if that was your intention, sir, you should have called on Lord Lambert before you approached my daughter so intimately. To be so lost to decency as to *embrace* Lizzie, and in such a coarse, fondling way, before you were married; I have never been so shocked. Furthermore, who are *you* to aspire to a Lambert? I have never heard of your family; there could be no question of marriage between two of such unequal station. Why, Elizabeth numbers two bishops on her family tree, besides innumerable members of the peerage. How dare you, sir, be so presumptuous?"

"But surely, when two people are in love, there can be no thought of consequence and the inequality of our stations in life," Mr. Bates declared, and then made the fatal mistake of adding, "And you must be aware, Lady Lambert, that in the sight of God we are all equal!"

Lady Lambert's eyes widened in shock, and she looked completely nonplussed at being preached to in such a manner. It was plain to see that Mr. Bates, besides being a most unworthy member of the clergy, was so naive as to imagine that the Lord did not recognize the superiority of the Lamberts over the rest of mankind, but she had no intention of arguing the matter with one so far steeped in sin and iniquity.

"Elizabeth! Without passing through the ballroom, you will go immediately to the ladies' withdrawing room, and you will remain there until I have assembled the rest of the family and taken our leave of Lord and Lady Justin."

Lizzie hung her head and turned very pale, for she had never heard quite that tone of voice from her mother before, and she was terrified.

"Go! At once!" Lady Lambert said, and her daughter pulled away from Mr. Bates and almost ran from the room.

"Please, m'lady," the curate begged, "do not be angry with your daughter. We are only human after all—"

"Human?" Lady Lambert asked in an awful voice. "You may be as 'human' as you like, sir, but you will do me the kindness of not being so 'human' around my daughter!" With this, she swept from the room, muttering "Sodom! Gomorrah!" and left the young curate mopping his face with his handkerchief and wondering if it were any use to call on Lord Lambert and plead his suit. He was not at all sure that the gentleman would not horsewhip him—or worse—if he were so bold. In honor, he knew he should offer for Elizabeth immediately, but even though he really did wish to marry her and had never considered himself a coward, he was not looking forward to the coming interview at all.

As it turned out, he was spared this ordeal, for Lord Lambert came to the manse early the next morning and was closeted with the rector for some time. After he left, Mr. Bates was summoned and told that under no circumstance was he ever to set foot in Aylesford Grange again, for his suit was abhorrent to the Lamberts and would not be contemplated under any conditions. He was also forbidden to write to Miss Elizabeth. It was the rector's considered opinion that his curate should begin looking at once for another parish, for it appeared that the Lamberts would not rest until he had left the county permanently. Mr. Bates tried to beg for the rector's intervention, and promised to be the soul of discretion if he were allowed to stay, but his superior shook his old silvered head sadly.

"It is no use, my boy, and I am sorry. You have been of great assistance to me here, and I believe you to be a true Christian gentleman with a real vocation for the ministry, but the Lamberts carry great weight, you know, very great weight. If they have decided you have become *persona non grata*, believe me it would be most undesirable for you to remain in the county. Write to your friends and any influential people you may know who might help you to a new post. Indeed, I hope it will be possible for you to even remain in the church; I shall endeavor to restrain the family's vindictiveness to that extent, and I shall be glad to recommend you without mentioning this . . . er, falling from grace. I am sure you have learned a bitter lesson!"

It was not many more weeks before Mr. Bates was gone for good, but until he left the parish, not one Lambert attended church. Lady Lambert had written the family bishops, which did much to hasten the curate's departure, but it is fair to say that Christmas in the year 1810 was a very unhappy one, not only for the unfortunate Mr. Bates but also for most of the Lambert family. They were stunned and shocked by the unworthy behaviour of one of their members. Other families had these problems—never the Lamberts!

As for Lizzie, no one spoke to her on the ten-mile drive home the evening of the ball, and when they reached the Grange, she was ordered to her room and told to remain there until Lady Lambert should see her in the morning. Whether she slept at all that night is questionable, and Janet, watching her hurry up the stairs with tears running down her face, felt sincere pity for her sister. She did not know exactly what had happened, but from Lord Lambert's heightened color, and Lady Lambert's tight-lipped frown, she could guess, and she knew the consequences of Lizzie's flirtation were sure to be considerable.

The punishment was swift and severe. Although Lady Lambert did not beat her, which Lizzie quite expected, she was told that she was not to accept any invitations to parties or appear in company for an indefinite length of time. While the rest of the family attended dances and dinner parties, Miss Elizabeth was going to be confined to her room with an infectious cold and putrid sore throat which would linger most distressingly. Furthermore, she was not to leave the Hall for any reason whatsoever when she had recovered from her fictitious malady, unless she were accompanied by her mother. The chaperonage of her sister or a servant was not deemed sufficient for one so lost to decorum and the need to uphold the Lambert name.

Janet watched and listened and shivered a little. It had been very bad, that is true, but after all, there had been no scandal. No one in the county was aware of Lizzie's wanton behaviour, nor did they have the slightest idea there was any connection between her indisposed state and the fact that Mr. Bates had left so hurriedly for a poor church in Scotland, so that most horrendous occurrence—that the Lamberts should be gossiped about and pitied and laughed at—never came to pass. But Lady Lambert remained stern and unyielding, and her children were very careful not to offend her in any way in the weeks that followed. Janet even reduced her piano practice until she noticed that her mother did not seem to care quite so much whether she practiced or not. Lady Lambert appeared to have weightier matters on her mind and was often preoccupied.

One afternoon when Lady Lambert had gone to take tea with an old friend, Janet spent two happy hours at the piano. She was idly playing *"Für Elise"* in different tempos, transposing chords and notes for her own amusement, when suddenly she noticed that she had written a melody of her own. Tentatively she played again the song that had come into her head. Yes! It was different, not merely a parody of Beethoven. She began to work out the chords and timing until she heard the carriage bringing Lady Lambert home come around the gravel drive in front of the Grange. She had several lines of music memorized, and she ran up to her room so she might get them down on paper before she forgot. After that day, she worked on several pieces of music, and was happier than anyone else in the family, for when Lizzie's sniffles or her mother's frowns quelled everyone's spirits, Janet was composing in her head and did not hear half of what was said. This pastime made up in a small way for the promised music that had never arrived.

In March, after a considerable exchange of letters, a

Mrs. Rustin and her son William arrived at the Grange. Vaguely Janet remembered that they were distant cousins of Lady Lambert's, but they had never visited before, and after only a very few days, Janet did not care if they ever came again. Mrs. Rustin was just as imposing a matron as Lady Lambert, stern and cold in manner, but even so it was plain to see that she doted on her son and treated him as if he were some precious treasure that had to be coddled and cosseted. Why this was necessary, Janet had no idea, for the young man was the prototype of healthy English squire, and thought very well of himself without any assistance. He was somewhat short in stature, with a heavy build. His lank brown hair topped a red face in which there was nothing of refined good looks, for his nose was bulbous and his thick lips were wet and loose. Janet thought him coarse, not only in his physical appearance, but also in his manner and conversation. His large hands were as red as his face, and he had a grating laugh which he brayed loudly and often, generally in response to some witticism he himself had made.

It appeared that the Rustins were to stay at the Grange for some time, although why they were so honored was a mystery, for even Lord Lambert looked offended when Mr. Rustin insisted, one evening at the dinner table, in describing in great and gory detail a freak calf that had been born on his estate the previous year.

The family was not kept in the dark for long, however, and soon everyone knew that William Rustin had been chosen by the Lamberts as Elizabeth's future husband. When Lizzie rushed to her sister's room to tell her of this astonishing ultimatum, she was in tears. "How *can* Mama?" she wailed. "I will not marry such a horrible person; I hate him, and the thought of his touch makes me ill. I won't! I won't!"

But of course there was no gainsaying Lady Lambert's wishes, especially when her mind was made up, and it was only a short, if turbulent, two weeks later that Elizabeth's engagement was announced. There were to be no festivities attending this nuptial, no parties or balls, for Mr. Rustin had no desire for a long engagement and wished to be married before he returned to his home. Lord and Lady Lambert were agreeable, perhaps because they felt a mere reading of the banns sufficient for such an unworthy Lambert, or perhaps because the sooner she was safely bestowed in matrimony, the better.

It seemed a very short time later that Janet was once again standing beside a sister in church. Lizzie was very pale and spoke her promises in a soft, failing voice, while William Rustin leered at her in such an intimate way that Janet was shocked. She noticed the new curate was thin and elderly, and she wondered if Lizzie was comparing him—and her new husband as well—to Mr. Bates's tall, handsome blondness.

Janet had only a few moments of private conversation with her sister while she was helping her change to her travelling costume. The new Mr. and Mrs. Rustin were to leave immediately for Hillside, their estate in Sussex. There was to be no wedding journey, for Mr. Rustin did not believe in travel or the Season in town, considering such activities tomfoolery for light-heads. They were to be accompanied by his mother, of course, for she intended to remain in residence with the newlyweds indefinitely.

Janet squeezed her sister's hand in sympathy, and Lizzie said as her eyes filled with tears, "Be very careful, Janet. Do not offend Mama, for you have seen what will come of it, and you, like I, might very well be tied to such a man for the rest of your life. I do not know how I am to bear it, indeed I do not!"

Before she could break down completely, Lady Lambert arrived to see that the trunks were securely fastened and her daughter correctly attired for her journey. She did not kiss her good-bye, not even when Elizabeth went up to her, but only took her hand and said coldly, "I shall expect you to do just as you ought, Elizabeth. Perhaps as a married woman your character will improve, for now, at least, your curiosity about the opposite sex can be satisfied. Let us hear nothing to your discredit, for that way you can best please your parents. Come, your husband and his mother are anxious to be off."

Janet wished she had someone she might talk to about

Lizzie's wedding and her own future, but outside of Henry there was no one in the family to serve as confidant, and since he was a boy, she felt unable to initiate a conversation. She wondered in the days that followed about her own possible fate. Mama, it seemed, was not content to merely raise her children with an iron hand, she was determined to choose their mates for them as well. And since Janet and her mother seldom agreed, it did not augur well for her, and for some time thereafter she felt uneasy whenever she thought of it.

It was not much longer before Wilbert also brought shame to the Lambert name, and in doing so caused Janet to forget her fears, at least temporarily. It must have begun to seem to the elder Lamberts that some evil fairy was at work, for never before had they had to deal with children as wayward and unpraiseworthy as Elizabeth and Wilbert.

This time it was Lord Lambert who bore the brunt of his son's folly, although it was not long before everyone in the house knew of it. It seemed that Wilbert had graduated from the barmaid at the Leaping Hare to a young dairy maid employed by his father. Molly Beekins was a ripe, pretty girl with flashing eyes and an abundance of dark curls, and it was no wonder that Wilbert's eyes should light on such a tempting armful, especially since his mother had managed to send Meg, the barmaid, on her way, richer by several guineas.

It was most unfortunate that Lady Lambert felt called upon to take this step, for Wilbert's dalliance with a willing partner wise in the ways of the world was vastly different from his forcing the pretty Molly to succumb to him. When she became pregnant, she hurried to tell her father and that man lost no time cleaning himself up and dressing in his best for a visit to the Grange, where he demanded to see Lord Lambert.

Of course Janet did not hear in detail what happened between the two men, but shortly thereafter Miss Molly Beekins left Aylesford Grange, her pretty face distorted by weeping and her thickening waistline concealed by a long frieze cape as she sat on the hard bench in her father's cart, her bundles around her. As a result of his daughter's downfall, Mr. Beekins was able to purchase a small piece of land that spring that he had had his eye on for some time, and as for Molly, she eventually gave birth to a lusty son whom she insisted on calling Lambert Beekins, much to Lady Lambert's disgust.

As for Wilbert, he had already been sent up to town and the army. His father had purchased his commission for him and consigned him to his uncle the general's care, and both Lord and Lady Lambert prayed that all would be well and army life be the making of dear Wilbert. He came very little to the Grange after that, preferring on his infrequent leaves to visit the many friends he had made, or to travel about to race meetings and prizefights. No Lambert was aware of it, but Wilbert was supremely happy with his lot, and determined never to return to the Grange to live again. If he prayed at all, it was for the continued good health of Horace Junior! And instead of Meg or Molly, there were now any number of pretty little light-skirts to share his life; Ann and Joan and Clorinda and Harriet, none of whom ever caused him a moment's pang of conscience or concern. The army suited Wilbert to a T.

Throughout all this turmoil, Janet had been growing up and noticing everything, and she was very careful to remain in her parents' good graces. After watching her older brother and sister and their punishment, she was more than a little afraid of her parents, and most especially Lady Lambert. Whereas at thirteen she had been rebellious and outspoken, now she was quiet and subdued. On the rare occasions that the Lamberts had guests or were invited to others' homes, she remained so much in the background that Lady Lambert was sure that here at least was another daughter who would never bring shame to the family escutcheon. She even went so far as to wish Janet would be a little more sprightly in company, "for," as she told her husband, "she is so unusual-looking that I do not see how any gentleman would be attracted to her unless she begins to show some strategy—a few smiles and a willingness to enter into conversation!"

Lord Lambert agreed. When he had to talk to Janet he found it very heavy going. He had no idea that his daughter found it so as well.

She was the only Lambert daughter left at home now, of course, and to her lot fell all the work that Agatha and Lizzie had previously done, but she hid a sense of indignation that she had no free time for her music or her books and worked without complaint. When her seventeenth birthday came, she caught her mother looking at her speculatively, and she became even quieter, afraid that Lady Lambert might very well begin to cast about her for a suitable husband to spare the inconvenience and expense of a Season in town.

Although Janet did not feel at all ready to marry, she had sometimes daydreamed a little in the past about what being in love might be like. In her imaginings she was swept into a strong pair of arms, kissed and adored, and by some coincidence, her lover was the exact image of the Marquess of Hallowsfield, Anthony Northbridge!

She had never forgotten him, not really, although she was aware by this time that he had forgotten her, and most completely. It saddened her to think that her first friend had been so false, and she told herself that she would never trust anyone again, or open up her heart, because that was to leave yourself vulnerable to hurt. She might dream of a man who would love her, but she did not really believe that it would ever happen. The relationships that she had observed, from her mother and father's marriage, to Agatha and Percival, and poor Elizabeth and the revolting Mr. Rustin, were not such as to give her any idea of conjugal bliss. Marriage was a business arrangement, there was little of love in it, and so when she caught herself dreaming, she was quick to shake herself mentally. If she had not become so frightened of her mother and her power, she might still have had thoughts of rebellion, but now she told herself she was resigned, and only hoped that when the time came, the husband that was chosen for her would not be too repulsive, and if there was no possibility of love, that at least there might be respect and companionship.

Letters came with great regularity from Agatha, who was now in what she called "an interesting condition," which unfortunately would prevent her from visiting her family in the fall as she had planned to do. She did not sound at all like the old Aggie, Janet thought as she listened to her mother reading her letters; she had begun to sound just like Lady Lambert, stiff and proud and serious. Every letter was full of "Percival says," "Percival has decided," and "Lord Farquhar requires," so it appeared she was happy with her lot. From Elizabeth, communication was much more irregular. Janet had had one letter written shortly after her wedding, and although she had answered it promptly, Lizzie did not write again. There had been nothing in this letter that could not be read aloud to the family, but Janet knew that Lizzie was miserably unhappy. She and her husband were not asked to visit, nor did she ask anyone from the Grange to come to her, so Janet was unable to see for herself what state her sister was in.

In July, Lady Lambert decided that since her eldest daughter could not come to them, she would go to the Farquhars herself to be sure that dear Agatha was in good health. Janet was to go with her, and she looked forward to the trip, since she had never travelled farther from the Grange than the twenty miles to the nearest large market town. There had been no mention of a Season in town for her that spring; perhaps, she thought as she began to get her clothes ready for the visit, her mother had decided to wait until she was a year older. After all, she was only just turned seventeen, and with Agatha about to make Lady Lambert a grandmother, perhaps that lady had forgotten her third daughter for a while. Janet could only hope that such a happy state of affairs would continue indefinitely.

❧ 5 ❧

But alas, it was not to be. Far from forgetting Janet, Lady Lambert had written a long letter to her eldest daughter, and the very interesting reply she had to this epistle was the reason Janet was to accompany her on her visit.

In due course, one fine September morning Janet and Lady Lambert arrived at Lord Farquhar's estate and principal seat, Rundell Court at Melton Mowbray. After the initial welcome, Janet was able to look around and stare. Certainly her sister lived in a great state, for the Court was a huge building of several stories and many wings, and it was surrounded by acres of lawn, a large lake, and several pretty streams. Made of rosy brick that glowed in the sunlight, the Court was fronted by terraces and formal gardens, as well as an extensive maze of boxwood fashioned into fantastic animal shapes, and all in all it was a most impressive and noble home.

Lord Farquhar, who still stuttered badly, was delighted to show Janet around while her mother was deep in conversation with her daughter, Lady Farquhar. This was a new Agatha indeed, for she had become very proud and formal, and with the weight she had gained since her marriage, she was a force to be reckoned with. Janet noticed to her surprise, in the days that followed, that Lady Lambert deferred to her daughter and treated her with the utmost respect. It seemed that being very rich had its advantages after all, and not just the joy of being so wealthy you could spend any amount of money you wished, at any time. But if Janet had hoped to have some good talks with her sister, and confide some of the things that had been troubling her, she soon realized that this would be impossible, for the new Agatha was sure to tell her to obey her mama, do just as she ought, and to put all such silly megrims from her mind. Never mind Lizzie, she had got just what she deserved, and it was a very lucky thing that any suitable man had been found to marry her at all after her behaviour. As for Wilbert, she was sure to agree with Lady Lambert that he would eventually come about and make the family proud of him, but for now it was clearly her sister's duty to be led by that excellent woman her mother, and behave as a Lambert should.

Actually, Agatha agreed with her mother that Janet, at seventeen, had turned out much better than anyone had expected when she was a child. True, she still had that disconcerting manner of staring at her family with her large dark blue eyes intent and unsmiling, but she had completely stopped annoying Lady Lambert by answering back or trying to interject her own ideas and wishes, and although she was still of an independent nature, both Lady Lambert and her eldest daughter considered that compared to the bad behaviour of Elizabeth and Wilbert, Janet was become most meek and amenable, with all expressions of rebellion gone from her nature.

Lady Lambert was sure she had brought this strange and willful daughter under her thumb at last, but if she had not been such a self-satisfied woman, so sure of her power, she might have wondered a little at her success. You may tame a tiger after all, but any trainer will tell you it is most unwise to turn your back on him, for he may revert to his wild state at any moment. Miss Janet Rose Lambert was not a tiger, of course, but she was not nearly the domesticated tabby her mother believed her to be.

Because of Agatha's "interesting condition," life at the Court was placid and regimented. There were no large parties, no late nights, no strenuous dancing, in spite of the fact that there were several months to go before confinement. Janet was disappointed, even though a few small dinner parties were planned, and some friends of the Farquhars were shortly to visit for a couple of weeks. At that time, Percival confided to his sister-in-law, things would p-p-pick up a bit, and she would see how lively they would all become. Janet smiled and nodded, but she knew that Lord and Lady Farquhar's idea of liveliness would not be hers, for their entertaining was sure to be distressingly Lambert-like.

But still she was not unhappy. She enjoyed the gardens and the lake, and the small folly that was placed on its shores, and many a warm afternoon she would wander down there with a book, for although Lord Farquhar had inherited a most impressive library from his father, he had no use for it himself, and insisted she make free of it. There was also a beautiful music room, far enough away from the bedrooms and the main salons and drawing rooms so that Janet could play as much as she liked, without disturbing her mother or her sister. Lady Lambert left her very much to her own devices, for she was busy discussing births, pregnancies, labor, and nurseries with her married daughter, and taking a great delight in being shown all the housekeeping arrangements of the Court, as well as such changes and additions Agatha had made since her last visit.

Agatha had given up riding, so Janet was not forced to endure that pastime. "I consider it much too dangerous at this time," Agatha announced one evening when they were dining *en famille*. "It is my duty to consider *the heir*. No, no, my dear Lord Farquhar," she said as that gentleman opened his mouth to speak, "there is no need to repine! I do not regret it for I am sure I know that my duty to *the heir* comes first!"

Lady Lambert smiled and nodded at such noble sentiments, Lord Farquhar subsided without saying what he had in his mind, and Janet, accepting a helping of queen's pudding, wondered wickedly what horrible breast beatings and cries of disbelief would occur if *the heir* turned out to

72

be a little Agatha instead of a miniature Percival. Whichever sex, she sincerely hoped it would not inherit its papa's stammer and beak of a nose, nor its mama's puffed-up conceit!

The day came that Lord Faquhar's guests were expected. Both Agatha and Lady Lambert had been busy making sure that all was ready to receive them, and although Janet offered to help, she was denied. "That is most kind of you, Janet," her sister said seriously, "but Mama and I have everything in train, and with some fifty servants—or is it now fifty-two?—in the Court alone, not to mention those about the stables, the farms, and the gardens and grounds, I am sure we can dispense with your assistance. Do go and amuse yourself—but stay! Perhaps you might talk to Lord Farquhar? I am too busy to attend to him right now."

Obediently Janet went to the main hall, but the butler, Hemmings, told her that m'lord had gone out to the stables. She did not feel it necessary to seek him out there, and feeling she had done her duty after all, repaired to the music room. It was unfortunate that Lord Farquhar's library had not included any scores, nor were there any here to learn, but she had for so long played all the études and concerti she knew, that it was no hardship to sit down and play from memory. If I were Agatha, she thought as she began her scales, I should order every piece of music ever written! That is *my* idea of luxury.

As she often did, she became lost in her music, and it was not until the sun shone in through the windows that she was recalled to the time. It must be very late, she thought as she started up, for the sun is so low in the sky! She hurried as fast as she could to her room, where she found the maid her sister had assigned to her in a state of distress, for the second dressing bell had long since sounded and she had no idea where Miss was! Janet dressed quickly, and since she had no time for fuss, for it would not do to be late the first evening that the guests arrived, she only bade the maid to brush her long black hair smooth and fasten it into a coil low on her neck. She was wearing a pretty, modest gown of deep blue muslin, and since she had with her a knot of ribbons the exact same shade, she fastened them above her chignon before she ran down the stairs. She only slowed her steps at the bottom of the flight when she saw Hemmings raising an eyebrow and one of the young footmen hiding a grin.

Hemmings moved majestically to open the drawing-room doors for her, and as she went in, she saw she was the last to arrive. She was embarrassed, for everyone turned to stare at her, but when she saw the identical haughty frowns of her sister and her mother, seated together on a velvet sofa, she could not help but smile, bringing into view the deep dimple in her cheek. Lord Farquhar came forward, and taking her hand, introduced her to his guests. There was a Colonel Baker and his wife, a Lord Wharton, a Mr. and Mrs. Reginald Utley, and a Lord and Lady Sanders. Janet smiled and curtsied and said she was pleased, and all the while her mind was summing up the new arrivals.

The colonel, who had a wooden leg and a fierce white mustache, was a man of few words, and his pale little wife, who was dressed in dowdy brown, a woman of none. She did, however, nod slightly. Lord Wharton was a young man with a pleasant smile and an open, good-looking face who had been to school with his host, and Janet liked him immediately. Mr. and Mrs. Utley might have been a middle-aged brother and sister. They were both very tall and robust, with rosy complexions, and Janet recognized the type. Country people, and probably bruising riders to hounds. Even though they were both correctly attired in evening dress, it was not difficult to see that they would be more comfortable in their habits, swinging crops and trailing a large pack of hounds. "How-de-do?" asked Mr. Utley. "Tally-ho!" his wife added, somewhat irrelevantly.

The last couple was the most unusual. Introduced as Lord Sanders, Viscount Broughten, the gentleman was a tall man in his early thirties, with straight reddish hair and the high complexion that often accompanies this type of coloring. Janet wondered, even as she smiled and curtsied

74

to him, why you could not call him a good-looking man. His features were regular, his eyes a light clear blue framed with sandy lashes that seemed almost nonexistent, and there was nothing particularly disturbing about his face, but somehow he seemed bland and featureless, with the kind of face one has difficulty in calling to mind when its owner is absent. Lady Sanders was gray-haired and stout and she raised a pince-nez so she might inspect Janet with piercing eyes as blue as her son's. After she had nodded distantly, she turned to her host and began to tell him about their journey.

"I do not know why it is, Percival," she exclaimed in a loud and plummy voice, "that whenever we come to Rundell Court, it always commences to rain. And there, in a thunderstorm of terrible proportions, was Ernest, riding his hunter alongside the carriage instead of being dry inside with me. We must sincerely hope that he has not taken a chill; time out of mind I have told him that that is why we employ grooms, for no one cares if they become ill. Ernest!" And here she turned to her son, who was standing beside her chair and staring at Janet. "You must tell me at once if you begin to feel indisposed. I shall never forgive myself, no, never, for not insisting that you ride in the carriage this morning."

"Of course, Mother," Lord Sanders replied in a curiously light tenor voice. "But it is only a few miles to the Court and the rain did not last for more than a few moments. You may be calm."

"It is so important that Ernest take care of himself!" his fond mother now informed the company, ignoring his last remark. "Now that my poor husband has passed away, Ernest, as his only son, is the heir to Willows! Indeed, he came into his title when he was only nineteen, but I have always taken the greatest care of him."

She smiled triumphantly at the others, but no one had anything to add in response. Janet wondered if Willows was as magnificent as Rundell Court as she excused herself and moved to her mother's side in response to her beckoning hand.

Several times during the long and formal dinner, Janet,

who had been placed between Lord Wharton and Mr. Utley, looked up to see Lord Sanders studying her face. She felt it very rude of him, for not only was he making her uncomfortable, he was ignoring his hostess, at whose right hand he sat, as well as those guests who had been placed near him. She had been chatting with Lord Wharton about the London theatre, and enjoying the conversation, but now she turned away to Mr. Utley and asked him about his estate, her color slightly heightened. She was determined that she would not look Lord Sanders' way again, no, not even if Mr. Utley continued to bore her by prosing on and on about his stables.

Janet would have been astounded if she had known that the heir to Willows had fallen violently in love with her. After living three and thirty years without feeling any emotion stronger than a slight liking toward those of the fair sex, he had succumbed to Miss Janet Rose Lambert in a matter of minutes. He had always known it was his duty to marry and set up his nursery some day, but now he was glad that the few times he had seriously considered it, his mother had dissuaded him from his choice. Miss Franklin was too tall and had a silly simper, she pointed out; Lady Peck was willful, and there was something about her mouth that showed a shrewish nature; and it was plain to see that Miss Veronica Botley was going to be obese before she was thirty, besides having such a shrill unpleasant voice. So far from in love with all these young ladies had Lord Sanders been that he had accepted his mother's appraisals without question and had withdrawn his attentions, but now he could hardly wait to tell her of his excellent choice of a wife. Thank heavens he had waited. How pleased Lady Sanders would be.

From the moment that Janet had entered the drawing room, he had been struck by her. Those beautiful dark blue eyes, that graceful slim figure in its modest gown, and her soft musical voice, so low and refreshing. He thought her generous mouth and that intriguing dimple in her cheek when she smiled entrancing, and he admired her midnight-black hair, as smooth as a crow's wing, dressed so unusually in a simple style without any of the fussy curls and puffs the other ladies affected. He wished he might see her take it down and let him run his fingers through its silken length.

If you had told Lord Sanders there was such a thing as love at first sight, he would have stared at you in disbelief, before this evening. Romantic longings were for the lower orders, not for a man in his station of life. And so he had firmly believed before Janet made her entrance.

But here he was, unable to take his eyes from the young lady, although when Janet turned away, a blush on that delicate cheek, he recalled himself. He would seek her out after dinner, but for now he would converse with her sister and find out all about her life. He was aware that his friend Lord Farquhar had married a girl of excellent breeding and demeanour, and although Miss Janet Lambert did not look at all like her sister, she was sure to be of just the same excellent type. Since Lady Sanders had many times pointed out Agatha's fine qualities and bemoaned the fact that there was no woman to compare with her for her son, he knew she would be astounded at his good fortune. He was not acute enough to have noticed that the women Lady Sanders generally found admirable were all most permanently married already.

At last the ladies withdrew and left the gentlemen to their port, and Janet took leave of her dinner partners—from Mr. Utley pleasantly and with relief, and from Lord Wharton with smiling reluctance. He was a nice young man, she thought as she entered the drawing room. Agatha beckoned to her and led her over to where Mrs. Baker was seated, somewhat forlornly alone, and Janet realized that it was to be her duty to converse with the lady. This she did not have to do for very long, however: very shortly silence fell as all the ladies became aware that two of their number were deep in a match of wits, a game Janet had often called "Can You Best This?"

Lady Lambert opened fire with a description of Aylesford Grange, the spaciousness of its hall, its fertile lands and clear streams, and Lady Sanders replied that Willows was a most superior seat, as large as Rundell Court and with considerably more land. Round one to

Lady Sanders. Then Lady Sanders spoke of her son, and Lady Lambert was not slow to bring to her attention all *six* of her children, including *three* sons, and investing all of them with such qualities that Janet could only stare. Horace Junior was extolled as the very epitome of handsome English manhood and his father's right-hand man; Wilbert was a stalwart and upright soldier of the crown; Elizabeth had made an excellent marriage—perhaps Lady Sanders was acquainted with the Rustins of Sussex? On hearing that she had not had that pleasure, Lady Lambert felt free to add several hundred acres to Mr. Rustin's holdings and several members of the peerage to his family tree. Agatha of course was known to the lady, so her mother said that she would not put her daughter to the blush by complimenting her, for that was surely unnecessary when Lady Sanders could see her excellence with her own eyes. And as for Janet—and here everyone's eyes were turned to this young lady as she lowered her eyes in seeming modesty, although it was only that she was afraid the others might see the incredulous disbelief there— Janet, besides being trained in every detail of running a household of the *largest* kind, was also notable for her needlepoint, and a musician of great talent besides. She concluded by remarking that her youngest, Henry, was a dear little boy who had never caused his parents a moment's qualm. Lady Sanders retired from the lists vanquished, and Janet had the insane desire to applaud. She found the lady absurd, even more offensive than her mother with her haughty manners, and that was going some.

By the time the gentlemen returned to the drawing room, the battle lines had been drawn up. On Lady Lambert's side were her two daughters, and on Lady Sanders' were ranged her old acquaintances Mrs. Baker and Mrs. Utley. Of course, none of this was apparent as the men entered and came to converse with the ladies. Lord Sanders hastened to Janet's side, and she was unable to stifle a feeling of unease as he smiled at her and asked permission to share the sofa, for Mrs. Baker had bustled over to join his mother shortly before.

"You must not think me bold, Miss Lambert, when I tell you I have seldom been so taken with any young lady on such a short acquaintance!" he began in a heavy, playful way that reminded Janet forcibly of her eldest brother's pleasantries.

"M'lord?" she inquired, her large blue eyes going swiftly to his face, even as she folded her hands composedly in her lap.

"You must have noticed how I have been staring at you all evening!" Lord Sanders explained. "I do apologize if I have offended you!"

"Not at all, m'lord!" Janet said, looking about for someone—anyone—to save her from this unusual *tête-à-tête*.

"I daresay I have shocked you!" he continued, bending closer to her. "Well, well, of course it would be so with a protected young girl of your gentility. I shall hold myself in check, my dear Miss Lambert, until we have had a chance to become better acquaintances. Yes, Wharton?"

Janet looked up in gratitude to see Lord Wharton standing before them, and she smiled warmly at him. She had no idea what to make of Lord Sanders' expressions of interest in her, and could only think he had had too much port in the short time that was all her sister Agatha allowed Lord Farquhar to entertain his gentlemen guests alone. Agatha had no intention of having them staggering into her drawing room after a drunken hour or so, as was common in other households.

But Janet was confused. That the son of the same Lady Sanders who had just been expounding his virtues, his nobility, his marvelous sense of rightness, and his nicety of taste, should speak to her in such a way was most certainly astounding. She was still wondering whether she could possibly have misinterpreted his remarks when Lord Wharton began to speak again of the London theatre. This young man had quickly assessed the company and had decided that attendance on Miss Lambert was the only thing that would make his stay bearable, and he was not about to be bilked of his prize by that damned Sanders. The two men stared at each other, and then

Lord Sanders shrugged. What did it matter if his bride-to-be spoke for a while with young Wharton? He had a title, it was true, but his estates were in considerable disarray, he had not a tenth of Lord Sanders' wealth, and his family was nowhere near as old or noble. Besides, Lord Sanders could not conceive of anyone refusing his suit; he had listened to his mother extolling his virtues for too many years to have any doubt that he was the catch of the century. He was sure Miss Lambert must agree, but for now he was content to bow and take his leave of her, much to his mother's relief. To see her son speaking so confidingly to *that woman's* daughter had given her a nasty palpitation.

There were two other interested observers to Lord Sanders' direct path to Janet's side: Lady Lambert, who widened her eyes in shock; and Agatha, who was not so old and staid that she could resist looking at her mother in conjecture, eyebrows raised. Janet had been brought to Rundell Court for the express purpose of arranging a match with Lord Wharton, Lady Lambert feeling that he was the best she could hope for for such an unusual, unattractive daughter, and Agatha had promised to do everything in her power to bring this alliance to fruition. But there was Lord Sanders at her side, smiling and chatting and bending toward her so solicitously! Lady Lambert looked at her third daughter with new eyes. What a coup if she could pull this off. She was very quiet for the remainder of the evening, not even responding to some of the very provocative statements made by her new rival, for she was thinking deeply about what she might do to bring such a desirable *parti* into the Lambert fold.

Janet was surprised the next morning when her mother greeted her in the breakfast room with a kiss and a fond exclamation. "Dear girl!" she said softly, and Janet was sure it was only for Lady Sanders' benefit that she was so honored, for her mama was not given to embraces or kind salutations. She looked at her askance, and under cover of the table Lady Lambert pinched her hand. "Did you rest well, my dear?" she asked. "I recommend the sardines, or perhaps the kippers. I expressly desired Agatha to serve them, for I know how fond of them you are. And here is Lady Sanders to share our repast. Could anything be more pleasant?"

"No, Mama," Janet said, obediently taking a kipper, although she would have preferred the coddled eggs and one of the delicious pastries the chef had made early that morning. "A very good day to you, Lady Sanders," she added as she took her seat, and watched her mama pour her out a cup of coffee, in a most solicitous way.

Stranger and stranger, she thought, as Lady Sanders nodded distantly and sniffed.

"And what are you plans for the day, dear?" her mother persisted. "I believe that Percival—Lord Farquhar, of course," she added with a kind sideways glance at Lady Sanders, who was not blessed with such a desirable son-in-law. "I believe that Percival is planning a gala picnic for us by the home wood later today. You will of course wish to attend—that is, if you can spare the time from helping your sister or practicing your music."

Janet choked a little on a mouthful of kippers. *This*—this was her mama? Wonder of wonders! When she was able to speak, she said, "I shall be delighted to attend the picnic, mama. I do not think that Agatha has any commissions for me this morning that one of her many servants cannot undertake." Janet lowered her eyes when she saw her mother frown.

"Be sure to wear your primrose gown, my dear," that lady said next. "I declare, Lady Sanders, that Janet is ravishing in primrose, with her dark hair. But of course, you will see for yourself."

Lady Sanders rose from the breakfast table. "I do not believe I shall attend the picnic, thank you so much, Lady Lambert," she said. "I am feeling a little low after our journey yesterday, and I think I can safely say that dear Ernest will not be present either, not when he learns of his mother's indisposition."

"How very unfortunate," Lady Lambert murmured as Lady Sanders swept to the door, but to her daughter she did not sound at all distressed. Lady Lambert might have spent a few minutes explaining her most unusual behaviour to her daughter if just then Mr. and Mrs. Utley had not come in, dressed for riding, and bringing a strong odor of the stables with them.

" 'Mornin', ladies!" Mr. Utley said, making a beeline for the buffet. "Good-oh! Kippers!"

Mrs. Utley sank into her chair and beamed at the Lamberts. "Glorious mornin' for a ride! Reggie and I have been over most of the estate already. Surprised to see you still within doors, Miss Janet."

She accepted the heavily laden plate her husband brought her and tucked into it with a will, so Janet was not required to answer.

Later that morning, Janet donned the primrose gown, as requested, and was just about to go downstairs to join the other guests assembling in the front hall for the picnic, when her sister came in with a very fetching wide-brimmed straw hat decorated with daisies and moss-green velvet ribbons. It all but proclaimed the smartest London shop. Agatha also carried a soft gossamer shawl of white cashmere which Janet knew she had only recently acquired. It was so unlike Agatha to be generous with her possessions that Janet could only stare as her sister pressed her to try on the hat. "I am sure it will be ravishing with that gown, Janet," she said, and then could not restrain a tiny sigh. "I was wearing it the day that Percival discovered I was *the one!*"

"But, Aggie, perhaps I should not . . . what if he recognizes it? And the shawl too! Did you not tell me that it was a gift from your husband?"

Agatha colored a little but answered her in an even tone. "Yes, that is true, but he will not remember it. Gentlemen, dear sister, are very unobservant when it comes to what ladies wear. Besides, it will finish off your toilette to perfection. There!" she exclaimed as she tied the ribbons in a fetching bow under Janet's chin. "I have never seen you in such looks, Janet."

Janet admired the effect in the pier glass, but she was not to be deterred from asking her sister a few questions. "What is going on, Aggie? First there was Mama this morning at breakfast, all smiles and kisses, and calling me 'dear' every other thing, which you know very well she has never done in her life, and now you appear bearing your very best hat and a most expensive shawl, and insisting that I wear them. I do not understand."

"Ungrateful wretch!" her sister said, turning away to adjust an errant curl in the glass so Janet could not see her face. "Why should I not wish to see you well dressed? Your appearance reflects on me, you know, and we both know that Mama has never been exactly generous with our outfits; in fact, I intend to lend you my pearls this evening, to dress up your white evening gown. But come, no more questions or we will be late for the picnic. Percival has had the pony carts brought around, and there will be strawberries, and chicken in biscuits, and the most delicious little frosted cakes. Do come at once."

She went quickly to the door, and Janet was forced to follow her, still very much in the dark as to why she had been so honoured by her family.

With the exception of Lady Sanders, all the guests were already assembled in the hall as the two sisters came down the stairs. That lady had been unable to convince Ernest that he should bear her company, for, for the first time, he was not to be deterred from his plan to spend as much time with Miss Lambert as possible. He had come to his mother's room that morning with the express wish of telling her his good news, but when he found she was not feeling well, he decided he would wait, and when his mother begged for his attendance, saying how distraught and lonely she would be without his company, he only replied, "You shall be in much better hands with your maid, Mother, than with me, if you are not feeling up to snuff. I shall of course come and see how you are when I return from the picnic; for now, why don't you try to rest? I am sure you will feel more the thing shortly."

He had kissed her cheek before he left, but Lady Sanders was not mollified by this, and even now, instead of taking his advice and resting, she was hiding behind the curtains at her window and watching the guests come down the shallow steps of the terrace and climb into the pony carts. The Utleys had elected to ride, of course, but all the others were being helped to their places by some of the footmen. She was distressed to see that dear Ernest had been seated next to Miss Lambert, while across from them the Farquhars were taking their places.

It was no lucky chance that Lord Sanders was so situated, for he had been very adroit when Janet first appeared. He was stunned afresh with her unusual beauty in the primrose gown and that glorious hat, and had hastened to her side before Lord Wharton could end a conversation with the colonel that he had been so foolish as to get involved in. Carefully helping Janet down the steps, he made sure he was seated next to her in the cart, talking gaily all the while to Lord and Lady Farquhar.

The little cavalcade was soon under way. Somewhat ahead went a large wagon with the food, the wine, some folding chairs and rugs, several footmen and maids to wait on them, and whatever else the guests might require in the short time they would be away from the Court, and then followed the two pony carts bearing the guests, and the Utleys on horseback.

Lady Sanders sniffed and went back to her bed. As long as she was left here alone, she might as well recoup her strength, she thought as she climbed into bed. She had a strong premonition that there was to be a major battle before long, for which it would be most important to be in the very best condition.

Janet chatted lightly with her sister and brother-in-law, and tried to ignore the way Lord Sanders kept looking at her. She was glad now that she had the hat on, for the wide brim made it possible for her to hide her face every so often. It was a lovely day, still so warm even in September as to make it seem almost summery. There were only a few puffy clouds in the sky, and the light breeze was delicately scented with all the flowers blooming in the gardens. Janet wished she did not feel such a sense of unease, even as she wondered why this should be so.

When they reached the spot that Lord Farquhar had chosen, they found the servants there to help them down, and already several chairs and cushions had been placed around the little clearing in the woods. A small stream meandered along one side, and it was so delightfully sylvan, with the sun peeking through the trees overhead, that Janet was charmed.

"What a perfect place, Percival!" she could not help exclaiming. "And what a lovely idea. I am so glad it did not come on to rain."

"As if it would dare, when *you* were desirous of a picnic, Miss Lambert!" Lord Sanders exclaimed as he held out his arm. "Shall we stroll awhile? I am sure you will wish to see more of the wood."

Janet glanced at her sister, and saw her nod and smile. "Yes, do, my dear. It will be some time before we are ready to serve, and it is such a pleasant day for a walk. I am sorry I cannot join you, but I do not feel it would be wise. If I should miss my step . . ."

Janet was forced to take Lord Sanders' arm while she heard Lord Farquhar ask her sister in some distress if she felt quite the thing, did she think she had better sit down, did she wish a cushion for her back, and numerous other questions that Agatha parried by saying that she only felt a little tired and wished to rest. Unspoken, but palpably in the air, was her concern for *the heir*.

Lord Sanders tucked Janet's hand through the crook in his arm and patted it lightly with his other hand as he helped her over a fallen tree trunk. There was a narrow path heading deeper into the woods, and it necessitated his walking much closer to her than was comfortable, for Janet at least.

As they went out of sight of the others around a bend in the path, she said anxiously, "I hope we shall not become lost, m'lord. I have not been in this part of the woods before."

"I shall take the greatest care of you, Miss Lambert. The very greatest care," Lord Sanders said in such a serious and protective tone of voice that Janet felt the urge to giggle. Lord Sanders seemed prepared to battle on her behalf, whatever ferocious creatures the Farquhars' woods might harbour, and since the only animals that she had seen were a chipmunk and a squirrel who chittered noisily at them for making him climb a tree trunk, she did not think this fervor at all necessary. They strolled in silence for a while, Janet wondering what on earth she was supposed to say to this strange man, and Lord Sanders admiring the sunlight and shade that dappled her cheeks, and telling himself what a restful girl she was, not constantly chattering or laughing as other, less wonderful young ladies were wont to do.

At last he woke from his reverie, and reminded that he had told her he wished to know her better, began to ask her about her home. Janet was glad to tell him about the Grange and all her brothers and sisters.

"How I envy you!" Lord Sanders said. "It was very lonely being an only child, in spite of all my mother's tender and loving care. I wish I might have had such companions when I was growing up."

Janet nodded, although remembering how her brothers and sisters had teased her and made fun of her, she could not easily see them as advantages.

"And do you believe in large families, Miss Lambert?" Lord Sanders asked next, pressing her hand again more intimately.

"I . . . I had not thought. I mean, I suppose so, but that is such a long way away," Janet stammered, feeling a blush on her cheeks and wishing she did not sound like such an idiot. Or was it that Lord Sanders brought out the idiot in her? She did not know, but she wished he would stop!

He laughed a little at her confusion. "I wish you might see Willows, Miss Lambert," he said, kindly changing the subject after they had gone a few more steps. "I pride myself that it is the most beautiful spot in England, and I am sure you will agree. Perhaps we might ride over some morning, and have a nuncheon, and then I can show you the grounds and the house. Well, not *all* the house, of course, for that would take too long. I cannot tell you how happy I would be to see you at Willows."

Janet thanked him for the invitation but said firmly, "It is so kind of you, m'lord, but I cannot accept. My sister is unable to ride at the present time, and I do not think my mother would wish me to go without her."

There, she thought, that takes care of that. But then she peeped up at him from under her hat brim and was surprised to see him smiling and nodding at her refusal. "Of course! We shall make up a party. May I say, Miss Lambert, that the delicacy of your mind, your modesty, your girlish charms, and the integrity of your character are such that they can only be applauded. I kneel at your feet in admiration."

Janet looked startled, as if he might do just that, but Lord Sanders had no intention of ruining his buff kersey-mere pantaloons, and had been speaking figuratively. Kneel he would, and as soon as he could contrive it, but only on one of Lady Farquhar's well-brushed rugs.

"Tell me about Willows," she said desperately. "Your mother was speaking of it last evening, and it sounds most impressive."

For the remainder of the walk, her companion spoke of his estate, and even after Janet suggested that perhaps they should turn back and rejoin the others, he continued. Of course, there was a great deal to Willows; it was not a subject to be tossed off in a few careless sentences, and Janet was delighted she had found such an absorbing top-ic of conversation. She did not realize that Lord Sanders thought she was inquiring with an eye to her future home, for if she had, she would not have been able to continue so nonchalantly, interjecting a leading question every now and then, and relaxing for the first time since they had been alone together.

When they reached the clearing again, it was to find the other guests being served by the footmen, and Janet hur-ried to her sister's side, where a chair had been placed for her. One of the footmen brought her a plate. Janet saw Lord Wharton glaring and saying something to Lord Sanders, but in the general conversation she was unable to hear what it was.

"Did you have a pleasant walk, Janet?" her sister asked, and then whispered, "What did Lord Sanders talk about?"

"Mostly about Willows," Janet said, taking a bite of her biscuit, for she was hungry. She missed the satisfied little nod her sister gave as she continued, "But, Aggie, is he all right? I mean, he is not a little lacking, is he? I cannot understand him in the least, and I find him the strangest man."

"A little lacking? *Lord Sanders*?" her sister asked, putting her cucumber sandwich back on her plate in disbelief. "Never say so, Janet. Of course he is all right, and not in the least strange."

Janet accepted a glass of champagne from the footman, and her sister was so distraught that she did not even notice this unprecedented move. Then Janet whispered, "I must talk to you, Aggie. There is something going on that I do not in the least understand."

"But not here," her sister hissed, rising and brushing off her skirts. "I must see to my guests. But, oh, my dear, how wonderful if you can . . . Why, Mama will be so pleased."

Janet watched her as she moved away to chat lightly to this one and that one of her guests, but then Lord Wharton came to take the chair she had vacated, and in a few moments she forgot the strangeness of both her sister and Lord Sanders, for he began to tell her of some concerts he had attended, and to ask her if she enjoyed music. Her face became more animated as she replied, and across the clearing, Lord Sanders, who was sitting with the Bakers, smiled to himself. She was perfect! He could sit here all day and admire her—her lilting laugh, her delicate smile, those expressive eyes. He felt he had made great strides on their walk and was perfectly agreeable to letting Lord Wharton sit with her, for surely he had made himself very clear, and this good humour and animation were due, no doubt, to her joy that she had been chosen to be the wife of such an exalted and superior person.

❧ 6 ❧

True to her promise, Agatha appeared with her pearl set as Janet was dressing for dinner, and she brought her own London maid with her as well. There was no opportunity for Janet to question her with that severe and superior lady there, bustling around, dismissing the young maid who had been assigned to her, and taking complete charge of the proceedings. The white gown was donned and adjusted, and the silver sandals put on, a perfect match for the ribbon that was threaded through the lace trim of the gown's neckline. Then Miss Lambert was bade to sit at the dressing table so Miss Simpton could do up her hair.

Janet looked thoughtfully at her sister in the mirror as the maid was brushing, but Agatha, catching her questioning look, only shook her head and turned away. Janet had to admit her hair had never looked so well. Instead of just pulling it back tightly, Miss Simpton brushed it up on the back of her head in soft waves, and the chignon she finished with was much larger and softer than usual. Agatha had two pearl-and-silver combs to set on each side, and when the necklace, brooch, and bracelets were added, Janet was sure she was dressed as grandly as any London lady. Fleetingly, as she appraised herself in the mirror, Janet wondered if Northbridge would recognize in the elegant figure reflected there the shy young girl with hair in plaits whom he had befriended. Then she was ordered to rise and turn slowly, and the thought vanished as she wondered why the dresser frowned. "If I may be so bold as to say so, m'lady," Miss Simpton said, ignoring Janet as completely as if she had been a bisque doll, "I would suggest removing the brooch and all but one bracelet. It is too much for *une jeune fille*, if you take my meaning, m'lady."

Agatha nodded. "Quite right, Simpton. As it is now, there is not that air of purity and innocence, or becoming modesty." She bustled over to her sister and unpinned the brooch, and Janet reluctantly removed the bracelets she indicated, leaving only one slender band. She was more than a little annoyed at not even being asked her opinion in the matter, and said a little tartly, "Lizzie always wore pretty jewelry. Why should not I?"

"And we all know what became of her, do we not?" Agatha reminded her in a severe voice. "It is just what you might expect of Lizzie, so forward and bold. Simpton, put the jewels away at once. And now I must go down so I will be ready to receive my guests. Janet, you are to remain here until the second bell."

Before Janet had a chance to ask why she must remain abovestairs when she was all ready to join the others, Agatha went to the door, which a curtsying Simpton held open for her. After she had gone, the dresser came back to the table and put one or two more hairpins in Janet's chignon, and then she said with a knowing smile, "It will not be much longer, miss, before you can wear as many jewels as you care to!"

Janet stared at her, perplexed. As the dresser continued to fuss with her hair, she added, "Indeed, with your fair complexion, you should never wear a white gown without some flashing stones. Pearls are all very well for a young girl, but you will look much more attractive in diamonds or sapphires to match your eyes."

Simpton stepped back to admire her work, and Janet said, "Thank you. It is very kind of you to help me. As for diamonds, or even sapphires, I shall never see the day. My family is not given to ostentatious display."

Simpton curtsied and smiled coyly. "Oh, miss," she said, "but when you become 'your ladyship,' the bride of a wealthy man, why, then you shall have all manner of jewels. And instead of white muslin, I suggest a scarlet silk or a deep blue satin. Stunning!"

Janet would have demanded to know what on earth she was talking about, but the maid went just then to answer an imperious knock on the door, and to admit Lady Lambert, regal in purple. Her daughter rose hastily and curtsied. Her mama bade her turn, and when she had made another slow circle, she looked at her and was astonished to see mama smiling. No, almost beaming!

"Dear girl!" Lady Lambert said fondly. "The picnic has brought some most becoming color to your face, I am glad to see. Why, you are in exceptional looks this evening, Janet. I am glad I thought to come to escort you to the drawing room."

"Thank you, Mama," Janet stammered.

Then Lady Lambert added, "Agatha wishes you to play for her guests this evening, after dinner. I trust you remembered to bring your music from the Grange?"

"That is not necessary, Mama," she replied, her mind whirling over this unexpected command performance. "I can play from memory; indeed, I have been doing so for many years."

"How impressive that will be!" Lady Lambert agreed cordially. "As long as you do not make any errors, for that would be fatal."

Janet agreed that she would do her best and went meekly down the stairs in her mother's wake, while that lady instructed her over her shoulder, " 'Good, better, best! Never let it rest! Till the good is better, and the better best!' Of course, as a Lambert, you will always strive for the 'best'!"

The other guests were all assembled, and Lady Lambert had the satisfaction of making a grand entrance with her daughter. She noticed both Lord Wharton and Lord Sanders rising hastily to their feet as Janet entered, her hand tucked into her mother's arm. Lord Sanders hurried forward, leaving his mother alone, in mid-sentence. A frown came to her face at this unprecedented rudeness.

"My dear Lady Lambert! Miss Lambert!" he said, bowing slowly. Both ladies curtsied, and then Lady Lambert excused herself, saying there was something she must ask her daughter, Lady Farquhar, about immediately. Lord Sanders led Janet to a sofa near his mother and seated her.

"You have met Miss Lambert, Mother, of course," he said, taking the seat next to Janet and beaming. Lady Sanders sniffed. There was a moment of silence.

"I do hope you are feeling better, Lady Sanders?" Janet remembered to ask, when it appeared that the lady was not about to enter into conversation with her.

Lady Sanders inclined her head, and left it to her son to say, "Yes, the rest did her much good, and she said that on no account would she think of missing dinner, which is fortunate, for I understand we are to have a special treat this evening, are we not, Miss Lambert?"

Janet looked at him questioningly.

"I understand from Lady Farquhar that you are to honor us with some music after dinner. I am sure we all look forward to it!"

His expression was so eager, and he smiled so warmly, that Lady Sanders felt a distinct quiver of alarm, and her intention of ignoring Miss Lambert was put aside. She cleared her throat. "How kind of you, Miss Lambert! Of course *we* are only used to hearing the finest European musicians, true professionals, but I am sure you will do your best." She sighed heavily as if she wished she had asked for a tray in her room after all, rather than be subjected to such an ordeal. Janet felt a spurt of anger. What a very rude woman Lady Sanders is, she thought, even as she determined to play better than she ever had before. Lord Sanders stared at his mother for a moment before he turned again to Janet and began to discuss the picnic they had both attended. Janet was not sorry to see Lord Wharton approaching, and gave him her best smile. Just then Percival came over and begged Lord Sanders to come and settle a dispute with Colonel Baker as to the exact date of the Battle of Hastings, and Lord Sanders was forced to relinquish his place, albeit reluctantly.

Janet was horrified to see Lord Wharton waylaid by Mrs. Utley, who grasped his arm and engaged him in conversation, for it left her alone with Lady Sanders and there was no way she could rise and leave her without being impolite.

"Yes," Lady Sanders continued in an even ruder tone now they were alone, "I have always felt it disgusting when parents, so eager to show off marriageable daughters, push them forward in a most unbecoming way and expect the rest of the company to suffer through an amateur performance. I expect you shall sing, as well."

This was said in such a tone of foreboding that Janet lowered her eyes, sure they were flashing with the anger she felt. "I shall try my best not to disgust you, m'lady!" she murmured. This meek answer did nothing to placate the older lady, who twitched at her skirts impatiently, her narrowed eyes studying Janet intently.

"How very unfortunate that you do not have your sister's looks!" she said next. "Such a lovely woman, so typically English with her light brown curls and rosy cheeks."

Janet looked over to where Agatha was seated. "She is very pretty, ma'am," she agreed calmly.

"But where did you get such foreign looks?" Lady Sanders persisted. "So very dark and Italian, or even Spanish. That black hair, for instance . . ."

By this time Janet had had enough, and she rose from her seat. "You will have to ask my mother, m'lady," she said as coldly as she dared. "I have no idea. And now, if you will excuse me . . ." She sketched the shallowest curtsy she dared, and moved away, her head high. She had no idea why Lady Sanders had taken her in such obvious dislike, but she decided to avoid her company as much as possible in the future.

It seemed all too soon before dinner was over, and the ladies returned to the drawing room. Janet had had the same partners as before, and since Mr. Utley was intent on talking to Mrs. Baker on his left, she was free to converse with Lord Wharton, whose obvious admiration of her looks did much to restore her self-esteem. He did not care that she looked foreign! Lord Sanders, too, sent her many a smile, nodding his head approvingly, and even though Janet was sure that no matter what anyone said, the man obviously had a screw loose in his brain-box, that too was comforting.

Agatha led her sister to the grand piano, instructing a footman to open it and arrange the candelabrum so a becoming light would fall on Janet's face. "Perhaps you would like to practice, Janet?" she asked in an undertone. "It is most important that you play well!"

Her sister flexed her fingers and then took her seat, adjusting the bench so she could reach the keyboard and the pedals easily, and when she looked up, Agatha was still hovering over her, an anxious expression on her face.

Janet smiled. "Do not worry, Aggie! I won't disgrace you, I promise. Indeed, I have a special reason for playing my very best this evening."

At that her sister bent and kissed her, a smile glowing on her face.

"Dear Janet, I was sure you knew! How happy we shall all be."

She went away to make certain the older ladies were comfortably seated and did not require a shawl, or a cushion for their backs, and Janet softly played some warming-up exercises. As she did so, she noticed Lady Sanders talking in a very animated way with Mrs. Baker and Mrs. Utley, her voice overly loud, and she had to smile to herself. Ignore me all you wish, m'lady, she thought to herself, *for now*. These are only scales, and your inattendance does not distress me in the least.

When the gentlemen came in, she was ready. Agatha clapped her hands and announced that her sister would now play for their enjoyment, and Lady Sanders was forced to end her conversation and turn toward the piano, since her son kindly told her that the chair she had chosen quite put her back to Miss Lambert, and he was sure she would wish to change her seat. Janet waited until everyone was quiet, her head bowed, and then she began to play.

It was almost an hour later before the last notes of the concerto she had chosen to finish her program died away. She had expected that the guests would chat quietly together while she was playing, as they had done at Aylesford, and at first the attentive silence made her a little nervous, but she was soon able to forget it as the music wove its spell. She forgot the guests, Lady Sanders' rudeness, and the fact that she was not to bend over the keys or sway to the music, and quite unwittingly she presented a beautiful, graceful picture. Lady Lambert risked a sideways glance at Lord Sanders, afraid that Janet's behaviour—so unladylike! so foreign—had offended him, and was delighted to see his fond expression, his eager air of attendance, and his delighted smiles when Janet at last rose from the bench. Everyone applauded her soundly, even the colonel and Mr. Utley, who had dozed off during the slow passages and even, at one point, snored in unison.

"But, Miss Lambert," Lord Wharton exclaimed, coming forward to shake her hand. "You did not tell me you were such an accomplished musician. What talent!" As she thanked him, he added in an undertone, "I was sure we were to be treated to the performance of a rank amateur. You have no idea how many young girls I have had to hear torture the harp and abuse the piano! There was even one who thought she had mastered the flute. Bah! But to hear you was a joy."

He was able to say no more, for everyone, with the exception of Lady Sanders, was congratulating her and begging for an encore, but Janet, catching her mother's eye, was quick to see her shake her head.

"I thank you—so kind!—but I think I have monopolized the evening too much already!" she stammered, suddenly remembering swaying and bending, and sure she was to be read a mighty scold before she went to bed. And no matter how much Lord Wharton entreated her or Lord Sanders begged to hear her sing, she remained adamant, and went to sit by her mother's side.

"Excellent, my dear!" Lady Lambert said, patting her hand, to Janet's surprise. "I am most pleased with you, and it was not a bit too long, as I originally feared. And if that does not do the trick, I shall be very much surprised." Janet turned to look at her sharply, and Lady Lambert added in what could only be called a voice of complete satisfaction. "*Dear* Lady Sanders does not look at all well this evening, does she? Perhaps her indisposition has returned."

The next morning Janet rose early. She had been elated at the compliments, and her mother's new attitude, and found that not only had it been hard to fall asleep, she came awake with the birds. Running to the window, she saw it was going to be another lovely day, and decided to dress quickly, without summoning her maid, and go out for a stroll while she could still be alone. She wanted to remember all the wonderful things the guests had said about her performance. It was such a complete change from being derided for her talent, and ordered to forget such worthless fripperies as music, that it was no wonder that she felt so elated.

She was walking through the garden sometime later, wondering if she had missed breakfast, when she heard herself hailed by Lord Wharton, and turned to wait for him.

"Miss Lambert," he said, bowing low. "Well met. Do me the honor of walking with me for a bit. How very fortunate for me to find you alone, for it seems that whenever we meet, Lor . . . I mean, the others are clustered around you. And how are we to become better acquainted in that case?"

Janet did not know whether she should refuse, but when she looked at him she saw him smiling down at her lightly, with a twinkle in his eye, and she had to laugh. They went along the paths, admiring the flowers and chatting easily, until suddenly they found themselves at the entrance to the maze.

"Shall we?" Lord Wharton asked, extending his arm. "Do you dare to try to figure out Percy's puzzle, Miss Lambert?"

"I have never ventured inside, m'lord," Janet replied, "for I was afraid I would lose my way and never be found again. Percival says it is so difficult, really formidable."

"He does, does he?" Lord Wharton answered, opening the gate. "Then let us accept the challenge! I am sure that between the two of us we shall have no trouble at all, and won't Percy be as mad as fire that we have beaten him? He is very proud of his maze, you know."

As they disappeared around the first turn, Lady Lambert was even then entering the library, where she had arranged to meet Lord Sanders after he begged the indulgence of an interview. She smiled smugly as the butler bowed and closed the doors, and Lord Sanders came to meet her, and she was smiling even more broadly sometime later when she left the room and asked to have her daughter summoned and sent to her immediately. It had been agreed that Lady Lambert would speak to her daughter alone first, even though Lord Sanders assured her that Miss Lambert knew what was on his mind. Lady Lambert was not so positive, and she invented a maidenly shyness that would have astounded Janet if she had known of it. "So young, m'lord. So innocent," she simpered. "Let me explain to her and allow her blushes and tears of joy to subside before she joins you. I promise you, she will not be long." The truth of the matter was that Lady Lambert had no confidence that Janet would not ruin everything by a wild statement of disbelief and dismay, or a hasty refusal of the honour that Lord Sanders was prepared to bestow, such as would give the gentleman a disgust of her. No, much better for her to be prepared and brought to a sense of her great good fortune before m'lord saw her alone. And if necessary, Lady Lambert thought triumphantly as she climbed the stairs to her room to await her daughter, I shall insist on being present for the proposal, citing her tender years, in case she should wish to refuse. She did not really expect Janet to do anything but agree meekly, but just to be on the safe side . . .

The butler dispatched maids and footmen throughout Rundell Court. Miss Lambert was not to be found anywhere. Soon the search spread to the gardens and grounds, and even to the stables, although everyone knew she never went there. Lady Lambert became impatient, and hearing from a frightened maid that her daughter had completely disappeared, very agitated. She took to pacing up and down her room, even as Lord Sanders was doing in the library, a frown on his face as he wondered whatever could be delaying his bride-to-be. He had risen early, to find Lady Lambert at the breakfast table, although his mother was nowhere in sight. Lady Sanders had overslept, something she rarely did, and would forever bemoan after this fateful morning, so he could not speak to her as he had planned to do, of his intention of proposing to Miss Lambert. But the proximity of Lady Lambert, and their privacy, had made him forget his mother in his eagerness to settle the matter.

At this point, a very tired Janet was sinking down on a marble bench, somewhere deep in the maze, and saying somewhat desperately, "But, Lord Wharton! I am sure we passed that monkey—or was it an ostrich?—a few moments ago!" She pointed to the corner of the hedge with an accusing finger.

"Perhaps you are right! And Percy has placed so many of these dratted benches about, that I am not at all sure that we have not rested here before, too!"

"Do you mean we are lost?" Janet asked, her blue eyes wide. "Oh, I should have asked Aggie for the key to the maze! I am sure we have been missed, and *what* will Mama think?"

She moaned, and Lord Wharton wiped his brow. "Now, now, my dear Miss Lambert, there is nothing to fear!" he said in a bracing way he did not at all feel. "I am sure we can get out if we put out heads together. Come, is there nothing we can use to mark our trail?"

Janet looked down at her simple morning dress. It was very plain, and there were no knots of ribbons or decorative rows of buttons that could be used, and since Lord Wharton was also dressed simply, there was nothing of use there.

"We shall have to break off pieces of the hedge!" she

said firmly, getting up and twisting off some twigs. "There is no need to destroy the sculptures, for the hedge must be all of eight feet high, and a few branches won't be missed!"

"My compliments, Miss Lambert," Lord Wharton said, coming to help. "You *are* a resourceful young lady."

Together they began to retrace their steps, leaving a branch behind them every now and then so they would know where they had been. Lord Farquhar had been a little carried away when he planned his maze with the famous landscape gardener who had been a student of Capability Brown, and had insisted the maze must be the largest and most difficult in England. Janet and Lord Wharton often found themselves at a dead end, or in coming around a corner would see one of their hedge branches ahead of them on a path that they had been sure would lead them out. It was almost an hour later when they thankfully reached the last turn and saw the gate ahead of them. They turned to each other in triumph, and then they heard loud voices.

"I say!" Lord Farquhar was exclaiming. "You cannot have searched throughly, Jenkins! Have the men spread out over the grounds again!"

Here Lord Wharton would have called, but Janet took hold of his arm and raised her finger to her lips for silence, as her sister said in a weak voice, "So unlike Janet! I pray she is not lying injured somewhere in the woods, or perhaps drowned in the lake."

"Never say so!" came the horrified tones of Lord Sanders, and Lady Lambert was heard to say sharply, "That is unworthy of you, Agatha. Remember how a Lambert behaves! Of course Janet is not at the bottom of the lake!" Her tone was so disbelieving that it was plain to all that no Lambert would ever do anything so ridiculous as falling into a lake, no matter how provocative the circumstances. "I am sure she is sitting somewhere secluded, reading a book, and has forgotten the time. She is a very educated young lady, Lord Sanders, and when she is reading or playing her music, she does tend to be a little absentminded."

Even from behind the hedge, Lady Sanders' sniff was very audible.

"I wonder if anyone has noticed that Lord Wharton is also absent?" this lady now asked the others in a satisfied purr. "I am sure they must be together, although such a *tête-à-tête*, so forward for a single young lady, can only be deplored."

Janet put her hands to her hot cheeks and moaned softly. In her mind's eye, she could envision only too plainly her mother's bristle at this slur.

"Glad to ride with the men, Percy!" Mr. Utley offered, and his wife eagerly chimed in. "We've run many a fox to his earth, y'know! Sure to find the gel!"

Even Colonel and Mrs. Baker were present, for Janet could hear him talking about sorties and patrols and the need of a good map of the estate so he might deploy his troops. She stared at the now completely silent Lord Wharton in horror. That gentleman, thinking quickly, grabbed her hand and led her around a few bends, picking up the twigs as he went, one finger to his lips to ensure her silence. When they were again deep in the maze, he whispered, "We are safe here. You go on a little farther and then let us call for help. I will wait until you are some distance from me before I begin!"

"But . . . but . . ." Janet sputtered. "I cannot let my mother know I was in here alone with you all this time. Why, you heard Lady Sanders. So improper!"

Lord Wharton was just as tired as she was, and he had missed his breakfast as well, and he had no intention of hiding here indefinitely until everyone went away. "Never fear, Miss Lambert!" he said. "I have a plan, and all will be well if you follow my lead. Now, go!"

Janet saw that there was nothing to do but face the music, and although she was not looking forward to it in the slightest, now she hurried away, deeper into the maze, hearing Lord Wharton calling "Halloo? Halloo? Is anyone there?"

When she felt she was far enough away from him, she also began to call for help.

"Janet! Is that *you* in here?" she heard her mother ask. "It cannot be."

"Just as I suspected!" Lady Sanders said smugly. "Alone and together."

"Is that you, Wh-Wh-Wharton?" Percival called. "Stay where you are, both of you! I'll get the head g-g-gardener and he can climb up to the chair and direct you out."

It seemed a very short time later before Janet and Lord Wharton had been directed out of the maze by the grinning gardener, and Lady Lambert came forward to fold her daughter in her arms, a little stiffly to be sure, but still in such a way as to appear unconcerned with this very un-Lambert-like adventure. Lord Wharton spoke up before the others had a chance to question them.

"Thank heavens! I had no idea your maze was so difficult, Percy, and when I heard Miss Lambert calling just a few minutes ago, I went to her aid, little dreaming I would not be able to lead her out in a trice. Why, I am ashamed to admit, I could not even locate her!"

Janet, her head bent on her mother's massive bosom, could only applaud this quick thinking as she felt Lady Lambert relax.

"But what were you doing in the maze, sister?" Agatha asked in a puzzled voice. "It was most unwise for you to venture in there alone, without the key."

Janet sighed and raised her head. "I have heard Percival speak of it so often, that when I found the gate ajar this morning, I could not resist trying a few turns. But then I really became confused! And I must say, Percival, that if you had to use animal shapes, it was not at all kind of you not to use several different ones. That way the maze would be so much easier to figure out. But all those monkeys!" She saw her brother-in-law beaming at his success, and continued, "I am very, very sorry to have caused all this worry and commotion, but oh, I am so tired!"

Lord Sanders came forward and bowed. "Allow me to take you back to the Court, Miss Lambert. Perhaps a glass of wine or a cup of tea will make you feel more the thing."

Janet noted Lady Sanders sniff, like some sort of doleful Greek chorus afflicted with a head cold, as her mother replied for her. She could see that her daughter had on one of her oldest gowns, her hair was coming down, and there were smudges on her face. The proposal of a viscount, who besides his title was the owner of such a magnificent estate as Willows, deserved better than that. Besides, she had yet to prepare Janet for this great event and instruct her in what she was to say when she accepted. She was, after all, only seventeen and a half, and had led a very sheltered life.

"I shall take my daughter to her room to freshen up, but thank you for your kindness, Lord Sanders. She will be able to return to y . . . to the company shortly."

The gentleman bowed in disappointment as Lady Lambert led Janet toward the terrace. Behind her, she heard Mrs. Utley say, "Well, what shall we do now, Reggie? Our fox hunt is over before it began!"

She sounded very disappointed, but not more so than the colonel as he exclaimed, "Looked forward to a good search!" And then he barked to the gardeners and groundskeepers lined up before him, "Company dismissed!"

Janet tried not to giggle, although when she thought of the scold her mother was probably taking her away to administer, she sobered quickly. When they reached the hall, Lady Lambert instructed Hemmings to have some tea sent to Miss Lambert's room, and went upstairs, her arm still around her daughter. She said not a word until the bedroom door was closed behind them, and this was so ominous that Janet turned fearfully toward her, to see a large broad smile creasing her mother's face. She sat down abruptly.

"No, no, my dear, we must make haste! The most wonderful thing has happened. Quickly, take off that terrible gown and wash. Your face is very dirty, and we must have Simpton to do your hair."

She does not sound at all angry, Janet thought as she obediently began to unhook her dress. Lady Lambert opened the wardrobe and began to flip through the gowns

102

there. "I wish we had thought to buy you more clothes, my dear," she said in a muffled voice from within the closet, "but of course I had no idea at all that such a wonderful thing would come of our visit. I tell you, Janet, I never hoped for such a distinguished match for you. No, not at all, but you have surprised us all, you sly little puss!"

Janet had removed her gown and, wrapped in her dressing robe, was bent over the washbasin. The water was barely warm now, but it was refreshing, and with her splashing, she missed the last part of her mother's declaration. When she was finished, she was astounded to find her mother beside her, holding out a towel in a most solicitous manner. I must have died and gone to heaven, she thought as she wiped her face and hands. Lady Lambert hurried her to the dressing table and quickly unpinned her chignon. She began to brush her hair, something her daughter could never remember her doing even when she was a little girl. She looked at her mother in the mirror with wide eyes.

"We shall summon Simpton presently, my dear, but for now, I wish to be alone with you, for we have much of a private nature to discuss. Both Agatha and I are so pleased for you. And I do not think you realize, even now, what a coup this is. Dear girl! So very satisfying, especially after Elizabeth. Wait until your father learns! I daresay he will be as happy as we are."

"Mama!" Janet finally broke in. "Why are you happy? And Aggie? And why will father be happy as well? About *what*?"

"Come, Janet! There is no need for such coyness. Surely you have been aware of the gentleman's distinguished attentions. It can come as no great surprise to you that he has spoken to me this very morning and asked permission to marry you."

"Marry me?" Janet asked, her heart sinking. There was only one unmarried man present who could have spoken so to her mother, for the other one had been lost in the maze with her.

"Of course! I must admit I was very, very angry with

you when you were nowhere to be found this morning. Not that I think Lord Sanders is about to change his mind, of course, but in matters of this nature, it is best to strike when the iron is hot. That is why you must put on your prettiest gown, have your hair done, and hurry down to the library, where he is waiting for you, as fast as you can manage it."

"But . . . but, Mama!" Janet exclaimed. "I really do not believe this! I hardly know Lord Sanders—or he, me. And I had no idea—truthfully—that he meant to propose. In fact, I was sure he must be slightly mad, the way he has been behaving. I don't want to marry him. I don't want to marry anyone yet!"

Just then the maid knocked and entered with a tray. Janet, who a short time ago had been famished, now could not bear the sight of food, her stomach was quivering so in shock, but she accepted a cup of tea and tried not to look at her mother's face. Lady Lambert sat down on a straight chair, and she did not speak until the maid curtsied and left the room.

"I cannot believe I have heard you correctly, miss!" she said in a cold, severe voice, quite unlike her exultant tones of a moment ago. "Of course you will marry Lord Sanders. He is an excellent man, titled and wealthy. You have only to observe the conjugal bliss your sister enjoys to see what your life will be like."

"But I do not even *know* him, Mama," Janet dared to whisper.

"I should most sincerely expect not!" her mother snapped. "There is no need for that. I hope I shall never see the day when a Lambert chooses his marriage partner because he has 'fallen in love.' Bah!" She sounded so disgusted at such a common notion that Janet shivered again. "You will be guided by your parents, of course, in this most important matter. We know, as we have always known, what is best for you. Do not be setting yourself up against me, my girl, for it is most unbecoming. I say you shall accept Lord Sanders, and so you shall."

She paused and stared at her daughter and added, "When you are married, you will find that an affection might possibly grow between you; not of course that that is at all necessary. Respect, unfailing kindness, concern for your well-being, and the politeness I am sure Lord Sanders will always treat you with are all that are required."

Janet still stared at her mother, her face so white that another mother might have feared she was about to faint. No Lambert ever would, of course, so Lady Lambert rose and went to shake out the pretty blue muslin she had taken from the wardrobe.

As she did so, she said in a more conversational way. "I shall be most displeased, Janet, if you disobey me and refuse Lord Sanders. We shall be forced to retire to Aylesford Grange immediately, and there will be no question of any more trips for you, or a Season in London of course. A daughter who is so rebellious that she refuses this most excellent offer can expect nothing further to be done for her, now or in the future. Of course, I have heard from Mrs. Rustin that her younger son, Charles, is on the lookout for a suitable bride. That might be a possibility."

Janet started up, her hands gripping the edge of the dressing table tightly. If this Mr. Rustin were anything like his brother, why, nothing could be worse!

Lady Lambert was rummaging through her daughter's small jewelry case for a suitable necklace for the blue gown. "There are those who say that he can become quite violent when there is a full moon, but I for one have never believed it. The Rustins are a good old family and distantly related to us as well, but some people delight in vicious gossip, and that need not concern us."

"Mama! You couldn't! You couldn't make me marry a Rustin!" Janet cried out.

"You say I couldn't?" Lady Lambert asked, fixing her with a stern, unsmiling expression. There was not a semblance of affection or sympathy there. "Think of Lizzie, Janet, and let us have no more of these girlish vapours! You always knew you would marry where we chose; be glad that such a fine, distinguished gentleman has met with our approval. It is a great deal more than you deserve. And now I am going to ring for Simpton, for we have wasted quite a lot of unnecessary time. You will be dressed, you will go down to the library where m'lord is waiting, and when he proposes, you will say, 'I thank you for the great honour you have bestowed on me, m'lord, and I should be pleased to accept.' "

She came up to the dressing table, and putting her hands on her daughter's shoulders, she squeezed them painfully. "What will you say to Lord Sanders, Janet?"

Slowly Janet repeated her mother's words, and was released instantly.

There was another person who was as horrified as Janet, and at precisely the same moment. Lord Sanders, knowing how long it took ladies to change their gowns and do their hair, had taken this opportunity to escort his mother to her room so he might tell her his wonderful news. To his surprise, she screamed in a most piercing manner and fainted dead away. In some distress, he summoned her maid and hovered over that woman while she held some burnt feathers under Lady Sanders' nose and waved her vinaigrette. At last Lady Sanders returned to her surroundings. When she caught sight of her son, she moaned piteously, and Lord Sanders dismissed the maid.

What occurred for the next thirty minutes was most unpleasant for both of them. Lady Sanders was stunned to discover that her feelings in the matter were of small regard to her hitherto adoring son, and Lord Sanders learned that his mother not only disliked his choice of bride, she positively loathed her. He was not to be swayed from his choice, however, not even when treated to his mother's assessment of her character as a pushy, forward young woman from a provincial family, who besides being a most unequal match for her glorious son was darkly foreign-looking and so musical as to smack of the stage, and had treated his mother to a severe snub only the evening before.

"I had such *hopes* for you, Ernest," she cried, wiping away her tears when at last she had been brought to a realization that he insisted on marrying Miss Lambert. "Such very great hopes, for I daresay even minor royalty was not impossible. And to choose such a nobody as a mere Miss Lambert—and I shall be forced to receive her family as well. I cannot bear it. Why, you might have had Lady Peck . . . or even Lady Grace! Say you will think it over, Ernest. It is such a serious step."

Lord Sanders soothed her and said all that was proper, but she noticed that his jaw was set firmly, reminding her forcibly of her late husband. And when George got that expression on his face, she had always known there was nothing she could do to change his mind. Finally she waved her son away and requested him to send in her maid. "Do not expect me to appear in company for some time, Ernest," she said faintly. "I am prostrate with grief. You may do as you please, of course, and I can see that my feelings do not matter to you in the slightest, but I will not come downstairs to congratulate that horrible Lambert woman and her insignificant daughter."

Lord Sanders stared at his mother and said firmly, "Nonsense! You will of course be present at dinner tonight, when I am sure the announcement will be made. If necessary, I will come and bring you down myself. You have all afternoon to rest and prepare yourself, and believe me when I say that you will appear, for I will not tolerate any slight to my chosen bride."

Lady Sanders moaned and turned her head away, and Lord Sanders went quickly out the door and down to the library. His mother must be contracting a contagious infection, he thought, to behave in such a way. When she came to know Janet—ah, Janet Rose! What a lovely name, so English, so very proper!—why, then she would come to love her, even as he did.

III

Music for a Trio

❧ 7 ❧

A very short time later, Janet found herself going slowly down the main staircase. Lady Lambert had not left her for a minute, hovering around while Simpton did her hair, and chatting lightly of inconsequentials. Janet glanced at her triumphant face every now and then, and could not help hating her. It was obvious that Mama was pleased, and it did not matter in the slightest to her that her daughter was miserable, and liable to remain so for the rest of her life. A successful marriage to a member of the peerage was all she cared about. *I wish I could tell her that no matter what she does, I shall not marry Lord Sanders; I wish I had the courage to stand up to her,* Janet thought as she trailed sadly down the stairs. But she could still feel her mother's hands bruising her shoulders, and she had been beaten too many times as a child not to realize that Lady Lambert would not hesitate to use physical punishment as a means to persuade her. And then, of course, there was the loathsome Mr. Rustin, who sounded even more ghastly than his brother. *I think I shall hate Mama all my life,* she told herself, *for what she is doing to me.* She sighed as she reached the bottom step. Besides being most reluctant to accept Lord Sanders, she felt quivers of alarm at the thought of promising to marry where she did not love. Suppose he asked her if she loved

111

him, what could she say? And suppose he wanted to make love to her? Surely a gentleman who had just had his hand accepted in marriage would expect some display of affection from his betrothed. She almost turned away in panic at the thought, but Hemmings, who knew the signs he had seen this morning better than anyone, was beaming at her in a fatherly way and holding the library door open for her.

This time Lord Sanders had not been waiting above a few minutes. The scene with his mother had delayed him to the point that he practically flew downstairs in a very undignified manner, for he was afraid that Miss Lambert would already be there in the uncomfortable position of standing about alone, wondering where he was.

Now Lord Sanders hurried toward her, beaming, his arms outstretched after Hemmings had softly closed the doors behind her. Janet watched him come, aghast, and only just remembered to curtsy as he reached eagerly for her hands.

"Come, my dear Miss Lambert. I cannot tell you how glad I am to see you here at last." He led her to a small sofa, and after she was seated, sat down close beside her and leaned toward her. Janet could not draw away, for it was a very small sofa.

"I was so sorry you were lost in the maze, for your sake of course, but more so for my own. Ah, my dear Miss Janet—I may call you 'Miss Janet'?—it was very painful to have to wait so long, wondering what ill fortune had overtaken you. And when I had something of such particular importance to ask you as well!"

This last was spoken in his heavy, playful way, but Janet kept her eyes firmly downcast, studying her clasped hands as they rested in her lap. There was a moment of silence, and Janet, who felt she had to contribute something to the conversation for politeness' sake, said softly, "I am so sorry to have alarmed you, m'lord."

"Well, no harm done," he exclaimed heartily. "All's well that ends well, eh? And now you are here, and we are alone at last."

He reached over and took her hands in his, and she

looked up into his face. There was such panic in her expression that it caused him to pause for a moment. She is frightened of me, he told himself, for she is very young and demure, and perhaps she is overcome with the honour I am about to bestow on her as well, and feels unworthy. He pressed her hands warmly and smiled down at her to reassure her that although he was far above her in consequence, it did not matter to him. Unfortunately, Janet missed his condescending smile, for she had lowered her eyes again, and all he could see was the top of her head and the tips of those delicate pink ears as she stared at their intertwined hands.

"Miss Janet, I assume your mother has spoken to you of what I wish to ask you? She has told you of what is in my heart, what I most ardently desire, and have desired ever since I first laid eyes on you the other evening? Oh, happy day when first we met!" he enthused, pressing her hands again.

"Yes," Janet answered baldly, somewhat stunned by this flight of fancy.

"Then I can understand your modesty and reticence. But come, my dear, will you not look at me?"

There was nothing Janet could do but obey. After all, she supposed it was customary when you were receiving a proposal to look at the gentleman in question. His blue eyes were so intent, and there was such an expression of ardor on his face that she felt a little ashamed. No matter how she felt, Lord Sanders did seem to really want her to be his wife, and since she was forced to accept him, she would try to do it with a good grace. She attempted a smile, but it was a tremulous thing and quickly gone. Lord Sanders saw it, however, and he went down on one knee before her and said, "My dear one, I have the good fortune to be able to ask you to do me the honour of becoming my wife, Lady Sanders, Viscountess Broughten, and mistress of Willows as well!"

He paused expectantly, and Janet made herself answer through stiff lips, "I thank you for the honour you have bestowed on me, m'lord. I should be most happy to accept."

Another, more perceptive man might have wondered at this point whether the lady was willing, in spite of her words, for she sounded so very unenthusiastic and wooden, but Lord Sanders was not at all perceptive. He smiled broadly and rose, drawing her up with him to pull her into his arms. "Janet! Dear one!" he exclaimed, and then he bent his sandy head and kissed her. Janet tried to stand quietly, but she had never been kissed before and she found it very uncomfortable and unpleasant. His face was so warm, his lips so dry and insistent, and his arms were holding her so closely against his chest that she thought she might faint, so she tried to pull away. He released her instantly and stared down at her white face.

"Whatever is the matter, my dear?" he asked, in some confusion now. "Are you feeling all right?"

He seemed genuinely concerned and perplexed, and Janet dared to whisper, "I beg your pardon, m'lord, I do feel a little faint. Perhaps it was all the exertion of the morning, and I have not eaten. . . ."

"Of course, I understand. Poor girl!" he said, seating her again before he went to the bell pull. Janet breathed a sigh of relief as he moved away. "I shall order some sandwiches and a glass of wine for you, and while you are eating, we can make our plans. We have a great many plans to make, you know! Ah, there you are, Hemmings. Some sandwiches for Miss Lambert, and two glasses of wine at once."

The butler bowed and left, and Lord Sanders came and sat down across from her. Janet was delighted he had not returned to the sofa.

"What a happy and auspicious occasion," he said, and she tried to smile at him again. "I must tell you how much I respect your maidenly reserve, Janet. You are so modest, so chaste. And I daresay you have never been kissed before, have you? But that is how it should be, of course. I must remember how very young you are, my dear. Forgive me if I have frightened you with my ardor, but I am sure you will return it in a very short time. I shall be patient."

Janet shook her head and would have tried to speak, but Lord Sanders rushed on, and she was glad the love-making seemed to be over, for now at least. "This very afternoon I shall ride over to Willows, Janet, for I want you to have the Sanders ancestral engagement ring before this evening. And even though I know how hard it will be for us to be parted, even for such a little while, I do not ask you to accompany me, you notice, for I am sure you will wish to rest after this morning's tiresome adventure. I expect you to be in your best looks this evening; I imagine Lady Farquhar will serve a festive dinner to celebrate our coming nuptials, and your mama—excellent woman, your mama!—will announce our betrothal to the others."

He paused, and Janet murmured, somewhat overcome by his verbosity, "Most kind. So considerate."

Lord Sanders beamed at her in a proprietary way and continued, "But we shall make a grand tour of Willows soon. I hope my mother will accompany us, but she is not feeling well at the moment, so it may have to be delayed for a few days."

"I am sorry to hear she is indisposed, m'lord—" she began.

He shook a playful finger at her and interrupted. "No, no, Janet. Not 'm'lord' anymore. My name is Ernest, you know. As an engaged young lady you are permitted to address me as Ernest."

Janet swallowed and whispered his name, and he beamed again. She decided that he had a very fatuous smile. Just then Hemmings and a footman knocked and entered the library bearing a plate of sandwiches and an iced bucket of champagne as well. The butler presented the bottle to Lord Sanders to approve.

"I took the liberty, m'lord," he said with the hint of a smile, "of being so bold as to think champagne was what was required. Of course, I can fetch the claret or Madeira if you wish . . ."

"Excellent thinking, Hemmings!" Lord Sanders nodded. "You are quite correct for Miss Lambert and I are indeed celebrating, are we not, my dear?"

115

Janet nodded. "As you say, m'l . . . Ernest," she answered.

When Hemmings had offered his congratulations and bowed himself out, Lord Sanders was quick to correct her.

"In the company of servants, my dear, it does not do to address me by my given name. You will notice that I was careful to call you 'Miss Lambert.' It is just a small thing, but I am sure that you are most desirous of doing the right thing at all times, as befits my chosen bride."

He smiled to remove the sting of his little lecture and Janet tried to eat her sandwiches. She was not in the least hungry, she felt she would never be hungry again, but it occurred to her that as long as she was chewing, Lord Sanders could not kiss her. He did, however, continue to make plans.

"I know you will want to do a great deal of shopping in London, Janet. I shall invite you and your mother to stay at my town house in Park Lane for the duration. That way I might be permitted to see you now and then when you are not engaged in fittings or trying on bonnets. I know you ladies."

He paused so she might applaud this pleasantry, and Janet took a large bite of her cucumber sandwich so she would not have to answer.

"Perhaps, since it is now September, we might be able to go to town for what remains of the Little Season. Would you like that, Janet? And then, what say you to a Christmas wedding?"

Janet swallowed her entire glass of champagne. "M'l . . . I mean, Ernest, that is very kind of you, but if I might venture to say . . . I mean, I do not wish to upset you, but . . . well . . ." Her voice trailed away into silence, and Lord Sanders threw out his hands in an expansive gesture. "Your desires are my command, dear one. I am longing to hear what you wish so I might instantly gratify you. Come, do not be shy, tell me," he commanded in ringing tones to show his sincerity, and Janet, wondering if the butler had his ear to the door, took a deep breath.

"Well, Ernest, it is just that I am barely seventeen, you know. Why, my eighteenth birthday is not until next spring!" She noticed that he had stopped smiling, and hurried on. "I should so love to see London during the Season, for I was never brought out, you know, and there are so many things I wish to do before I am a married lady. I have never been to a concert or the theatre, or seen any of the art galleries. Please, could we not have a longer engagement than three months? As you said, there is so much shopping to do, and I would not like to come to Willows without being correctly dressed, and so young and gauche it would give you a disgust of me. But if I have some experience in town and meet all your grand friends beforehand, I shall be so much happier and better able to manage, as befits your . . . your wife."

Lord Sanders had frowned all through this ingenuous speech, which Janet would never have found the courage to utter unless she had had two very quick glasses of Percival's excellent champagne. Lord Sanders thought of pointing out to her that as his wife she could attend theatres and concerts as much as she wished, but there was such a look of pleading in her eyes, and he was so very besotted, that he made himself nod.

"It shall be as you say, my dear. It is true that you are very young, and after you have done your 'raking' in town, we can be married in the spring. And you will find it all so much more comfortable, I am sure, with me beside you to tell you how to go on. And you are very wise to realize that as Lady Sanders you have standards to uphold; my mother will be delighted to instruct you. In fact, if your mother does not feel able to remain in town the entire time, I am sure that by then my mother will be delighted to chaperone you and guide you."

Janet did not miss his reference to his reluctant mother, but she put this disagreeable lady from her mind, and her instructive lectures as well, for she was feeling quite elated. She had not thought it would be so easy to get him to delay the wedding, nor had she dreamed he would take her to town. And since Lord Sanders wished it, Lady Lambert would be forced to acquiesce in the scheme.

117

Janet felt as if a great weight had been lifted from her, for May was such a long time away. She knew she had to marry Lord Sanders eventually, but now she had some precious months of freedom left. And Mama would be forced to deck her out in the finest style as well, for it would go against the grain for her to have a Lambert daughter looking provincial. When she considered how much this would cost, and how much her mother would dislike spending money on a *fait accompli*, she smiled again. Serves her right, she thought as Lord Sanders came and took the plate from her hands.

"What happiness to see you smile at me, m'dear. I know we shall deal extremely with each other, and you are not to worry your pretty little head over the disparity of our stations in life. Although I am far above you in consequence, *I* do not regard it, you know. And you must promise to tell me instantly if there is anything you wish, anything at all."

Janet found it easy to smile again and thank him prettily, but caution warned her not to mention several other things she had in mind to ask. One step at a time. Sanders kissed her cheek and then smothered her hands in kisses. "You have made me the happiest of men," he breathed.

Janet drew away and swept him a curtsy as she begged to be excused. "For I must tell Mama, you know, and Agatha and Percy as well."

"Of course. And I shall ride to Willows at once. You will promise to rest this afternoon, will you not, my dear?"

Janet agreed to do so, and went back to her room, to find not only her mother but also her sister there. They exclaimed over her and kissed her, Lady Lambert nodding approvingly, and then left her so they might talk to the chef and plan a festive party for the evening. Janet sank down on her window seat and stared out at the beautiful September day, wishing she did not feel so strange, almost as if she were standing outside herself, watching some other girl playact at being Miss Janet Rose Lambert.

In her heart she knew that she had had no choice but

to obey her mother; indeed, she had always known that her parents would choose her husband for her, and she would be forced to accept, no matter how she felt. Why, not even revulsion could be an excuse! Look what Mama had done to Lizzie! At least Lord Sanders was not ugly and coarse, and perhaps she would grow accustomed to him and even come to care for him a little in time. She sighed and leaned her head against the windowpane, her dark blue eyes pensive. But why, when she was being so sensible, did she keep seeing in her mind's eye that one handsome face with its white grin and piercing eyes? And why did she keep hearing that deep, resonant voice?

She rose abruptly from the window seat. The Marquess of Hallowsfield. Was he always to haunt her dreams? She wondered sadly where he was and what he was doing.

Unbeknownst to her, Anthony Northbridge was just then leaving his latest mistress, a handsome older woman who was much sought after for her blond beauty and voluptuous figure. She blew him a kiss as he stood at the door of her room, lying back amongst the lacy pillows and satin hangings of her bed. The duke thought Lottie looked especially handsome in the diamond eardrops he had brought her only that afternoon. Although her lacy peignoir was thrown across the foot of the bed, and the diamonds were her only adornment, she was languidly unconcerned with her nakedness. He grinned at her—the same grin that Janet remembered so well—and decided to bring her the matching diamond bracelet she had pleaded for, as well.

But as he left the house and strolled leisurely toward his club, Tony Northbridge reflected that not even the beauteous Lottie would amuse him for long. He could feel the boredom that she had kept at bay creeping back even now, and he resolved to make the diamond bracelet his final present to the lady. She had really grown much too demanding and greedy; it was so tiresome!

Janet slept most of the afternoon, and when it came time to dress, she found Simpton had been lent to her again. The dresser felt Miss Lambert was a boon from heaven. Since Lady Farquhar was *enceinte*, there would not be any more festivities worthy of her skill, or any more trips to town, and she had been thinking seriously of leaving. Now she had another young lady to dress, and if she made herself indispensable, she might even be able to transfer her duties from one sister to the other. To this end, she bent all her skill, and although Janet was pale, she was beautifully dressed and coiffed. All the while she worked, Simpton kept up a running monologue. How lucky Miss Lambert was to be marrying such a wealthy man; how very handsome the viscount was, besides being of such an exalted station; what wonderful clothes and jewels would soon be hers.

Janet was thinking her own thoughts and so was not paying much attention to this rosy picture being painted of her future. She was glad now she had not mentioned any of Lord Sanders' plans to her mother. Time enough for that when he was standing beside her and Lady Lambert could not object. Janet felt she was growing up very quickly, out of necessity, and was delighted that she was beginning to learn how to manipulate people and events to her own satisfaction. Mama did not hold all the cards in this game, she realized. She felt a little thrill of power when she remembered how easy it had been to get Lord Sanders—no, Ernest—to delay the wedding.

Just then a knock came at the door and the maid hurried to open it and admit the viscount's valet, who presented Janet with a large chest of jewels.

"M'lord said you are to choose whichever you prefer to wear this evening, miss."

Janet gasped as he held out the open chest. There were pearls and rubies, opals and sapphires, and a glorious diamond necklace and matching drops and bracelets.

"Good heavens, I cannot!" she exclaimed, and when both servants looked at her in disbelief, she drew herself up and said firmly, "Thank Lord Sanders for me, but tell him that I do not consider it appropriate to wear family jewels until after the ceremony."

The valet bowed low and prepared to take the chest away with him, but not until he said that his master wished a moment of her time in the library before she joined the other guests. Janet nodded and went back to the dressing table so Simpton could fasten her one small necklet of pearls around her throat.

When the first bell for dinner rang, she went reluctantly to the library, and was startled when Lord Sanders greeted her by going down on one knee before her again. She hoped this was not to become his customary form of address.

"Dear one! Such delicacy of mind. Such presence. I kneel in homage to your good taste."

Janet looked at him askance, and he added, "Of course I would wish to see you in the Sanders jewels as soon as possible, but I understand that to someone of your sensibilities, it would not be becoming before our wedding. However, I have no doubt that you will agree to wear *this*!"

He rose, took a box from his pocket, and opened it with a flourish. Janet gasped in amazement, and, reassured, he took it out and put it on her finger. She felt immediately as if her hand was going to drop off. Never in her life had she seen such a massive, ugly jewel! It was a huge yellow diamond, surrounded by clusters of other colored gems, all set in intricate swirls of heavy gold and filigree, and it covered her entire finger right down to the knuckle. She was glad she was right-handed, for she was sure she would never be able to lift a fork while wearing it. She also felt deeply uneasy; the heavy, ugly ring seemed to set a seal on the engagement that she had not truly acknowledged before. As she stared down at it, it seemed to be saying, "Now you are a Sanders—forever!"

Lord Sanders cleared his throat expectantly, so she broke off her reverie and thanked him by saying it was most unusual. Just then the second bell rang, which allowed Lord Sanders time for only a brief embrace before they had to join the others. True to his word, he had made sure his mother was present, and it was to this lady that he led his intended bride as soon as they entered the drawing room. Janet was surprised to find she was sorry for the lady, for she did look pale and ill, even though she murmured "So pleased" as Janet curtsied and took a seat beside her to chat lightly until dinner was served.

It was a festive meal, not even marred by Lord Farquhar's stammered announcement and toast, which came as no surprise to anyone, since Agatha had been very busy over the afternoon teacups.

After the ladies withdrew, Janet found herself seated between her mother and Lady Sanders in the drawing room, a reluctant shuttlecock in a fiercely played game of badminton. Lady Lambert would announce some plan for the happy couple, and Lady Sanders would deny her by saying that the Sanderses never did things that way. No matter what Lady Lambert proposed, Lady Sanders was sure to find something wrong with the scheme, from the bridal clothes to the honeymoon destination, or the number of attendants to the desirability of being married from the village church at Aylesford, which Lady Sanders implied was nowhere near grand enough for such a magnificent event as her son's wedding. Lady Lambert bridled and asked her daughter her opinion, and Janet began to gain some favor with her future mother-in-law by saying only that whatever Lord Sanders wished was her desire as well. She was very glad when the men rejoined them and Lord Sanders hurried to their side, for both ladies were glaring at each other openly across her and it was most uncomfortable.

"I have just been saying, m'lord," Lady Lambert opened the attack, "that I am sure Janet wishes to see Willows as soon as possible. And of course there are all the wedding plans to make. What date have you chosen, m'lord?"

"You must call me Ernest, Lady Lambert, now that we are to be related." Lord Sanders smiled, as his mother gritted her teeth. "Janet and I have decided that a spring wedding would be perfect."

"But that is such a long time away!" Lady Lambert exclaimed.

"*Late* spring?" Lady Sanders inquired.

Lord Sanders explained, with a fond smile for his betrothed, "You see, Janet has such a lot of shopping to do for her bride clothes, and I had the happy thought that she would enjoy a season in town, so we have planned the date for May, after she turns eighteen. I hope you will stay at my town house, Lady Lambert, when you bring Janet to London, and I know my mother adds her invitation as well, and would be delighted to chaperone her if you are unable to remain for such a long time."

Janet was careful not to look at her mother, for she knew she was being stared at in a very direct way. "How very kind of you, Ernest," Lady Lambert said at last. "But I hardly think such a long delay is at all necessary. Why, we can have Janet's clothes ready in a month. I have already married two daughters, you know, and in a much shorter span of time."

The words were said in her soft, pleasant way, but Janet heard the steel underneath.

"But you have never had the good fortune to have a daughter marry a Sanders," Lady Sanders interrupted. "That will require a longer time, for of course she must have everything of the best."

Lord Sanders changed the subject, since even he could see that the ladies had declared open warfare.

"We shall drive over to Willows this week, as soon as Mama is feeling more the thing, and of course you must accompany us, Lady Lambert, to see your daughter's future home. Forgive me for seeming immodest when I say I am sure you must approve. Shall we say Thursday?"

The day was agreed on, and Janet was glad to excuse herself and go and help Agatha hand around the teacups. As she gave Lord Wharton his, he whispered, "I suppose best wishes are in order, Miss Lambert, and I am glad our adventure in the maze did not disrupt the proceedings, but may I say how disappointed I am that you have made this decision so quickly?" There was such a rueful twinkle of regret in his eyes that Janet had to smile at him.

The carriage had been summoned for early Thursday morning, and both Lady Sanders and Lady Lambert were ready in plenty of time, since neither of them was willing to concede an inch to her rival. If Lady Lambert was going to Willows, you can be sure that Lady Sanders would have dragged herself from her deathbed to be one of the party. Janet was wearing the glorious bonnet again, and her primrose muslin, and Lord Sanders told her she looked as fresh as a daffodil as he squeezed her hands and helped her to her seat. Lady Sanders remarked to no one in particular that although the muslin was very pretty, it was obvious that Miss Lambert had a great deal of shopping to do, as she had worn that gown several times already.

Willows was very grand, and even Lady Lambert was impressed with the long drive that swept through the woods to a river lined with the trees that gave the estate its name, before the vista opened up and the hall could be seen before them, massive and elaborate with its grey stone walls and pillared front. She managed to hide her awe, however, by making several remarks, that although always prefaced by a compliment nevertheless contained some criticism. Lord Sanders seemed unaware of this, but Janet was amused to see that Lady Sanders did not miss a single veiled barb.

The blue drawing room was splendid, Lady Lambert declared, so large and beautifully furnished, but perhaps some new hangings might add to its charm? There was something about that shade of damask that jarred the eye, and didn't Janet agree? And then, the morning room—so sunny and pleasant—could certainly benefit from a new rug. She waxed enthusiastic about the spaciousness of the hall before she instructed Janet to remove some of the tables and chairs scattered about. And what a glorious display of paintings in the gallery. Most impressive. Lady Sanders smiled for the first time that morning, until Lady Lambert added kindly that she would be glad to send her a recipe for cleaning soot and dirt from valuable oil paintings which had obviously never come Lady Sanders' way.

Lady Sanders countered all these remarks by saying that Willows had always had blue damask hangings, the rug was a very rare Oriental pattern and she was surprised Lady Lambert was not acquainted with it, and that she always sent the family paintings to a London dealer since they were so irreplaceable she would never consider homemade cleaning remedies.

Finally, when both ladies paused to regroup, Janet entered the conversation. "Excuse me, Ernest, but I was just wondering, where is the music room? I do not recall seeing one."

Lord Sanders admitted that Willows did not boast a music room, but that that could be easily rectified. "And perhaps when we are in town, you will accompany me and help me choose a piano for you, my dear," he said, delighted to be able to give her such a magnificent gift. Janet had only a moment to thank him before Lady Lambert was suggesting that dear Lady Sanders' personal sitting room would be ideal as a music room, and Janet quickly broke in and said she would never hear of inconveniencing the lady. Perhaps Lady Sanders could advise her in the best location? By the time the four of them rose from the luncheon table, Janet had the beginnings of a headache from acting as peacemaker, and Lady Sanders had begun to feel that perhaps Miss Lambert would prove to be more amenable and more easily guided than she had supposed.

As they were driving away, Lady Lambert asked where the dower house was, causing Lady Sanders to glare at her again. When Lord Sanders pointed out a pretty three-story building some distance away, Lady Lambert nodded and smiled. "Perhaps it was wise to plan a spring wedding after all," she said, "for I am sure your dear mother has a great deal of renovation and redecorating to do to make the dower house over to her satisfaction. Of course she will wish to remove there before the wedding."

Lord Sanders mumbled that it had not been decided since his mother appeared to be struck dumb with shock. He was sure she had no intention of removing from the seat of power she had always occupied, and he hoped Janet would not ask it of her. He felt unable to deny his fiancée anything, but he did not wish his mother to be unhappy. Besides, he had thought that since Janet was so very young, she would need his mother's guidance for some years to come. He stole a glance at Janet, but her eyes were lowered as she smoothed her kid gloves, and she had nothing to add to the conversation.

In a very few more days, the Lambert ladies left for Aylesford Grange, where they would spend some little time before travelling up to London. Lady Lambert had denied Lord Sanders, to his mother's relief, declaring that either of her sisters-in-law, the duchess or Mrs. Meccleston, would be delighted to house them. Janet was as relieved as Lady Sanders was, for she was looking forward to a respite from her fiancé's attentions. She had become used to his kisses by now, but although they did not precisely repulse her, neither did they attract her, and she did not like to be touched by him. When he took her hand or put his arm around her waist, it was all she could do not to pull away, and she could not refrain from stiffening a little at his lovemaking. If he felt she was less than affectionate, he told himself it was maidenly modesty, and she would soon return his love.

Lady Lambert had it in her mind to ask Mrs. Meccleston to chaperone Janet after the essential shopping had been accomplished. Now she was safely engaged, she felt she could leave her to her aunt's attentions, especially since she wished to return to Rundell Court for Agatha's confinement, and felt she had neglected her duties at the Grange for too long a period as well. She did not foresee that it would take very long to rig her daughter out; a few ball gowns, some day dresses, and one or two hats would suffice. Let Lord Sanders buy her clothes when they were married. And as for the wedding gown, there was either Agatha's or Lizzie's that could be made over, for Lord Sanders had never seen either one of them.

These small economies made it easier for her to bear her defeat in trying to force Lord Sanders to an earlier wedding date. She was distressed to see that he became stubborn, in spite of her most caressing manner and pleasant smiles. "No, no, dear Lady Lambert," he said firmly. "I have promised Janet a May wedding, and to that I hold resolutely. Ah, spring . . . and Janet!" In the face of such romantic sentiments, Lady Lambert was forced to admit defeat.

The Lambert ladies remained at the Grange for a week. A letter had been sent to Mrs. Meccleston, who declared she would be delighted to have them visit; such a good match. Ada must be most pleased. She added in a postscript that perhaps her dear sister would be kind enough to tell her how she managed so well for all her daughters, for both Cynthia and Adele showed no signs of going off, and refused to even contemplate the young men she introduced them to as suitable *partis*.

Janet smiled grimly when she read this part of the letter, and felt sorry for both her cousins should Lady Lambert impart her secrets of matchmaking to their mother.

❧ 8 ❧

Janet and Lady Lambert were in London by the end of
the third week of October, and had not been in residence
at Mrs. Meccleston's house on Charles Street above an
hour before Lord Sanders was announced. He had come
to make the acquaintance of these new relatives, and to
invite the Lamberts to dinner at his house the following
evening before attending a concert as his guests.

"I was sure you would wish to hear Maestro Roccani,
Janet," he said as he was taking his leave of her privately,
Lady Lambert kindly allowing him a few minutes alone
with his fiancée. "He is considered one of our finest pian-
ists, although to my prejudiced ears he is not a whit better
than you."

Janet was thrilled, and was able to smile at him warmly
for his kindness and even to press his hand as he left, and
Ernest went home walking on air, sure that she had
missed him as much as he had missed her.

Mrs. Meccleston begged Lady Lambert to tell her all
the news of home and most especially of this new engagement, and Janet was excused so she might rest and un-
pack. In this she was aided by a triumphant Simpton, who
had travelled to London before them. Lady Lambert had
had no intention of employing a lady's maid for her young
daughter, but she was forced to do so when Lady Sanders

heard her discussing the matter with Agatha, who mentioned her maid wished other employment.

"But of course you will provide a lady's maid for Janet, *dear* Lady Lambert. It will not do to have her looking so countrified in her simple toilettes, you know. Not the future bride of a Sanders. And dear Ernest is so used to the most beautifully dressed ladies; he might make comparisons if Janet is not turned out in the finest style."

Lady Sanders smiled triumphantly as she said this, and Lady Lambert was forced to engage Simpton.

As Janet was getting reacquainted with her new maid, Adele and Cynthia Meccleston came home from their afternoon's outing, and were quick to join her to learn all about her fiancé. They had been driving in the park with two dashing young officers, "So handsome, you would stare to see them, Janet!" Adele assured her, but since Janet did not attempt to praise Lord Sanders to them in return, they went away to dress for dinner much perplexed. They had expected all kinds of boasts and confidences, such as they had shared with Lizzie, but this cousin barely mentioned her intended husband, and Adele confided to Cynthia that she had always found Janet a most unusual girl, and difficult to know. Cynthia agreed. "I am sure, dear sister, that if I were engaged, I could not stop talking about the gentleman for hours on end! How strange she is! I hope we will all get on together!"

Since her son was away visiting friends, only Mrs. Meccleston and her daughters and Lady Lambert and Janet sat down to dinner that evening. Adele and Cynthia chatted easily all through dinner and completely missed the speculative eye their mama bent on them. She had found her sister-in-law's instructions about the best way to secure engagements to be most interesting.

The following evening, the Lamberts were admitted to the Sanders town house by a dignified butler, grown old in the service of the family. Lady Lambert looked about her with interest. The house was in the best part of town, and impressively large, and she nodded to herself as the butler announced them. Lord Sanders came forward quickly and begged them to be seated near the fire. "Such a bite to the air," he said. "Winter will soon be upon us, and then we must hope for an early spring, must we not, dear Janet?" Before she could think of a reply to this pleasantry, he continued, "And here is my dear mama to join us. What a happy occasion that finds us all together again!" Lady Lambert bowed stiffly, Lady Sanders nodded and sniffed, but Ernest was so happy to have Janet beside him again that he did not remember the ladies' feud. Instead he asked what the Lamberts had done that day and how Janet found London.

"It is very large and confusing . . . ah, Ernest," she said, "but I am sure I shall soon grow accustomed. Mama and I began our shopping today."

"I am so glad to hear that, Janet," Lady Sanders said with a smile. "I know how hard it must be for you to appear in public, still dressed in those simple little country gowns. When will your new ones be ready?"

Lady Lambert was quick to break in and tell Lady Sanders that the gown her daughter was wearing was brand-new today, and Lady Sanders raised her pince-nez and stared. "Really?" she asked in disbelief. "You mean you were able to find one ready-made? How quaint. Of course I expect you have ordered any number of gowns to be fitted to Janet, and by the finest modistes, of course. But perhaps you have not yet seen Mme. Ninette, and for hats, may I suggest Bonheure?"

These were the most expensive outfitters in London, of which Lady Lambert was perfectly aware, but she did not contradict her hostess. She intended to do most of Janet's shopping at the Parthenon Bazarr, and between them and that very expensive maid, she was sure that they could add any touches of lace or trimmings that might be needed to turn Janet out in acceptable style. She regretted very much that Lady Sanders had somehow stumbled onto her ideas of economy and never lost an opportunity to twit her about them.

Janet did not really begin to enjoy herself until she was in the concert hall awaiting the arrival of the Maestro Roccani. Ernest had seated both older ladies first, and followed her in from the aisle, and now he leaned closer to her and whispered, "My dear. What a delight to see you again. We must plan a drive in the park tomorrow, for I wish all my acquaintances to see you as soon as possible. And the night after that, there is a ball at Lady Gordon's. My mother will see that you have an invitation." Janet nodded and agreed to everything he said, but she was much more interested in looking around the hall. There were so many beautiful women in London, and their gowns and jewels were each more outstanding than the next. And the men were so impeccably dressed, so suave and sophisticated. She had to admit that Ernest did not appear to advantage with his straight sandy hair and colorless eyelashes. For example, he appeared insignificant in comparison with the very striking dark gentleman seated somewhat ahead of them across the aisle. Suddenly she raised her hand to her face and turned quite pale. Could it be? Just then, the gentleman in question turned away from his elderly companion and scanned the seats filling up behind him, and she could see it was Anthony Northbridge.

For a moment she felt her heart might stop beating, she was so stunned. At first glance he appeared to be unchanged, but then she noted the sardonic droop of his eyelids and the bored twist to his mouth. He was older, of course; perhaps that was what had tempered his handsome good looks and left behind this weary, blasé stranger. She took a deep breath to steady herself, and as she stared at him, his eyes swept over her without pausing, and the hand she had raised slightly in greeting dropped to her lap. Now her face reddened, for it appeared that m'lord did not remember her anywhere near as well as she remembered him. Through her tumultuous thoughts, Ernest continued chatting, pointing out this personage and that for her instruction.

There was some polite applause when the maestro finally took the stage, and for the next hour, of all the audience, Janet was the most transformed and attentive, even able to forget Anthony Northbridge and her horrified disappointment at the behaviour of a man she had counted at least a friend.

How perfectly the maestro played, and with what beautiful interpretation, she thought. When Ernest took her hand in his, she was not even aware of the intimacy, but gripped it tightly in her delight in the music. When the last chords had died away, she applauded eagerly, and then she turned to Lord Sanders with stars in her eyes. "Dear Ernest. How can I ever thank you for such a marvelous evening? I shall never forget it, no, never, in all my life. He is a superb musician. Oh, if I could only play a tenth as well!"

Lord Sanders beamed, well pleased with her reaction. "You play very well, my dear," he assured her as he helped her adjust the sarcenet stole she was wearing. "And of course after we are married, it will be a delight for me to hear you play—whenever you can find the time from your duties, of course! Willows is so very demanding."

Janet did not answer as she followed him out to the aisle. Nothing he said could dampen her siprits after the performance she had just heard. Then, as she turned to allow her mother and Lady Sanders to precede her, she heard a familiar voice behind her say, "I beg your pardon, if we might pass through?" and she turned to find Lord Northbridge looking down at her as coldly as if they had never met. "Servant, Sanders!" he said carelessly in his deep voice as he ushered the elderly lady with him past the Sanders party. Suddenly all her enjoyment in the beautiful music left her. Her heart had given such a lurch when she looked up into that handsome dark face, she was glad for the support of Ernest's arm, for she felt she might fall. Lord Northbridge's dark eyes had been narrowed and there was a petulant frown on his face as he surveyed the crowded aisle. "Your Grace!" Ernest replied, ponderously bowing, but Northbridge barely nodded before he pushed past them and was gone. Lady Sanders was introducing Lady Lambert to a friend of hers, and had not noticed the exchange, and Ernest made no move to stop Northbridge and introduce him to his fiancé. Indeed, Janet saw his face was red from the encounter, and wondered why. She was not to know that Ernest had no intention of presenting her to such a great rake, so unworthy of meeting the future bride of a Sanders, even though he had attained a dukedom on the death of his father the year before.

Anthony Northbridge was indeed bored; in fact it seemed he had been bored for as long as he could remember, and even the accomplished musical performance he had been treated to this evening had no way of elevating his spirits. He had been in so many concert halls, had attended so many dances and masquerades and balls, had watched so many prizefights and racing meets, had danced and flirted and made love to so many lovely women that there appeared to be nothing left in the world that he had not done times without number. His aunt was still his favourite companion, and in her company he was at least fairly content, for she never pulled any of her punches, nor did she tonight. At Grillon's, where he took her to supper after the concert, she was not slow to tell him that she was ashamed of him. One black eyebrow rose in disbelief. "And what have I done to earn such censure, Countess?" he asked. "I assure you, every move I make is copied instantly by the highest sticklers of the *haut ton!*"

"More fools they!" she snapped, cutting her veal marsala impatiently. "It is what you have *not* done! Look at you! Twenty-six years old and you act as if you had lived to be a hundred. How is it possible to be so blasé at only twenty-six? *I* was never bored at that age, dear nephew." She sighed, remembering past glories, and her nephew curled his lip, which she was quick to notice. "And there is no need for such scorn, Tony. At your age you should be living life to the fullest. Why have you not married? And have you given up travelling forever? Even with the state of the world, there are several places on the globe that are not at war—go and see 'em. Take an interest in your estates, learn more of the arts. But for heaven's sake, stop dragging around sneering at everything in that superior way you have begun to cultivate."

Northbridge had the grace to redden a little. "I was not aware it was so obvious, dear aunt," he said. "You are right, I *am* bored. Perhaps it is a shame that I am so wealthy there is no need for me to be gainfully employed. Would you like me better as a lawyer's clerk, ma'am? Or perhaps as a horse trader or a furniture dealer?"

She rapped his knuckles with her fork. "Do not be absurd! All I ask is that you look about you with fresh eyes. Surely there is some young lady in London that does not weary you completely. I begin to think that marriage would be the making of you, my man, and I shall cast about me for a suitable bride. Yes, that might be the very thing."

She looked so fierce and determined that Tony became alarmed. "Please do not trouble yourself. I assure you I am perfectly capable of finding a bride for myself, when I decide to marry, but that time is not yet upon me. And do not start lecturing me about my duty to the title and the estates. Surely at twenty-six I have a few more years in which I will be capable of begetting an heir!"

Lady Ralston did not blush, for she and her nephew had talked freely for years. Instead she said gloomily, "No doubt you do, but if you continue as you have been going on, you will not be able to get anyone decent to marry you, and unless things have changed considerably since I was a girl, it still requires two people, one of each sex, to beget heirs."

Tony laughed and agreed. They chatted of the latest gossip as their plates were removed, and then, when the waiters had left to fetch the next course, the countess said suddenly, "Miss Wharlington!"

Tony was not confused by her abruptness. "No conversation!" he snapped.

"Lady Wrotham?"

"Her laugh grates on my ears."

"Miss Phoebe Randall? You notice I do not mention the eldest Miss Randall; you could never abide her prosiness or her freckles."

"Nor Miss Phoebe's lisp either."

His aunt sighed. "I see you are going to be difficult, Tony, as were all the previous Dukes of Stour. Pray tell me, what would you like in a wife, provided you were interested in acquiring one?" she added.

Tony idly took a sip of wine as he thought. "If I were on the lookout, which I have told you I am not, I suppose I would be searching for someone who was intelligent and had some degree of wit. She would have to be from an excellent family, and wealthy as well, so that I could be sure she was not marrying me for my title or my money. Oh, and of course she must be beautiful, with an excellent figure, and absolutely no faults of any kind. And if she could manage to amuse me for more than a se'en-night, that would be helpful as well."

Lady Ralston laughed out loud. "A paragon, to be sure. But such a girl would not be allowed anywhere near you, you know. You have such a bad reputation as a rake, Tony."

"As to that, I have never found it matters in the slightest to a matchmaking mama; they still pursue me, sure that marriage to their eligible offspring is the one thing that is needed to reform me." He sighed and signalled the waiter for more wine.

"Indeed!" the countess snapped. "And now I must add insufferable conceit to your other estimable qualities. I hope I shall live to see the day that you are humbled, Tony. It would do you so much good."

"I am sure you are right," he agreed, so cordially that she longed to hit him. She said no more of the matter, but began to discuss the performance of a Bach fugue they had heard that evening, but in her mind she was determined to look about her and try to find Tony a bride. When he was married to some healthy Englishwoman of good breeding, with a parcel of babies tumbling around him, he would not have time to be bored. She was certain she could find just the girl. Tony, deep in praising the maestro's skill, was unaware that she was settling his future, and perhaps that was just as well: had he known, he might have begun planning an immediate trip abroad. When she made up her mind, Lady Ralston was just as stubborn as the rest of the Northbridges.

Two evenings later, Lord Sanders appeared to escort the Lamberts to Lady Gordon's ball. Lady Lambert had been so stung by his mother's comments about Janet's appearance before the concert that she had gone over her budget and purchased a most expensive deep-sapphire-blue gown for her daughter. She did not consider anything but pastels appropriate for a debutante, but Simpton, who had accompanied the ladies to carry their parcels, had enthused over the colour, which exactly matched Janet's eyes, and had pointed out that as an engaged young lady she was allowed more latitude in her dress than other young misses her age. Finally Lady Lambert had given in and had even gone so far as to lend her daughter a small sapphire necklace and eardrops to match. Lord Sanders had sent a bouquet of white flowers that morning, a few of which Simpton fastened skillfully above the soft waves of Janet's chignon. With her matching satin sandals and long white kid gloves, she looked very beautiful, and Lord Sanders' heart swelled with pride as he presented her to their hostess. Janet thanked her nicely for inviting her, a complete stranger to her ball, and Lady Gordon, a good-natured woman of middle years, complimented them both on their engagement, and was most gracious to Lady Lambert as well.

Ernest of course wrote his name on her card for many dances, but he did unbend far enough to allow some of his particular friends to sign her dance card as well.

"Not, of course, for any of the waltzes, Janet," he said sternly. "I do not approve of the waltz. If the musicians should begin to play one, I expect you to excuse yourself and rejoin your mother. A Sanders does not romp about in such an intimate way in public."

Janet tried hard not to be disappointed. Lizzie had introduced her to the intricacies of the dance, and she had been anxious to try it with a real partner, for it looked very dashing. Surely as an engaged lady . . . But, no, she thought, catching sight of Ernest's disapproving face. He would definitely say no. Better not to ask.

She enjoyed her first London ball nevertheless, even though most of her partners were as prosy and ponderous as her fiancé. She did not have to concentrate very hard to follow their innocuous chatter, and so she was free to observe the other guests. She wondered who that very lovely blond lady was, dressed all in gold, and the elderly gentleman with all the honors and medals across his chest, and the blue of the garter adorning his calf.

Sometime after supper, at which she had been introduced to the marvels of Dunstable oysters and lobster patties, as well as iced claret cup, she was sitting out a waltz with her fiancé, and was taking the opportunity to inquire about the identity of some of the more fascinating guests, when she heard a familiar deep drawl behind her, and stiffened.

"Gregory! Happy to see you in town again, my friend! And how did you find the country?"

"As boring as ever," Lord Wells replied. "It is a desert, Tony, 'pon rep! And my journey was all for nought as well." He sighed heavily and then added, "Great-Aunt Ciddy appears to be good for another twenty years at least. This new doctor chappie had her back on her feet in no time. I can tell you there were some gloomy faces at the dinner table when she tottered in and joined us. So I hastened back to town, claiming urgent business. And urgent it is, too, now that I am not about to inherit her fortune, as I had been given every reason to expect this time."

"Moneylenders, Gregory? Or could the real reason be that very pretty little blonde from the Gaiety Club that drew you back so promptly?"

Janet felt Lord Sanders stiffen before he rose and held out his hand.

"Let us remove to another part of the ballroom, my dear," he said, and it was obvious that he did not wish his betrothed to have to listen to such a disgusting conversation. Janet rose obediently, although she would have loved to hear Gregory's reply. It was quite the most interesting exchange she had listened to all evening.

"I say, your pardon, Sanders," the deep voice drawled. "Didn't see you . . . or the lady."

Ernest was forced to bow, and Janet turned as well and

137

stared at the duke. He returned her stare, a small frown creasing his brow as he contemplated this new face. Before Lord Sanders could draw her away into safety, the duke raised one elegant hand. "I do not believe I have had the pleasure of the lady's acquaintance; you must be new to London, Miss . . . Miss . . . ?"

He turned and looked at Lord Sanders, one eyebrow raised, and Ernest was forced to make the introduction. He might not approve of the duke and Lord Wells or any of the Corinthian set, but he could not be rude.

"My fiancée, Your Grace, Miss Janet Rose Lambert," he said, holding her arm tightly as if he felt she were in danger of being snatched away by this dissolute duke. "Janet, the Duke of Stour; Lord Wells."

"Miss Lambert? Now, where . . . ?" mused the duke. "I am sure I have heard the name, but in what connection I have no idea. My lamentable memory. You must forgive me, Miss Lambert, if we have been introduced previously."

He spoke so lightly, as if the matter was of small importance to him, that Janet became furious, and it brought a sparkle to her deep blue eyes that quite drove Miss Esmeralda of the Gaiety Club from Lord Wells's mind. He had seldom seen such a handsome gel as this Miss Lambert. Pity she had to be engaged to Stuffy Sanders.

Janet curtsied, holding her head high. "Your Grace," she murmured. "Yes, we have met before, although I agree it was an entirely forgettable occasion." Her smile glittered, and Lord Sanders drew in his breath at her rudeness as she explained, "You were visiting my father, Lord Lambert, at our home at Aylesford Grange, with your uncle, Lord Baggeston. I am sure I do not know why you should have bothered to remember me, any more than you might have remembered Princess Patty."

Lord Sanders pressed her arm in warning, and she stopped, even though Tony Northbridge's eyes were lit up now with laughter. "Of course, the pig. But, Miss Lambert, you must allow me to tell you that you have changed a great deal. When I saw you at the Grange you were a mere child, a funny little girl intent on her piano and trying to avoid her father's horses. You see, I *do* recall you."

He had looked her up and down while he was talking, openly insolent, and now he smiled as if he expected to be congratulated for this feat of memory. Janet, remembering all the weeks she had waited for the music he had promised to send her, all the hours she had dreamed about him, and the sadness she had felt at his betrayal of their friendship, was more angry than ever. She turned aside without another word and said to her fiancé, "Ernest, may we retire? I must speak to my mother at once."

Lord Sanders was not at all loath to obey her, and promptly, but he made a note to speak to her about her abruptness to one of the duke's importance. He was glad to see that she appeared to dislike Northbridge, since he knew that all too many young girls found him fascinating, but even though Janet came into society armed with the impressive credentials of being his chosen bride, it would not do for her to be impolite to such a leader of fashion. If Northbridge should take her in dislike, all the rest of the *haut ton* would follow his lead. Accordingly, he bowed very deeply to the two men to remove the sting of her words, before he led her away to her mother.

"Brrr!" Lord Wells said as the couple moved away. "Now, whatever did you do on that visit to make the young lady dislike you so much, Tony?"

"I have no idea!" Northbridge replied, his eyes still on the slender figure in blue. "I thought she liked me then, for she confided in me most openly. I remember feeling sorry for her, such an odd little mite, and so different from the rest of her family. I was there only a year and a half ago, as I remember, just before my father died. My mother sent me along with my uncle, hoping to interest me in the bucolic life and estate matters."

Lord Wells laughed until the tears came to his eyes. "*You?* Interested in farming? Your mother is the most incredible optimist, dear boy."

"I think she has finally admitted defeat at this point," Tony said. "But to think it was such a short time ago, and now here is Miss Lambert, with her hair up and wearing a smart London gown, and engaged as well. I wonder where she met Sanders? She told me something then, but I cannot recall what it was, about the Lamberts and marriage. . . ."

"Perhaps you will get a chance to ask her," Lord Wells said as he waved to an acquaintance across the room.

"Perhaps I shall," his friend mused. "But what odds would you take that she would not cut me dead if I tried? I wonder why she has taken me in dislike, I most sincerely wonder why. It is a mystery, dear Gregory, and perhaps I will pursue the matter! After all, solving a mystery might relieve the boredom and feeling of *ennui* that I have been afflicted with these past months." He did not add that Miss Lambert's beauty also intrigued him. What a change a year or so could make. Comparing the big-eyed child in pigtails, dressed in an insipid pink gown, to this stunning young woman, elegantly coiffed and wearing a modish blue gown that clung delightfully to her suddenly mature figure, he found the transformation miraculous. His interest was decidedly captured.

"Shame about Sanders, though," Lord Wells added as he watched the gentleman bending over Miss Lambert possessively. "She doesn't look a day over eighteen, and I have never seen her in town before, for those eyes I would surely remember. He must have met her in the country, and sealed the bargain before she was even brought out."

"Perhaps. I myself would have thought Ernest Sanders would have chosen a more conventional bride, being so stuffy himself. Miss Lambert is not at all in the usual style, and she looks as if she will lead him a merry dance."

From across the room, Janet was careful not to look the duke's way again. Insolent man! Conceited idiot! she thought as she smiled and chatted with her mother and Lady Sanders. At last her heart stopped pounding and her breathing slowed, and she was glad that no one seemed to have noticed her agitation as she prepared to join a set of country dances with her betrothed. The duke left the ball shortly thereafter, and even though she was trying hard not to look at him, she was instantly aware of his departure and of a feeling of dissatisfaction. Ernest, in the meantime, was taking her to task for her rudeness and pointing out how dangerous such behaviour was, but although she nodded, she was not listening.

The following days she seemed to see Northbridge everywhere. If Ernest took her for a drive in his carriage, there was the Duke of Stour riding a black gelding and tipping his hat to her with a wicked grin; at the theatre he was with a party in the box directly opposite the Sanders party, staring at her openly through his opera glasses; and at Ranelagh he was again present at a concert she attended with Lord Sanders. He made no move to single her out or speak to her again, for which she told herself she was very glad, as it saved her the trouble of cutting him, no matter what Ernest had told her, but she somehow always found herself looking about her eagerly when she was in company to determine if Northbridge was present. It was amazing how many evenings proved to be boring when the duke was not in attendance.

Lady Lambert eventually completed her shopping, and being promised by Mrs. Meccleston that she would take the greatest care of Janet, prepared to rejoin the rest of the family at Aylesford Grange. Janet was forced to spend a final afternoon being instructed by her mother, who, although she remarked on how pleased she was to see her daughter had settled down in her engagement just as she had predicted she would, still had a long list of dos and don'ts for her. Janet heard one last time how a Lambert was expected to conduct herself; whom she should acknowledge, and whom avoid. She was warned to be thrifty, although how she could be anything else with the small amount of pin money her mother left her was not explained; she was urged to help her aunt and work diligently on her needlepoint; to be attentive to her future mother-in-law and most especially to that excellent man her fiancé; avoid sloth, pursue goodness and purity of heart, and . . . and . . . and! When she had kissed the cool cheek her mother extended, and had seen her to the Lambert travelling carriage, Janet drew a sigh of relief.

She had several schemes in mind that had been impossible to execute under her mother's watchful eyes, but now at last she was ready to begin. She had noticed that Aunt Meccleston allowed her daughters a great deal more freedom than Lady Lambert would have considered proper, and she intended to take full advantage of this happy state of affairs while she was able.

It had been arranged that Janet would stay in town until Christmas, and then travel to Rundell Court for the holiday season. That way she would be able to see her new nephew, and be close enough for Lord Sanders to visit whenever he could spare the time. Lady Sanders said she would be delighted to escort Janet to the country, glad to be seeing the back of Lady Lambert at last. Time had done nothing to endear these ladies to each other, and the state of affairs between them now resembled an armed truce. With Lady Lambert's departure, Lady Sanders had every intention of stepping up her campaign to rid herself of her son's chosen bride, pointing out Miss Lambert's many faults to her son, and her unworthiness to occupy her present position. After all, an engagement was not a marriage, and many a one of them had been broken in the past. Although she could not like it for a Sanders, it was vastly preferable to an alliance with *that* family.

The same afternoon her mother left for home, Janet went to her Aunt Jane and told her that she would like to pay her respects to her other aunt, the Duchess of Meresly.

"That is well-thought-on, Janet, most proper you should!" Mrs. Meccleston said, rummaging through her workbasket. "Now, where did I put the pink silk? If that isn't the way of things, always disappearing when you need them! Tchh! So annoying!" Janet found the silk on the table next to her aunt's chair, and went away to get ready for her call. The Mecclestons did not have a piano, and she missed practicing very much, especially now that she had heard so many fine musicians. It occurred to her that perhaps the duchess possessed one, so when she was admitted to the lady's drawing room, she curtsied and tried not to look around her too obviously.

The duchess eyed this new niece with interest. She had not been attracted to either Agatha or Elizabeth Lambert, for they reminded her too much of their mother, and she had never been a fan of Lady Lambert's. But this slim, dark girl with the large dark eyes and pointed face was completely different. She patted the sofa beside her, and before long was questioning Janet most particularly. What she learned was enough to pique her interest, and she made a point of asking Janet and her fiancé to dine in a few days' time.

Anne Ellis, née Lambert, although she looked somewhat like her brother with her stout figure and ruddy complexion, was nothing like him in disposition. She enjoyed London as much as she disliked the country, rarely left town, and had none of the Lambert stuffiness or conventionality. When she learned that her niece loved music, reading, and the arts, her heart warmed to her, for she, off all people, was most aware that to anyone so inclined, being brought up as a Lambert had to have been a distinct hardship. And when Janet confided shyly that of all things she loved the piano, her aunt was quick to ask her to bring her music the evening of the dinner. "I am sure we will all be delighted to hear you play, my dear!" Janet agreed, although she warned her aunt that she had been unable to practice since arriving in town, and was woefully rusty, and the duchess insisted she make free of her piano whenever she had the time, and instructed her butler to this effect. As Janet strolled home, trailing a respectful Simpton, she felt she had accomplished a great deal that afternoon.

The next day she declined to drive out with Lord Sanders when he called, saying she felt tired from all the parties they had attended. He was disappointed, but told her instead that he would look forward to seeing her, as fresh as a daisy, at Mrs. McCree's reception that evening. As he kissed her good-bye, Janet closed her eyes and wondered why it was that Ernest always managed to make the most ordinary statement sound trite. Fresh as a daisy indeed! Did the man never have an original thought? she wondered, and then she put him from her mind and ran upstairs to put on her bonnet and instruct the long-suffering Simpton, who would much prefer to see her mistress off on an afternoon's outing so she might take a discreet nap in the sewing room, that she was once again to have the treat of accompanying Miss Lambert on another cultural expedition. Together they took a hackney cab to the Royal Academy.

Lord Sanders had escorted Janet and his mother to the latest show some days previously, but his idea of looking at art was to walk very briskly, not neglecting a single painting, but never stopping to admire any but the largest works by the best-known artists, at which he would raise his quizzing glass and murmur, "Excellent. Very like," before hastening on. Lady Sanders was even worse, for she conversed without pause and barely looked at the paintings, although later, of course, she would chat knowledgeably about them to all her acquaintance. To the Sanderses, a painting was only successful if it portrayed nature most faithfully, and there were some landscapes by a new Academician that Janet wished to study more closely, for they were almost fanciful in their use of colour and line. Accordingly, she spent a long time before a London street scene. She could not have told you why just the suggestion of mass was more exciting to her than a detailed architectural drawing that showed every line and crevice, but it was. She noticed at once that if you stood too close to these paintings, they seemed to be nothing but colorful blobs of paint, but if you retreated a bit, the whole painting became clear, springing to life from the canvas and reminding you forcibly of a particular day when the light so clear, the shadows so sharp. She moved on to the next painting by the same artist, a study of nymphs that she had no way of knowing had caused quite a furor in the Academy. You could hardly call these ladies classical beauties; instead Janet was reminded of the members of the muslin company she sometimes caught sight of in the park or the streets. They were young and pretty, but there was something common and coarse about them, and an alarming fragility as well, as if their tenure as beauties was to be of very short duration.

She backed up a bit, her head tilted to one side as she studied the painting with intent blue eyes, and could not help murmuring, "But how sad!"

Beside her, an older woman turned to her and stared and then said, "So you see them that way too! How very alarming to have your mind read, for I was thinking the very same thing. The man has talent—and an acute eye!"

Janet smiled and nodded, and would have spoken if she had not seen the Duke of Stour behind the lady. The duke smiled at her gently.

"Miss Lambert, well met," he said. "Allow me to present you to my aunt, the Countess of Grant. Aunt, Miss Janet Rose Lambert."

"M'lady," Janet said as she curtsied, trying to ignore the wicked twinkle in the duke's eye. The countess looked at her keenly and smiled.

"I am delighted to meet you, Miss Lambert," she said, "and to discover that your taste in art so closely parallels mine. It is unfortunate that Stine is so poorly hung, but there are several who do not admire his work, you know; they feel it is too radical for the other old fogies of the Academy!" She laughed out loud, causing another visitor to stare, until she raised her pince-nez and surveyed him in such a way that the gentleman took a hurried leave. Janet decided she liked the lady, in spite of her relationship with the duke. That gentleman pointed his quizzing glass at the nymphs and asked, "But what do you think of his talent, Miss Lambert?"

He did not sound particularly interested in her opinion, and Janet felt a tiny spurt of anger. "I consider him most talented, Your Grace, and by far the most superior artist of the exhibition. The use of colour, the way he suggests his subjects, leaving the viewer to supply the details. Oh, I am not saying it well, but I do consider him extremely skilled."

She paused in confusion, feeling she had been much too verbose, but the countess did not seem to find anything amiss. "Stine would enjoy your comments, Miss Lambert. Perhaps you would care to meet him? He some-

times comes to my salons, and every artist likes his admirers. Poor man, he has so few of us."

Janet said she would be most pleased, and smiled until
the duke said, "But you are not here with your fiancé,
Miss Lambert. I do not think Ernest Sanders would be at
all pleased to find you rubbing elbows with all the common artists and musicians that my Aunt Ralston so rashly
encourages. Perhaps you should ask his permission first?"

He seemed to delight in baiting her, Janet thought as
she put up her chin and remarked, most untruthfully, "As
to that, Your Grace, we are not always together, and if
Lord Sanders should not enjoy the experience, I can assure you that I would—and very, very much. I thank you,
Lady Ralston, for your kind invitation; I will make it a
point to attend. But your nephew reminds me that it is
growing late, and I have an engagement. Lady Ralston
. . . Sir . . . if you will excuse me . . . ?"

She curtsied again and took her leave after the countess
said she would send her a card, and beckoned to Simp-
tom, who was sitting on a marble bench some distance
away, resting her feet. The countess watched her leave,
and then swung around to her nephew and demanded to
know who this young lady was, and why he seemed to
take such a delight in teasing her.

As they strolled down the gallery, Tony told her all he
knew of Miss Lambert, little aware that his aunt found his
description very interesting. It was unfortunate that the
gel was engaged; however, she would wait and see
whether there was any love between the couple, for if
there was not, she did not see any reason why Tony
should not have this girl, who was as intelligent as she
was beautiful. She knew the Lambert family; boring
though they might be, they had impeccable bloodlines
and credentials, and the girl's aunt, the Duchess of
Meresly, was a very good friend of hers. Of course,
she thought to herself as she took her place in Tony's
carriage for the drive home, Miss Lambert is a most
unusual type, with that black hair and those huge eyes,
not at all the sort Tony generally chooses, and she is
lamentably young as well. Lottie, now, whose tenure as

his mistress had run its course, was blond and mature, and before her there had been a robust redhead, and a lady with ash-brown curls. But then, she thought, smiling at her nephew as he took up the reins, what man knows what he wants in a wife until it is pointed out to him? And Miss Lambert is not at all in the common style— perhaps she might even amuse him for more than a se'en-night! She chuckled to herself, but although Tony raised one brow in inquiry, she did not bother to explain the joke.

❧ 9 ❦

It would have been wonderful indeed if Lord Sanders had been able to ignore all his mother's derogatory comments about a fiancée who continued so cool toward him. True, he still loved Janet, he told himself, but it was tiresome to be constantly correcting her. She seemed to have no idea how to go on, and what was worse, she rarely paid any attention to his teasing, gentle lectures. Why, only the other day while they had been strolling in the park, he had had to take her to task for laughing so uproariously at the antics of a little boy and his dog. After he had pointed out that it was not at all ladylike and had attracted the attention of two starchy dowagers who were well-known to his mother as well, she had only looked up at him and said, "I beg your pardon, Ernest, did you say something? I was not attending. What a dear little boy!" And then he had had to give his lecture all over again. Lady Sanders was able to put in many a barb at the breakfast table, over the teacups, and on their drives to and from Mrs. Meccleston's house. She was clever enough to pose these criticisms as casual conversation, commiserating with her son on the difficult task before them, so that Ernest began to believe that his mother was at last on his side, and would leave no stone unturned (as he himself would have put it) to aid him with this very young, very un-Sanders-like bride. He had not seen much of Janet since her mother had left town, for she always seemed to be busy in the afternoons, and sometimes he found she had left the house before he called in the morning. He was not to know that Janet was taking full advantage of her aunt's piano, and since he always arrived on the doorstep promptly at ten-thirty, it was easy for her to escape the house before he called.

Lady Sanders had not been included in the invitation to dinner at the Duchess of Meresly's, and after Ernest had had a chance to survey the other guests, he could only be glad. There was that rake Northbridge and his aunt; Lord Wells and several others he could not like and had never acknowledged; and there were even some out-and-out cits whose only claim to gentility was the fact that they were patrons of the arts. Standing in the duchess's drawing room, his hand possessively under Janet's arm, he grew stiff and formal. No one would dare to criticize the duchess of her choice of guests, but surely his fiancée was much too young and naive to be exposed to such outrageous bohemians. Tony Northbridge noted his expression with amusement. His aunt watched the engaged couple very carefully as well, all through dinner. There were no smiles between them, no melting glances or blushes, but what was most interesting was how very still Miss Lambert's face became whenever Lord Sanders deigned to speak, almost as if she were consciously repressing any emotion, either of delight or of disgust. It was all very encouraging, she thought.

After dinner, which was a long, noisy affair accompanied by sparkling conversation, political commentary, and hearty laughter at the *bon mots* of the cleverer wits, the guests were escorted to the music room, and their hostess clapped her hands for attention.

"We are to have a special treat this evening. My niece, Miss Lambert, has been persuaded to play for us!" There were a few murmurs as Janet took her seat at the piano, until her aunt added, "There is absolutely no need for that long-suffering expression, Pierre. You will see."

At that, the guests laughed and settled down to listen.

Janet removed her heavy engagement ring and placed it carefully to one side before she bent over the keys and began to play. Wisely, she did not try to perform anything too difficult, for she was still out of practice, but even with the simpler études and sonatas, it was clear she had an outstanding talent, and she was heartily applauded at the close of her performance. Lord Sanders watched in horror as everyone crowded around her to compliment her. He could not help remembering his mother's comment that Janet's talent smacked of the stage, and he wished she had not felt it necessary to move about so as she played, for it was really rather theatrical. He continued to feel uneasy as he went up to lead her away from the instrument. What was correct at a small country-house party of good friends would not do in town. To think she had played for complete strangers, and such strangers, too. He resolved to speak to her about it on the way home.

Janet was able to ignore his disapproving face, for Tony Northbridge was before him at her side, bending his dark head to speak to her. Ernest would have intervened, but he found himself captured by the duke's aunt, and led away to a sofa quite removed from the center of the room, where he was forced to answer all her questions about his mother, Willows, and a second cousin he did not even remember, as well as giving her his opinion of the current exhibition at the Royal Academy. He had never been so honored by the countess before.

The duke led a suddenly breathless Janet to some chairs a little removed from the other guests. "My dear Miss Lambert," he said as he took a seat next to her, "what dramatic strides you have made with your music. My congratulations."

His voice was warm with admiration, and she inclined her head in thanks, but he hurried on before she could reply. "I suddenly remember a commission for you that I never completed, to my shame. To think that I forgot to send you the music I promised. I do hope you have forgiven me?"

Janet looked straight at him, and he was struck again

by the beauty of those sparkling blue eyes, now dark and stormy.

"There is no need to apologize, Your Grace," she managed to say. "I am sure you had some pressing business that drove any promise to me quite from your mind."

She sounded so stiff and hurt, the duke hurried to explain.

"It *was* very pressing, and very sad as well," he said. "When I arrived back in town after my stay at Aylesford, it was to discover my father taken ill, and I was forced to hasten to Stour. Unfortunately, he died before I could reach his bedside."

Janet's eyes softened in concern and sympathy, and without thinking, she put her hand on his arm to comfort him. The duke stared down at her hand, burdened by the ugly betrothal ring of the Sanders family as Janet said in heartfelt tones, "Forgive me, Your Grace, I did not know. You must have thought me unfeeling to be concerned about a few pieces of music when you have suffered such a loss."

The duke looked into her blue eyes, now so full of compassion, and he felt a pang—but of what, he did not know. In the silence that followed, Janet removed her hand and blushed. How could she have thought him indifferent and rude? Of course his father's death took all such petty promises from his mind! She was ashamed of herself for being angry at him.

But the duke was speaking again. "Yes, I loved and revered my father, but I am still sorry I forgot to send you those scores. You must have found a more reliable source than I, however, for I have never heard that last sonata before, and when I tried to identify the composer, I could not place him. It was not Mozart, and definitely not Bach, nor even Beethoven . . ."

Janet was glad to follow his lead. "An unknown composer, your Grace. You would not know the name."

The duke stared at her for a moment, struck by the sparkle that now filled her eyes, and then he exclaimed as her smile brought the deep dimple in her cheek into display, "*You* wrote it, didn't you? I *am* impressed!"

Janet lifted one hand as if to deny him. "But, Your Grace, how can you say so? *I*, write music? Remember, it is only Janet Lambert you speak to; only that 'funny little girl,' as I believe you called me. You are mistaken, Sir, surely!"

The duke bent his head closer and murmured in a low voice, "But how you have grown up, Miss Lambert! There is nothing of the little girl left, for you have become so sophisticated and beautiful, and your talent as a musician must be applauded, for it shows such maturity."

Janet dropped him a mock curtsy. "How kind of you to compliment me, Your Grace," she replied. "I hope it will not turn my head."

The duke raised an eyebrow in astonishment, unused to being answered so coolly, for generally his attentions reduced young debutantes to blushing, incoherent confusion. Janet nodded, as if she quite understood his surprise, while to herself she said: Oh, no, my fine duke you will not make me stammer like an idiot, no matter what you say! She found she was enjoying herself immensely, and smiled at him daring him to do his worst, but in a second her expression changed as the duke asked abruptly, "Whatever made you consent to have Ernest Sanders? He will drive you insane in a month. Or perhaps it would be wiser to say that you will drive *him* insane. I cannot think of a single thing you have in common."

There was no way to answer this impertinence, and Janet drew a breath to steady her and said lightly, as if she did not care a jot what he thought, "Perhaps we are in love, Your Grace? I believe engaged couples generally are, and I have heard it said that love removes all barriers."

He shook his head impatiently. "So I have always understood, but still it would be easier to believe this was to be a marriage of convenience." While Janet stared at him, he added, "I do see that Sanders might imagine himself in love with you, but that that love is returned—no. You are so dissimilar. Have you thought of what your life will be like, married to a man with his stern, staid outlook? I daresay he has never laughed out loud in his life, or indulged in the witty conversation and innuendos which I see *you* enjoy so much. And he does not like your talent, you know. I watched him while you were playing, and he looked most uncomfortable and disapproving. It was plain to see that he will insist that you give up your music after you are married."

Janet clasped her hands together to keep them from trembling. Every word the duke said was true, but to be discussing her fiancé with him went far beyond the dictates of good taste. And even though his eyes were kind and not mocking, and he appeared to feel a genuine compassion for her, she reminded herself that her affairs and Lord Sanders' were of small moment to him; he must be asking idly, perhaps thinking to amuse himself in a flirtation with her. He was, after all, a great rake. She looked straight into his eyes and said with a tinge of ice to her tone, "You must see that I cannot answer you, sir, for your questions go too far. Suffice it to say we are engaged, and the wedding is planned for May. There is nothing that can stop it; I will be Ernest Sanders' bride at that time."

With that she curtsied and gave the duke her cool hand before she excused herself and went back to her aunt. He was not to know that under that straight, slim back her heart was beating strangely, nor that in that high-held head her thoughts were tumbling around in disarray. He wondered why he felt so sorry for her, and why a sense of desolate emptiness had come over him as she left him, and his brows drew together in a frown, an expression not missed by his aunt, Lady Ralston, who was delighted to terminate her conversation with Lord Sanders and go to join her nephew. He did not speak of his *tête-à-tête* with Janet, but he was distracted for the remainder of the evening. His aunt resolved that tomorrow she would send an invitation to Miss Lambert to attend her very next Sunday salon.

Lord Sanders lost no time in persuading Janet to leave the party, although they were the first guests to do so. If Janet had not been thinking of the duke and his words, she might have considered it rude, but as it was, she allowed him to escort her to his carriage and drive her home without comment. Lord Sanders spoke most eloquently now they were alone, about Janet's behaviour and his feelings of seeing his future bride on such public display; the undesirablity of most of the guests present; and the need for Janet to be more modest and retiring. Janet, staring with unseeing eyes out the carriage window, did not hear a word, although when he paused to help her down at Mrs. Meccleston's door, she murmured, "Thank you, Ernest. I am sure you are right." She had found in the past that this was a very safe answer to give when she had not been attending, and Ernest, slightly mollified by her meekness, kissed her cheek before he rang the bell.

Janet did not sleep well that night. She kept seeing the duke's dark head so close to hers, his black brows and keen eyes, and the way his mouth twisted wryly whenever she did not reply to him in a satsifactory way. It was a long time before she fell into an exhausted slumber, and it was quite late when she made her way to the breakfast table the next morning. She found her aunt and both her cousins in the middle of an argument, and would have left except that Mrs. Meccleston beckoned her to come in. "Do join us, my dear," the lady said, twisting her napkin and looking distraught. "Perhaps you can help me put some sense into these silly girls' heads."

Janet took a seat reluctantly, and poured herself a cup of coffee while Adele tossed her head and Cynthia said hotly, "It will not do, Mama. You're all about in your head. Marry Mr. Lincoln indeed! I shall not."

"Nor I Mr. Botkins," Adele added. "I cannot imagine where you got the idea that they would be at all acceptable to us, Mama."

"Well, they are acceptable to *me*—" Mrs. Meccleston replied.

Before she could explain, Adele interrupted, "But we are the ones who would have to live with them for the rest of our lives. Mr. Botkins is a bore; he has no conversation and he talks only of his business. Furthermore, he is not at all handsome."

"But he is very wealthy," her mother said, trying to recoup her losses, "And of an excellent family."

"And Mr. Lincoln is very wealthy, too, is he not, Mama?" Cynthia asked.

"Yes, he is, and second in line for an earldom as well," Mrs. Meccleston agreed, throwing down her napkin and pointing a stern finger at her daughters. "I have made up my mind, you bad girls, and I say you shall marry where I choose."

This was so unlike their dithery, easygoing mother that both girls could only stare. Taking heart from their silence, Mrs. Meccleston continued. "You should learn to emulate your cousin, both of you. She is marrying the man her parents selected, as a dutiful daughter should. Would that I had such a one."

"Well, you do not, and I beg you to put such silly megrims from your mind," Adele said pertly. "You cannot *make* us marry them."

"I certainly can," Mrs. Meccleston replied, nodding her head so vigorously that both her chins wobbled and her morning cap became tilted over one ear, adding nothing to an expression she tried to make stern and frightening. "I can feed you on bread and water and lock you in your rooms until you agree. So there."

Both Adele and Cynthia looked at each other in horror, and Mrs. Meccleston, seeing their expressions, settled back in her chair more comfortably, sure she had convinced them at last of her determination. Janet looked from one to the other in confusion. Suddenly Adele giggled, and Cynthia burst into a trill of laughter, and before long, both girls were in each other's arms, helpless with amusement.

"Stop that at once, girls!" Mrs. Meccleston commanded, much confused. "You find such a plan *funny*?"

"Oh, Mama," Cynthia gasped, wiping her eyes. "As if you could. Why, you would be knocking on our doors within an hour, bearing a cup of tea and a plate of sandwiches, and asking if we were all right."

"Or letting us out so we might find your reticule or sewing basket," Adele contributed.

"Or coming to share the latest gossip you had heard. Give over, Mama. You know you could never sustain such punishment. Besides, why is it so important that we marry men of your choice when we tell you we do not love them?"

Before Mrs. Meccleston could reply, Adele said, "I daresay you wouldn't want to marry either of them yourself, Mama, if you just thought about it for a minute."

Mrs. Meccleston tipped her head to one side and considered this challenge. "Well, no," she said finally, "I must admit I cannot like Mr. Lincoln's red hands and coarse laugh, and to be sure, Mr. Botkins has a very distracting sniff—have you noticed it, girls? Besides, and although I should not mention it, I would be afraid all my children would be bow-legged."

At these candid comments on the husbands she had chosen for them, the girls dissolved in laughter again, and Janet had to smile as her aunt shook her head sadly. "I fear I am not a good mother. Your Aunt Lambert has married off two daughters, and here is Janet, engaged to a most suitable man, and I cannot even convince *one* of you to do as you ought. Something has been lacking in your upbringing."

The two girls assured her she was a wonderful mother and they loved her dearly, and begged her not to worry, for when the time came they were sure she would like the husbands they chose. When they had gone away to get ready for a shopping trip, Mrs. Meccleston shook her head and sighed, and Janet said softly, "Indeed, dear aunt, I think my cousins are to be envied their mother."

Her aunt looked at her sharply and would have questioned her, but Janet, feeling she had said too much, rose from the table. "I am late, and I must put on my bonnet and be off."

"Where do you go, my dear?" Mrs. Meccleston asked. "We have all noticed you are seldom home these days, and it is so very uncomfortable to have to explain to Lord Sanders, when he comes to call, that you have already left the house."

"Have your butler send him away, then, aunt," Janet

told her as she came to kiss the soft grey curls that showed under the tipsy cap. "I am going to Aunt Jane's to practice the piano, but I shall leave a message for Ernest that I would be delighted to drive out with him this afternoon. That should reassure him."

As she climbed the stairs, she could not help comparing her own mother to Aunt Jane, who although she might be flighty and giddy, was kind and loved her daughters. How wonderful not to be afraid all the time. Imagine being able to talk about what you liked and disliked, freely expressing your own opinions, and being listened to as well. She shook her head. It was no use to repine, for her future was clearly decided, and envying her cousins was an exercise in futility. She could not help being somewhat sad and reflective in the days that followed, however, and Lord Sanders was much encouraged, sure that Janet had learned the errors of her ways at last.

The following Sunday, Janet presented herself at Lady Ralston's town house in Eaton Square. She had attended church that morning with the Sanderses, as had become their custom, but as they were returning home, she had excused herself from an afternoon tea party with Lady Sanders by saying she was not feeling well and dared not take the risk of passing her indisposition to her future mother-in-law. Neither Lady Sanders nor Ernest had any reason to believe she was anywhere but lying on her bed in a darkened room with a handkerchief soaked in lavender water on her brow.

She felt a lightness of heart to be free of their company even for such a short time, but when she had been admitted to the hall by Lady Ralston's butler, given her stole to a waiting maid, and been announced in loud ringing tones at the door of the salon, she felt suddenly shy. The room seemed to be full of people—strange people she had never met—and she was glad when her hostess came up and drew her forward so she might introduce her to the others. She met Mr. Stine and was able to tell him how much she admired his paintings, and when the young artist brightened up at her words and beamed at her, she felt more at ease. She also met a lady novelist and a poet whose verses she much admired, as well as several other interesting ladies and gentlemen, and she found them to be very kind and not at all starched up. She had been a-fraid that in such august company she would be scorned, but to her surprise, everyone accepted her without question as someone who was knowledgeable in the arts and whose opinion they would be glad to hear. When the countess took her over to the window where a short middle-aged man with flowing hair was talking with a small group of friends, she recognized Maestro Roccani at once. She curtsied as Lady Ralston told him her name, and he took her hand with a flourish and kissed it.

"Ah!" he said with a broad smile, "*Not* Mees Janet Lambert! 'Orrible! She is a *bella rosa!*"

Janet was returning his smile when that now familiar deep voice said from behind her, "How wise of you to see it, Miró! The name Janet, so terribly stiff and ordinary, is not at all like the lady, for she is, in addition to being lovely, unique as well."

Janet turned to find the duke at her side, and he grinned at her as he added, "But perhaps you like your name, Miss Lambert, and we have offended you?"

Janet replied more calmly than she felt, "Not at all, Your Grace, Maestro. I have always disliked my name, even though it has been used in my family for many generations."

"Still, one wonders why your worthy parents felt they had to perpetuate it, even in that case. I agree with the maestro; '*bella rosa*' would be much more appropriate."

Since Janet had nothing to add to this unexpected compliment, Lady Ralston said, "She is indeed more than just *bella*, Maestro! You should hear her play your instrument. I vow you would be astounded at her talent."

All thoughts of the duke's nearness and surprising conversation vanished in an instant as Janet exclaimed, "No, no! I could not play for him; he is so far above my poor skills, he would but laugh at me."

Her face was so pale and she looked so distraught that the Italian patted her hands to calm her. "I would never laugh at you, Mees Lambert, and if my good friend the *contessa* says you have talent, I can be sure you do. She has a—how you say?—a discerning ear. Please reconsider; I have a studio in Dorry Street, and I would be glad to give you an audition any day you choose."

"You are too kind," Janet murmured, hoping her face did not show so plainly her agitation at this honour. The others began to speak more generally, which gave her a chance to recover. She could only be glad that the duke did not mention that she had the effrontery to consider herself a composer as well.

The time flew by, for Janet had never been in company that she enjoyed more. To hear Mr. Stine explain why he had chosen the models he had for his painting of the nymphs and how he had posed his subjects; to be among the first to hear the poet read his latest lines; to be able to listen as Maestro Roccani discoursed on the interpretation of the Bach piece she had struggled to master for so long—it was heaven.

When she was finally recalled to the time, it was to find that the salon was thinning of guests, and she went to take her leave of her hostess. "I cannot tell you how much I have enjoyed myself, ma'am. Thank you," she exclaimed.

Her happy expression and sparkling eyes made Lady Ralston reach out and pat her cheek and say, "Dear girl, I am so glad."

Maestro Roccani came up to them then and said, "Remember, mees, I shall look forward to hearing you play, and since I am sure you will 'esitate to make the appointment, shall we say next Thursday afternoon at three?"

Janet agreed, her reluctance gone. Even if the maestro thought her a rank amateur, she could not resist a chance to hear his opinion of her skill. She did not even notice that Tony Northbridge was close enough to overhear the conversation, and had made a mental note to be in Dorry Street himself on that day. Maestro Roccani was oblivious of his surroundings, but his studio was not in a good part of town, and perhaps Miss Lambert would be glad of an escort home.

He stayed behind after the other guests had left to congratulate his aunt on the brilliant success of her salon. Lady Ralston sank into a chair and fanned her face, carefully not looking at him as she said, "Yes, it went very well this time, and a lot of it was due to that nice child. How did the Lamberts ever produce her? I have met the family, you know, and outside of her aunt, the Duchess of Meresly, there is not a one of them I would willingly spend five minutes with."

Tony, lounging against the mantel and staring down into the flames, agreed with her, and then was somehow disappointed when she changed the subject and asked him to remain to dine. The earl never came to her salons, but he would be present at dinner and he enjoyed Tony's company. Hours later, although no one had mentioned Miss Lambert again, Tony found himself thinking of her as he strolled to his club. She was such an odd mixture, he was fascinated. The way her expressive face changed from laughter and happiness to a tight, carefully controlled propriety in an instant was intriguing. He had heard her lilting laugh again that afternoon, and it reminded him of the day in her father's wood when they had laughed together at that ridiculous prize pig. And here she was, engaged to Ernest Sanders, and after her marriage would be buried in the country again. He shook his head impatiently. It was nothing to him, after all, and Miss Lambert, although she did not show any wild delight in the prospect of her marriage to the worthy Ernest, seemed perfectly content with her lot. But why did she continue to fascinate him this way?

She was beautiful and bewitching, but so were many other women; he could name a dozen or more who were as handsome, although none who were so talented, so clever; none who answered all his most outrageous statements with such a cool air of amused disbelief. Tony shook his head and resolved to put her from his mind. He might be a great rake, but tampering with the affections of engaged girls was not one of his failings.

He could not resist approaching her, however, the following afternoon when he came upon her and her two cousins as they were walking in the park. Cynthia and Adele were delighted by this attention, especially since the duke smiled at them so warmly, and pressed their hands with such a knowing air. For a few moments they all stood together, talking lightly of the Season, but when Mr. and Mrs. Smyth-Blaydon asked if they might be allowed to pass, the duke said, "Shall we walk on, ladies? I fear we are obstructing the flow of traffic. Go ahead of us, Miss Cynthia, Miss Adele, and Miss Lambert and I will bring up the rear until we reach a more open spot."

As the two girls obeyed him, they exchanged glances, their eyes brimming with merriment. They were both such accomplished flirts, they could only applaud the duke's quick thinking, even as they wished he might have honoured one of them with his arm.

Janet could not agree with her cousins. She knew that every moment she spent in Tony's company was dangerous. Dangerous because she was attracted to him still, dangerous because she realized, deep in her heart, that she was delighted to take his arm and remain by his side as long as she could, and she knew this feeling was wrong. She was engaged, and she was going to marry another. And what would Ernest and his mother think if they should see her with the duke? Then she remembered that Lady Sanders was closeted with the dentist this afternoon, and that Ernest had gone with her to support her through her ordeal. But the feeling of relief she felt lasted only a moment. Someone was sure to mention it, for the park was crowded at this time of day with all the fashionable world come to see and be seen, admire and condemn, and gossip and tell tales. By singling her out in this way the duke was leaving her open to all kinds of malicious speculation, and certainly a long and tedious explanation to her fiancé and Lady Sanders as well. At this thought she made a motion to remove her hand from the duke's arm, but he was quick to put his other hand over hers and keep it firmly in place. Janet opened her mouth to complain of such high-handed treatment, but the duke had turned a little aside to tip his hat to Lord Wells, who was trotting by accompanied by a lovely redhead.

"I see Gregory has captured Lady Wrotham this afternoon," the duke remarked. "How dashing she looks with her auburn hair matching her chestnut mare, don't you agree, Miss Lambert? There is something about a woman on horseback—a woman with a good seat, that is—that seems especially attractive."

The duke spoke almost in a musing tone, but Janet was not deceived. He was remembering her own aversion to horses, and she lowered her eyes so he might not see the anger there as she replied, "Most attractive, Sir! I have always thought Lady Wrotham not only dashing but vivacious as well. That distinctive laugh of hers must be admired!"

The duke chuckled. Lady Wrotham had a piercing crescendo of a laugh that grated on any discerning ear.

"It is surely . . . hmm . . . unusual," he agreed, and then asked, "Have you heard her perform on the harp, Miss Lambert? It would be a revelation to you. By the end of her performance I could not decide whether her laugh or her musical ability was her most . . . hmm . . . outstanding feature."

Janet admitted she had not had the pleasure of hearing the lady, as the duke bowed to a girl who was waving to get his attention from her seat besides her mama in an open landau.

"And there is Miss Wharlington. Have you made her acquaintance yet? There are some who say she is the wittiest young lady to appear in London for many a season."

Janet's eyebrows rose. "Say you so, Your Grace? Yes, I have met the lady. Perhaps she was not feeling well that day, for she spoke no more than four words to me—'charmed,' 'really?' 'indeed!' and 'good-day!' Of course, she said them in a very witty way."

The duke's face was alight with laughter. "Ah, Lord Russell! Now, there goes a great rake for you, Miss Lambert. My small accomplishments pale in comparison, but then, he has been at it so many more years than I, being all of three score years and five."

"Lord Russell was kind enough to pinch my cheek one evening at a ball, Your Grace," Janet confided. "He made

162

me feel I had arrived at last on the social scene. My heart beat most alarmingly for several minutes, I must confess."

She was aware that the duke was staring down at her as he asked, "And is that your inevitable reaction to rakes, Miss Lambert? I am delighted to hear that I have that affect on you."

He spoke in a light, teasing way, but Janet drew in an indignant breath. This was going too far! But before she could give him a setdown he was sure to remember, he bent his dark head toward her again and changed the subject.

"And where is the earnest Ernest this fine afternoon?"

"Lord Sanders is attending his mother, Sir. She has a most distressing toothache and had to visit her dentist. My cousins were kind enough to ask me to join them for a walk, but if I had known *you* were going to be here, I might not have agreed to accompany them so willingly."

The duke stopped suddenly and turned toward her in surprise. "Why, what is this, my dear Miss Lambert? Surely it cannot be that you have formed a distaste for my company? No—it must be that you are afraid that my attentions will cause unfavorable comments." He patted her hand to reassure her. "It is a common practice for gentlemen to do the same, and to take my arm for a few steps will not compromise you, y'know! Not with such throngs of people present. To stroll along in full view of all society can occasion no censure; even Lord Sanders could hardly disapprove. Of course, it would not do for us to seek a secluded spot; we must try to control ourselves to that extent."

Janet was angry that her outburst had given him the advantage, for although she had enjoyed sparring with the duke at first, this sophisticated *repartie* was now beginning to unnerve her. She noticed that her cousins had drawn ahead of them by some distance and were deep in conversation with two young officers, and she quickened her steps.

"I shall do my best to control myself, Your Grace," she murmured. "Let me reassure you that I at least have myself in firm control. You need not fear. A secluded spot in your company could only be repugnant to me!"

There! she thought. That will teach him a lesson. They walked along for a moment more before the duke said, in a thoughtful way, "It would not be so for me, Miss Lambert."

Janet stole a glance up at him, expecting to see his mocking smile, and was surprised to discover how intent and serious his eyes were. She drew in a startled breath as he tightened her arm against his side.

"I wonder what can have come over me?" he added, nodding to yet another of his acquaintances on the opposite side of the walk. "But since I am being so open, may I say that I doubt very much that you would find being alone with me 'repugnant'? What a terrible word that is. I think, if only you would be truthful too, you would be forced to agree it would not be displeasing to you at all. Come, admit it!"

Janet tried once again to free her hand, but the duke had no intention of letting her go. Her head was high and there were storm warnings flying in her cheeks as she answered him. "I see I must remind you once again, Sir, that I am engaged to marry another man, and as such, this conversation can only be distasteful to me. Please release my arm at once! Between the two of us there can be no intimacies, no 'perhapses' or 'if onlys.' The ending of the story has already been written, and it cannot be changed. I am promised to Lord Sanders; and you and I have nothing at all to say to each other."

"I see," the duke murmured, but he did not let her go as he continued, in a serious voice, "Perhaps I was mistaken in your feelings, but to find myself so in accord with you always, to feel our spirits and interests so closely aligned, to know that what I find amusing you will also laugh at with me, to acknowledge deep inside of me such a rightness about us . . . no, I cannot be wrong to that extent."

Janet was delighted to see her cousins directly ahead of them, and hastened her footsteps. There was nothing she could say in answer; indeed, her throat was so constricted with tears she could not have replied if she had the words. Fortunately, Adele and Cynthia were busy introducing the duke to their companions, so her silence went unnoticed, and it was only a moment longer before the duke took his leave.

"Miss Lambert," he said after he had bidden the others good-bye, "I thank you for your company. It was a delight, as always."

Janet curtsied with her eyes downcast, and when she looked up at last it was to see the duke striding away from her. She stared after him, glad he had not been able to look into her eyes again, for surely then he would have discovered how she had lied, and how much she was in love with him, no matter what high-flown words of denial she was forced by her circumstances to utter. Her heart felt bleak, and she did not know how she was to bear living the rest of her life apart from him.

Adele nudged her arm and winked at her, and she forced herself to accept Captain Adams' other arm as the party began to retrace their steps to the park gates.

In the days that followed, Janet spent every available minute at her aunt's piano, not only to prepare for her audition but also as a way of escaping her thoughts of the duke. She was glad she was not required to talk about him with Ernest or his mother, for by some lucky chance, no one had mentioned her companion that afternoon in the park, and Lady Sanders was so full of descriptions of the agonies she had endured in the dentist's chair that Janet's silences and faraway looks went unnoticed.

On the appointed afternoon, she left the Mecclestons' house well before time so she would not be late, and she did not take Simpton with her. She did not wish anyone to know of this adventure, and she knew her maid was wondering about the amount of time she had to spend accompanying Miss Lambert about when the lady had a perfectly good fiancé to do so in her place.

Janet was wearing a warm blue cloak, for the afternoon was chilly, and although she had no idea where 23 Dorry Street was, she was relieved that the hackney driver simply tipped his hat and nodded when she gave him the direction. She knew she was very early, and had thought she might stroll through the neighbourhood while she waited, but after she had paid the driver and surveyed the narrow street, she decided she should ring the bell at once. Dorry Street was poor and mean, crowded with ragged children and slatternly-looking women, and she could not like the way the men lounging about the sidewalk were staring at her. To her relief, the door was opened promptly by a short, elderly woman with grey hair, dressed all in black. She was almost as wide as she was tall, and her round face with its rosy cheeks beamed when Janet asked for Maestro Roccani. Without a word, the woman beckoned her in, but when a little boy who was near the step reached out to touch Janet's cloak, she loosened a torrent of Italian and shut the door behind them with a snap.

"*Scusa, scusa,* mees!" she said, holding open a door in the narrow hall. Janet entered a small sitting room, and taking the seat the woman indicated, soon found herself alone. Somewhere in the house someone was playing the piano, and she did not have to listen very long before she was sure it was not Roccani. The playing ceased, and another torrent of Italian could faintly be heard. Janet loosened the ties of her cloak and settled back. She had not imagined the maestro would have pupils, but she was sure this must be the case, and she felt immediately better as she realized that her own playing was vastly superior to that of the pupil now having a lesson.

It was almost half an hour later when she heard the front door close, and almost at the same time, the door of the sitting room open. "Mees Lambert. A thousand pardons to keep you waiting," the maestro said as he strode in and seized her hand to kiss. Janet dropped a curtsy and wondered if all Italians made such a practice of kissing young lady's hands.

"But come—to the studio. I am sorry you had to wait, but my pupil—ah, of a talent most forgettable—was before you. It is my penance on earth to 'ave to deal with such . . . such . . . but I cannot say the word in your company."

166

All the while he was running on, he was escorting her up a narrow flight of stairs and into a large front room with a grand piano near the largest window. He took her cloak and then went to the door and bellowed in Italian, *"Mamma, mamma! Vorremmo due espressi fra una mezz'ora, per favore!"*

Janet looked around the studio and was immediately at home. The piles of music, the exercise books strewn about, the music stands and chairs arranged for a trio— it was just what she had expected a studio to look like. The maestro returned and led her to the piano.

"Now, Mess Bella, to work. Let me hear you play."

He moved away to a large armchair near the fire, and Janet sat down after adjusting the bench. Her heart was pounding with nervousness, but still she went through her regular routine, removing her rings and bracelets and massaging her fingers before she played a few scales. At last she was ready, and turned toward the maestro, who nodded without a word, his chin propped up with one strong hand. Janet played a Beethoven sonata first, and could have wept at her mistakes. Her fingers were so wooden, her arms so stiff. When she had finished, she put her hands in her lap and bowed her head, tears coming behind her eyelids at her ineptitude.

"Again," came the command, and, surprised, she began the sonata once more. This time she did better, and was reassured when he asked her to play something more. She dearly wanted to play the Bach, but did not dare, so she began an étude she herself had written. This time she was able to forget her surroundings, and was only brought back to reality when she heard the applause as the final notes died away.

"Brava! Bravissima!" Roccani said, coming to her side. "I am surprised, even though the good *contessa* told me of your talent. I do not often 'ear such skill from one your age." He picked up both her hands and studied them. "Yes, yes, strong fingers, good span. But, Mees Bella, the fingernails, no no."

Janet looked at him perplexed. "Too long," he explained. "You must keep them *vairy* short—no vanity, eh,

167

mees? And you must not worry about the pads that come when you have practiced many years. See 'ere, my 'ands!" He held them out for her inspection, but before she could speak, he hurried on. "Yes, you must have more lessons. I can see 'ow you have practiced—so 'ard—but even such work will be of no avail without lessons. I myself, the great Roccani, will be your teacher."

Janet's head was whirling now, and she put one hand to her throat.

"But . . . but, Maestro, I have no money, and I am not allowed to practice as I should."

"What is this?" he asked, a frown on his face. Stammering, Janet explained, and the maestro shook his head sadly. "These *Engleesh*!" he said when her voice trailed away in silence, and she tried to swallow the large lump in her throat. "It is too bad, but unless you can practice, there is no sense to waste the time, yours or mine. So, you choose the *bambini* over the music, eh, Mees Bella? Well, never mind, perhaps it is best, for it is 'ard for women to be musicians; they do not 'ave the singleness of mind."

He patted her hand and led her to a chair near his, just as a knock came and the door opened to show his fat little mother waving her hands in agitation, and behind her the Duke of Stour. Janet felt her heart give a great leap and she pressed her hands together tightly to hide their trembling. Why had he come? How was she to bear being here with him? He nodded to her casually while the maestro put both hands on his hips and roared with laughter. The duke was, as always, impeccably dressed, his white cravat startling against the swarthiness of his face, but he looked more than a little incongruous, for he was bearing a large tray.

"Eh, Antonio! Now you are a waiter, *sì*?" the maestro asked while his mother began to speak rapidly. Even though Janet had no idea what the words meant, it was plain to see that she was very upset that the duke had taken her tray and cast himself in such a humble role. Under that torrent of words, Janet was able to gain control over her face and resolve to herself to behave normally. The maestro's mother fussed over them until after the espresso had been served, and when she finally left the room, her son asked the duke, "And why are you 'ere, Antonio? Not only to bring my coffee, I am sure."

The duke grinned and took a sip of the steaming liquid. "No, Miró, I am come to escort Miss Lambert home. You do not know how dangerous your neighborhood is for a young lady of quality."

"But Mees has 'er maid, no?" Roccani asked, looking around in confusion. Janet admitted she had not thought it necessary to bring that excellent watchdog. She was bitterly disappointed in the results of her audition, and nervous in the duke's company as well, but in listening to the two friends chat and tease each other, she was able to forget for a little while.

When at last she stood on the doorstep, and the duke had gone ahead to fetch a cab, the maestro kissed her hand in farewell.

"Do not be *così triste, bella mia!*" he said. "No one can take your music away from you, and even if you cannot play as you would like, it will—'ow do you say?—always be with you. And perhaps one of the *bambini* will inherit your talent, *sì?*"

Janet thanked him again for his kindness as the duke came back with a hackney. Her sense of unease returned then as he helped her into the elderly carriage. She could not help noticing how it smelled, of old age and brittle leather, and stale tobacco and dirt, but the duke did not show any disgust, for he was well aware that the better cabs did not frequent Dorry Street. They set off at a slow trot, and Janet, determined to be as offhand and normal as she could, turned to her escort, who was now leaning back against the soiled squabs, watching her face.

"I thank you, Your Grace, for your help. I did not think how I was to get home, I'm afraid, or I would not have dismissed my cab."

To her relief, the duke replied in a casual, slightly bored voice. "He would not have waited, child, not in that neighborhood. It is a wonder Miró gets any pupils, living where he does."

Janet could not help sighing. "It is because of who he

is, Sir. I myself would go there gladly every day, if . . . if I were able."

She turned away, afraid he would see the tears sparkling in her lashes, but she was not quick enough, and the duke could not resist reaching out for her gloved hands in sympathy.

Just then, there was a shout from the roadway, the horse whinnied in fright, and the carriage came to an abrupt halt as something struck the side of it with considerable force. Janet was thrown hard against the duke, who put both arms around her to steady her. The hackney shuddered and bucked as the horse tried to bolt, and they could hear loud voices outside raised in argument.

Suddenly all the noise and confusion faded away as Janet stared up at the duke from the shelter of his arms. She had never been so close to that dark, handsome face before, and she noticed that his elegant beaver hat had been knocked off his head in the collision and one lock of black hair had fallen in disarray on his broad forehead. Her eyes widened as he stared down at her intently, making no move to restore her to her place. Neither spoke, and the duke, still searching her face, raised one hand and wiped away the tears that still threatened to fall. Then he slowly tightened his grip until Janet felt she must cry out, even as he bent his head still closer so his lips could touch hers in a gentle kiss. Janet could feel a pulse beating in her throat, and quite without meaning to, grasped his arms more securely as her lips parted in a sigh of pure delight. At that, the duke kissed her more deeply and passionately. When he raised his head at last, it was only to rest his cheek against her hair, and she felt his warm breath as he murmured, "*Bella Rosa!*" Finally he sighed, and moved back a little so he could see her face. Her eyes were closed, and her face was so white, he was suddenly alarmed. "*Bella!*" he commanded in a harsh, strained voice. "Are you all right?"

Unable to speak, Janet nodded her head, and he released her. Immediately the world intruded and they were both aware that the hackney had come to a halt, and they

170

could hear the elderly driver involved in a loud argument with several other men.

"I shall see what is the matter," the duke said as he threw open the door and stepped down onto the cobbles. Janet leaned back against the seat, her breath coming in quick, shallow gasps. She was used to being kissed now by Lord Sanders, but never had he kissed her like *that*, and never had she felt the least desire to respond the way she had just done. She remembered to her shame the disappointment she had felt when the duke took his mouth away from hers; how she had wanted to remain close to him, to throw her arms around him and pull his handsome head down to hers again.

She found herself shaking, and tried to pull her cloak closer around her. Whatever is the matter with me, she wondered, to behave in such a strange way? She hugged her arms tight to her sides as she pondered the problem. How could there be such a difference between the duke's embrace and that of her fiancé, and whatever must the duke think of her to behave so wantonly, especially since only a few days ago in the park she had assured him that she found his company odious. She wondered how she was ever to look him in the face again! Hearing his deep voice outside the hackney, she knew she had only a few moments to compose herself. Suddenly the door of the cab sprang open and the duke's dark head appeared.

"It is all right, Miss Lambert," he said in a normal tone of voice. "We should be on our way as soon as this imbecile straightens out his horse. He ran into a dray, and the street is covered with potatoes."

It was a laughable situation, but all Janet could do was nod again before he turned away. She could hear his strong, authoritative voice giving orders, and somehow she knew they would be obeyed instantly.

By the time the fracas was over and the duke had taken his seat again beside her, she had steadied her breathing and regained some degree of her composure.

"I must beg your pardon, Miss Lambert," the duke said formally as the cab got under way again. "It was unforgivable of me to take advantage of you when you were so helpless. Believe me, I had no intention of distressing you. I beg you to put the incident from your mind."

The duke was trying hard to reassure her and put her at her ease, and in trying for a light touch, sounded almost indifferent. Janet felt a stab of anger that her kiss should mean so little to him, and before she thought, said hotly, "Oh, yes, I should have remembered! You are a premier rake, Sir, are you not? No doubt this is all just a pleasant way for you to pass the time, indulging me in a light flirtation. How kind of you!"

She was staring at him now, but surely it was only her imagination that one strong hand was raised slightly in protest before he answered.

"I fear you are right, Miss Lambert, for surely only a rake would take advantage of a young lady of your quality, and one who appears content to be engaged to another man as well. You would be wise to have nothing further to do with me."

Janet ignored his bitter tone. "I shall most certainly endeavour to follow such good advice, Your Grace!" she replied, and then she turned away and stared at the passing scene with unseeing eyes until the hackney finally reached Charles Street and she was home at last.

The duke got out first and offered her his hand, and she was forced to take it as she stepped down from the cab. She hoped he could not feel how her hand trembled as it lay in his, nor how very shaky her curtsy was, and she did not dare to speak again, for she did not trust her voice. In a moment she was up the shallow steps and knocking on the door, and by the time the duke had paid off the cab and turned around, she was gone.

IV

Movement Allegro

❧ 10 ❧

The fashionable world looked in vain for the Duke of Stour that evening, for he had sent his regrets to his cronies for a dinner and an evening at the theatre. Lord Wells asked Reggie Anderson if he knew what was up with Northbridge, but Mr. Anderson had no idea, nor had the fourth member of the party, Lord Fitch. After the theatre and a neat supper in Lord Wells's room, the three men decided it would be a good thing to call round at the duke's town house. "Might be ill . . . all alone . . . needin' friends!" Lord Fitch declaimed to the moon, having imbibed too many glasses of Lord Wells's excellent claret. The others solemnly agreed, and as they wended their slightly crooked way down St. James Street, Reggie Anderson treated them to a stirring soliloquy on the merits of friendship. But when their knock was answered by Stour's butler, they found that the duke, although he was within, had given orders that he was not to be disturbed for any reason whatsoever. The young men would have questioned Woods further, but that worthy butler, seeing the condition they were in, firmly shut the door on them.

The duke had dined alone and then had closeted himself in the library with a bottle of port. Woods was not alarmed; whenever the duke had a problem, he was apt to retreat from society this way, until he felt he had found a solution. Outside of making sure he was not disturbed, and no difficulties occurred in the running of the establishment, Woods left his master strictly alone unless he was summoned to serve him.

The duke sat before the fire and stared into the flames. Even after all these hours, he could still hear her voice, still see the anger and scorn in those magnificent blue eyes as they darkened at his attempt to make light of the situation. And he could still feel how her hand had trembled in his when he finally put her down at her aunt's house. It had been all he could do not to take her back into his arms again and tell her that he had not meant a word of it. He groaned, wondering what on earth was happening to him. Surely he was too old and wise to fall in love with a young miss who was not only promised to another but also showed every sign of planning to go through with her wedding. Then he remembered how she had returned his kiss. He had not expected such passion from one who was, he knew instinctively, so truly innocent, for he remembered her shocked white face when he looked down at her afterward. Perhaps Sanders did not kiss her that way. . . .

Suddenly he rose to his feet and began to pace the library. Damn the man! To think of him daring to touch Bella. His hands formed hard fists for a moment, and then he shook his head and sank back into his chair poured himself another glass of wine. You are being absurd, Stour, he told himself. They are engaged. Of course he kisses and embraces her, and you would be wise to put any such visions of them lost in each other's arms from your mind, for that will surely overset you. But Bella . . . and that stuffy, solemn, opinionated, worthy, *dull* man. It did not bear thinking about.

He put another log on the fire and went over the situation again. Perhaps he was feeling sorry for the girl, he thought, and brightened up a bit. That must be it. For any girl of Bella's quality and talent, marriage to a dullard such as Ernest Sanders could only be a disaster. She must realize that, he thought impatiently, and yet still she persists. So therefore she has decided to have him regardless. Poor, poor Bella. No, he corrected himself, poor, poor Janet Rose Lambert. It was easier to think of the match when he remembered her real name. Ernest Sanders and Janet Lambert deserved each other. The Bella whom he had held in his arms so briefly was just a figment of his imagination, not the real lady at all. Feeling a little better, the duke took himself off to bed, but it was obvious to Woods when the duke passed him without his usual pleasant "Good night!" that the problem had not been resolved that evening.

Janet was not so fortuante as to be able to spend the evening alone, for she had promised to attend a lecture with her fiancé. As they drove to the hall, he told her all about the treat she was to have, for the speaker was an authority on some new methods of farming which, as the coming mistress of Willows, she was sure to find fascinating. When she did not respond to this heavy playfulness he looked at her sharply. Surely she was very pale this evening. He hoped she was not going to be one of those sickly women, all headaches and megrims and moods. When he taxed her with it, she recalled herself and said that she thought London was too hectic for her, and as soon as she was back in the quiet countryside again, was sure she would regain her spirits. Ernest beamed, for she could have said nothing that would have pleased him more.

She was glad Ernest did not question her about the lecture as they returned home, for she had not heard a word. Fortunately, he himself had been so interested that he did not notice her abstraction, and she was free to go over endlessly the events of the afternoon. She was so ashamed of herself for her wantonness in returning the duke's kiss so passionately. Surely a better-bred lady would have fainted or slapped him, or cried out for help. The dimple in her cheek quivered for a moment as she considered the impossibility of finding anyone who would dare to slap Tony Northbridge. And if she was honest with herself, she had to admit that crying for help was the last thing she had wanted to do, and as for fainting, she would have hated herself forever after, for then she would have missed that one rapturous kiss. And since that is the only kiss I will ever have from him, perhaps I am not so bad after all, she told herself. I know I must marry Ernest; well, I will make the best of it and he will never know. And I do have my pride. It was plain to see that the duke regretted his impulse almost as soon as it was over, and wanted her to know that it had been a fleeting thing, an opportunity that any man would have seized and then thought nothing of again. So might he kiss a pretty housemaid, she thought bleakly, or one of the tempting *demimondes* who strolled the streets. She told herself she was much better off with Ernest Sanders: since she did not love him, he had no power to hurt her, as Tony Northbridge had done so many times.

Ernest was surprised at the fervor of her kiss when he put her down at the Mecclestons', and he went away delighted at this new evidence of her warming regard for him. He was not to know that she had resolved to do better by him, and so she had tried to copy the duke's kiss. For her, it was not a success. Ernest's lips were so thin and dry, and his hands on her back felt soft and limp. When she was safely in her room, she rubbed her lips with a cloth to remove his touch. She was so depressed that she did not summon Simpton, but undressed herself and crawled into bed, where she lay staring up at the canopy above her and thinking sad thoughts until almost dawn.

Two evenings later, Janet found herself face to face with Tony Northbridge again, at an evening reception at Lady Jersey's. She paled a little and looked right through him, and the duke, his mouth twisting wryly, did not attempt to speak to her. On either side of Janet, Lord Sanders and his mother nodded, pleased to see her so distant with a man they could never approve. They were not the only ones to notice the meeting. Across the room the Countess of Grant wondered whatever had occurred to cause this stiffness between the two people she had every intention of bringing together. They had been very easy with each other at her salon, as far as she remembered, so whatever had happened had occurred after that. She made her way across the room, stopping every now and then to speak to friends, and at last came to stand next to Lady Sanders. She was delighted to see that Lord Sanders had taken Miss Lambert away, and lost no time engaging his mother in conversation.

"Such a crush, don't you agree, Lady Sanders?" she began. "Why Lady Jersey feels she has to ask every single soul in London to her parties, I have never been able to understand. And how are you liking the Little Season?"

Lady Sanders sniffed and said she could recall several that had been a great deal more entertaining, and Lady Ralston got down to business.

"I have not had a chance to tell you how delighted I am to be able to offer my congratulations on your son's approaching marriage. Such a lovely girl; so unusual and so talented!"

She paused and did not miss Lady Sanders' sniff, although the lady inclined her head in thanks.

"From such a good family, as well!" Lady Ralston persisted. "You must be ecstatic that someone has been found who is so worthy of your son!" Careful there, she told herself, no need to empty the butterboat over her.

Lady Sanders sniffed again. "Most happy," she said faintly, and at this faint praise, delivered in such a doleful tone, Lady Ralston made bold to continue.

"We were all so pleased with Janet when she attended my salon last Sunday She was so easy and pleasant with all the guests. Mr. Stine, the artist who paints those intriguing nudes, spoke to her for such a long time, as did Mrs. Farrell—has her latest novel come your way? *Such* a naughty book! But as I was saying, Miss Lambert made quite a conquest of Maestro Roccani in particular; I know he asked her to come and play for him at his studio this week, and when I asked him how the audition had gone, he kissed his fingertips and said, *'Bravissima!'* Surely your son is fortunate to have such a talented fiancée!"

Lady Ralston stole a glance at her companion and was not surprised to see that Lady Sanders' face had turned an alarming shade of purple.

"Indeed? Indeed?" the lady sputtered, and then she

gathered her voluminous brocade skirts and rose, her massive bosom heaving in excitement. "You must excuse me, Lady Ralston! There is something of primary importance that I must speak to my son about."

She rushed away, and Lady Ralston mentally rubbed her hands. It was perfectly obvious that Lady Sanders, far from finding Janet a suitable *parti* for a Sanders, did not care for the girl at all, and would be delighted to wrench her son from her grasp. Better and better, the countess thought as she watched the lady bustle over to Lord Sanders. Janet may be in for a few bad minutes because of what I have done, but how much better to suffer their lectures and horror over her behaviour now than to spend the rest of her life tied to such a man!

"Ernest!" Lady Sanders hissed, tugging at his coat of grey superfine. "I must speak to you. At once!"

Her son turned away from the group he had been talking to and eyed his mother uneasily. "Will it not wait, Mother?" he asked in an undertone.

She pulled harder at his sleeve. "No, right now. I insist!"

Lord Sanders, who thought his mother's colour very unhealthy, felt it best to agree. Janet was talking to her Aunt Meccleston and one of her cousins, and he knew it was safe to leave her in their company, so he allowed his mother to lead him from the room and into a small antechamber where they could be alone. Over her wineglass, Lady Ralston watched them go, her eyes twinkling.

"Whatever is wrong, Mother?" Ernest asked as soon as he had shut the door.

"I have just been speaking to Lady Ralston," she began in a rush. "You remember, Ernest, that last Sunday Janet excused herself from attending a tea party with me on the grounds that she was unwell? You yourself spoke of how thoughtful she was not to insist on going and possibly passing her indisposition on to me."

She paused to take a breath, and Ernest agreed that he remembered.

"Well, *Well!* She was not indisposed at all. That . . . that bold chit had the audacity to go—and all by herself, mind you—to Lady Ralston's salon. And even though neither you nor I would ever *think* of attending one of her afternoons, we know, do we not, what kind of people are there? Musicians and artists and *poets*."

This last was said in such a voice of loathing that the cravat of any poet within hearing would have wilted immediately at her scorn.

"But that is not the worst of it. According to Lady Ralston, Janet was very popular with the guests, quite a pet in fact, and that Italian piano player asked her to come to his studio and play for him. *Ernest! To his studio!*"

Since Lady Sanders' eyes were all but bugging out in shock, and her breath was coming in horrified gasps, her son begged her to sit down. "No, Mama, not another word until I have fetched you some wine. You are distraught; I insist you control yourself."

Lady Sanders was forced to sit down and fan herself rapidly until her son returned with a glass. When she had taken a large gulp, she continued, as if there had not been any interruption, "To a *man's studio*, Ernest A foreigner, a *musician*. Oh, the shame of it! Such wanton behaviour, such flaunting of morality and all society's strictures. I cannot bear to think that you are promised to such a woman, for 'girl' I can call her no longer. I am sure that you take my meaning?"

Lord Sanders paled at this and sat down abruptly, wishing he had had the forethought to bring a glass of wine for himself as well.

"Perhaps she did not go, Mama," he said feebly. "Perhaps there is some explanation . . ."

"Lady Ralston told me she *did* go, but I am sure she will have a very reasonable explanation," Lady Sanders cried. "See how easy she has found it to lie to you, my son. Indisposed indeed! When all the time she never intended to go to the tea party with me, and was planning on attending that . . . that bohemian orgy. She knew we would never approve, so she lied to us. And after you took her to task for playing for her aunt's guests. You see how she values your good advice."

Ernest was forced to nod his head, but he was not required to speak, for his mother raced on. "I have never trusted her, you know. She is so foreign-looking herself, so theatrical. A young girl should always endeavor to remain in the background, never calling attention to herself, and here is this . . . this *person* pushing herself forward, performing in public, and at all times making a show of herself. She has taken you in, Ernest, but now we know she is not pure and modest; she lies, and visits men in their rooms. You must break your engagement at once!"

"But, Mother, I cannot do that. At least not until I have given Janet a chance to explain." His mother groaned piteously as she caught sight of the stubborn set of his jaw, and her son patted her hands. "No, she will not deceive me, I promise you, but you do see that I must be fair—"

"Fair!" Lady Sanders shrieked. "How like you, my son; so noble, so good. But when you find yourself tied to her, and she has wasted your inheritance and ruined your estates, then you will wonder why you did not listen to your mother. Besides," she added, somewhat ruining this sweeping statement, "can you really be looking forward to a lifetime of listening to the piano while your home lies dusty and neglected, your fields are unplowed, and your children are unborn?"

How Janet could be responsible for dust and unplowed fields, since Willows employed an abundance of servants to take care of these chores, or unborn heirs, since no one could play the piano all the time, Lord Sanders had no idea, but he felt it best not to contradict his mother when she was so upset.

"Very well, if you insist on nobility, bring the Jezebel here and question her." Lady Sanders put down her wineglass with a snap and folded her fat arms across her stomach, her face taking on a belligerent look that would have cowed the most hardened criminal, but her son refused, saying that he would question Janet alone later, and with that his mother had to be content.

Janet noticed that Lady Sanders looked very pleased with herself the remainder of the evening, and wondered why, even as she wondered at Lord Sanders' frowns and abrupt conversation. She was not sorry when he suggested they leave early, for not only was it impossible to enjoy herself with a Sanders on either elbow, but she could not help seeing the Duke of Stour as he chatted with his hostess, laughed with his friends, and flirted with a very pretty girl. She could not remember spending a more miserable evening.

She was surprised when Ernest drove his mother home first, and then went on with her to Charles Street, but when she questioned him about this unusual move and asked why his mother had refused to bid her good night, he only said through clenched teeth, "I have something of great importance to speak to you about, Janet, and I wish us to be private." This was said in such a stern tone that Janet spent the remainder of the drive wondering what she could possibly have done to so badly offend him.

She was not kept in suspense for long, for Ernest followed her into the house, and giving his hat and cane to the Mecclestons' butler, told him that he and Miss Lambert were going to the drawing room and did not wish to be disturbed. Janet found herself propelled into the room with a firm hand to her back, and she turned as the door closed to see her fiancé regarding her with a heavy scowl. "Whatever is the matter, Ernest?" she asked, sinking down onto a chair.

"I have heard some intelligence about you, Janet that does not please me at all. It appears that far from listening to my direct orders and clearly expressed wishes, you have done just as you pleased, and have even gone so far as to lie to me about your activities. You will not lie now, however! Tell me at once about your afternoon at the Countess of Grant's salon, and then explain, if you can, why you went to Maestro Roccani's studio this past week."

Janet paled a little, but her voice was steady as she answered. "I knew you would not approve of my accepting the countess's kind invitation, and I did so much want to go. It was very wrong of me to lie to you and Lady Sanders, but I thought you would never find out. And then, when I met Maestro Roccani and he so kindly asked me to play for him, I could not resist the opportunity."

"So! *So!* It was true!" Ernest sat down abruptly, and wiped his brow. "I cannot believe it even now that I hear it from your own lips. And what happened in this man's rooms?"

"Why, I played for him, but when he said I had talent and should have more lessons, I had to tell him it was impossible."

"And what else happened?" Lord Sanders persisted. "I insist on hearing the whole sordid story."

Janet paled a little as she thought of what had happened after she left Dorry Street, and decided that the last thing she could tell him was that the Duke of Stour had also been present.

"The maestro's mother brought us coffee, and after we had had a cup, I . . . I came home. That is all."

Lord Sanders' lip curled in scorn. "You would have me believe, Janet, that there was no impropriety? No lovemaking? That a foreigner who is not our sort at all, with undoubtedly loose morals, would not take advantage of a girl who was practically asking to be ravished by immodestly appearing there alone?"

"Of course he did not," Janet said, firmly putting Tony Northbridge from her mind. "How can you think such an awful thing? The maestro is an older man, and his mother was there all the time. Besides, being a foreigner does not necessarily mean a person has no morals; I daresay his morals are as good as yours."

Lord Sanders rose and came to pull her from her chair, his face white. "How dare you!" he said, and then he raised his hand and slapped her. "Wanton! Liar! How can I believe you? Give me your word that this time you are telling the truth! Your sacred word, or I shall beat you until you do." As he spoke, he grasped her arms tighter and tigher and shook her until Janet was unable to restrain a cry of pain. Lord Sanders had the grace to look a little ashamed of his loss of control and let her go. She staggered a little, her head reeling before she grasped one of the chair backs for support. Both her arms ached and she knew she would have bruises there by morning, and her cheek was still smarting from his blow. She swallowed and said with quiet dignity as tears ran down her face. "You have my word, Ernest, that nothing at all happened at Maestro Roccani's studio that the Bishop of London and all his clerics could fault. Let me go now; you have hurt me and I wish to retire."

Lord Sanders groaned and began to pace up and down in an agitated way. "No! You will not leave. If I have hurt you, Janet, your behaviour warranted it. Let it be a warning to you in the future." He paused and looked at her sternly. "Indeed, I see now I have been too lenient with you. Very well, I will believe you, *this time*, but I will see to it that you have no further opportunity to defy me. You are to cancel all your engagements and prepare to leave London as soon as possible. My mother and I will be ready to travel next Wednesday morning; see that you are ready as well. The sooner I have you safe at Rundell Court, the better. And as for a London Season, I think not. We will be married in February, and I shall inform your mother of my decision immediately. Furthermore, there will be no piano, no music room at Willows, for you have forfeited the right to any further indulgences from me."

Janet stared at him, horrified. His pale blue eyes were bleak, and there was a stubbornness in his face that told her he meant every word. She could not know that, having chosen her in the first place, he now found it impossible to admit he might have made a mistake, that they did not suit. Like the Lamberts, Lord Sanders did not err as lesser men were apt to do. If necessary, he would mold Janet to his will until she was the wife he had imagined, but he would not give her up.

Janet sat down in despair. No piano! Just Ernest and his mother, forever, and not even another half-year of freedom. She did not feel she could bear it, and wished again that she had the courage to break the engagement there and then. Remembering Lady Lambert, she bowed her head and stifled a sob.

Lord Sanders came up to her and took her hand, and she shivered.

"I shall not kiss you good night, Janet, for I am still very displeased with you. Do not leave this house tomorrow until I come for you. Do you understand?"

Janet nodded, not trusting herself to speak, and remained with her head bowed until he left the room. She did not move until she heard the butler close the outside door behind him, and then she went slowly up to her room. She felt like a prisoner in a jail from which there was to be no escape for the rest of her life.

She did not summon Simpton, for she could not bear to have the maid see her bruised cheek, nor did she feel up to inventing any stories about how she had come by it. As she undressed, she told herself she was resigned to her fate, although she could not help shedding a few hot tears as she bathed her aching cheek. It was so very hard, especially after meeting Tony Northbridge again, that she could not help feeling bitter. Her life was over before it even began! Now there was nothing but that February wedding date hanging over her head like a sword, and then Lord Sanders and his hateful mother—all of them imprisoned at Willows forever. And having struck her once, would not Ernest be more prone to do so again, if she displeased him? She shivered as she climbed into bed, but she could not sleep. For hours she stared up at the dark canopy above her, and in her mind a little voice whispered: "And no more music, not ever, ever again!"

The next morning she told her aunt that Lord Sanders wished to leave London immediately. Mrs. Meccleston looked at her shrewdly, for it was plain to see that Janet had not slept well, and in spite of some face powder, that one cheek was suspiciously red. "I shall be sorry to see you leave, my dear," she said, "But of course, you must abide by your fiancé's wishes!"

Janet went to the library and wrote some notes, excusing herself from attending a luncheon, a reception, two tea parties, and a ball. As she sanded these notes and wrote their direction, she suddenly resolved to write two more.

First she wrote to her aunt the duchess to thank her for all her kindnesses, telling her how much she would miss their visits together now that she was required to leave for the country. The note to the Countess of Grant was harder to write; indeed, she hoped the lady would not think it impertinent of her, but she had to tell her again how much she had enjoyed the Sunday salon, and how grateful she was for the opportunity to play for Maestro Roccani. She mentioned in closing that Lord and Lady Sanders were escorting her to her sister's home near Melton Mobray, and that she feared she would not be able to return for the regular London Season now that Lord Sanders wished their marriage to take place in February. There was nothing in the note to tell anyone of her despair, but Lady Ralston frowned as she read it. Her plan had definitely gone awry, for far from making Sanders give Miss Lambert up, it appeared to have precipitated the wedding she had hoped would never take place. The countess sat at her desk for a long time, lost in thought, and then she wrote a note to her nephew, asking him to call at the earliest opportunity.

The earl had an estate some fifteen miles from Rundell Court, and she resolved to persuade him to retire there for the Christmas season, taking Tony with them, and enough other guests so he would suspect nothing unusual. To this end she sent several invitations to such friends as would amuse her husband and her nephew, and when at last she rose from her desk, she felt much better for the course of action she had initiated.

Early Wednesday morning, Janet and the Sanderses left town. She had not had a moment to herself in the interim, for Lord Sanders made it very clear that she was not to go out unless he or his mother accompanied her. Lady Sanders was still not speaking to her, and the expression on her fat face did nothing to elevate Janet's spirits. At one posting house, when a young buck raised his curly beaver and smiled at Janet, she grasped her arm and spun her away so fast that she almost lost her balance. Almost as if, Janet thought as she took her seat in the coach again, she was so wanton that she might have rushed over to the stranger and thrown her arms around his neck.

By the time they reached Rundell Court, she was heartily sick of both her fiancé and his mother, and she fell into Agatha's arms and wept. Lady Farquhar patted her sister's back in distraction, her eyes going to Lord Sanders in inquiry.

"I shall do myself the honor of calling on you tomorrow, Lady Farquhar," he said without a smile, and Agatha could only nod at him wordlessly before the Sanderses took their leave to drive the final miles to Willows.

After a long tearful session with her sister, and an even more difficult morning call from Lord Sanders, Agatha sat down and wrote to her mother. She did not feel able to handle this delicate situation by herself and even felt put upon that she was called on to do so, when the arrival of the Farquhar heir grew ever closer, but she knew that Lady Lambert would know exactly what to do. Accordingly, a very agitated letter, heavily underlined, left in the afternoon post for Aylesford Grange. The Lamberts had had no intention of visiting the Court until Agatha had her baby, but Lady Lambert was quick to change her plans. Bustling about, she informed Lord Lambert of the necessity of their travelling immediately to Melton Mowbray.

"I might have known, Horace!" she said, after directing the footmen to bring the baggage down from the box room. "It was all too good to be true, and I have never liked these long engagements, for so much can go wrong. And Janet . . . such a difficult girl, so unlike the rest of the family. I should never have left her to her own devices with only that silly Jane Meccleston to look after her, not with that Sanders woman so eager to put a spoke in the wheel if she could."

Lord Lambert nodded, although he thought the whole thing a mare's nest and could not see of what possible use he would be in the whole proceeding. When he mentioned this, he was quickly brought to see reason. Just the presence of her husband would help, Lady Lambert knew, for her rival was a widow, and sheer weight of numbers might turn the trick, Agatha having her husband so firmly under her thumb. A few days later as the Lamberts began their journey, Lord Lambert stole a glance at his wife's militant expression and set jaw, and for a fleeting moment almost felt sorry for Janet. Ada would set her straight—that much was certain!

And set her straight Lady Lambert did. Not more than fifteen minutes passed after their arrival before Janet was summoned to her mother's rooms and without so much as a hello kiss was ordered to stand before her and tell her everything that had happened. This Janet did in halting sentences, and had her ears boxed for her waywardness. "How dared you behave in such a rattlebrained, pumpkinheaded way!" her mother exclaimed, shaking her as hard as she could. "No Lambert should ever do so! One can only hope that irremediable damage has not been done by your unseemly independence! I shall ask Agatha to invite the Sanderses to dine tomorrow evening, and I shall do my best to repair this rift, but I warn you, I will brook no more defiance; go to your room and remain there. I am very displeased and do not wish to see your face again today."

Janet sat at the window of her room and stared out at the gray December day, her heart heavy. She could not know that the Earl and Countess of Grant were even then taking up residence a few miles away, and that the Duke of Stour and the other guests were not far behind them. She was sure that the next time she saw the duke she would be Lady Sanders, but try as she would, she could not erase his dark, handsome face and brilliant smile, his deep voice, and his piercing eyes from her mind. Only in remembering her mother's threats was she able to forget him.

It was a very stiff and formal party that gathered in the dining room the following evening. Agatha was uncomfortable in company and resented having to play hostess, Lady Sanders was distant and cold, and in spite of Lady Lambert's smiles and blandishments, Lord Sanders refused to smile. His somber gaze often went to Janet's set white face, and he was seen to frown. Lord Lambert and his son-in-law exchanged rueful glances, and both decided an attack on the port bottle after dinner was the only thing that would make the evening at all bearable. Lord Lambert had the happy thought that perhaps a few glasses might make this Sanders chap a bit more amiable as well.

While the three men were thus engaged, the ladies repaired to the drawing room. Agatha and her mother conversed in a determinedly cheerful way, while Lady Sanders took no part in the conversation except to contribute her perpetual sniff. No one spoke to Janet, and it was plain that she was still in disgrace, and likely to remain so.

When at last the uncomfortable evening was over and the Sanderses had left for home, Lady Lambert followed her daughter to her room, and dismissing Simpton, took a chair by the fire.

"It is worse than I feared," she began in a colorless voice, "for I noticed that Lord Sanders did not kiss you good night, Janet. Indeed, he made no effort to be alone with you—a most unusual thing in a man about to be married. I am afraid that you are in need of instruction."

Here she paused and smoothed the pleats of her brocade gown, and her daughter wondered what on earth was coming.

"Your behaviour has been so bad that it has given Lord Sanders a disgust of you, but there are ways to return to his good graces," Lady Lambert said, and Janet was stunned to see that her mother was blushing and consciously not looking her in the eye.

"Yes, there are ways . . . especially at this stage of a relationship. What I mean to say, Janet, is that you must show your affection in a more physical way . . ." Lady Lambert faltered as Janet stared at her, her head tilted to one side and her big blue eyes intent and unsmiling. She wished that the girl would at least have the grace to colour up.

"You must kiss him warmly and sigh with delight, and caress him in such a way that no matter what Lady Sanders says, he will want you. Men are so often swayed by the opposite sex—indeed, even after marriage there are many things you can achieve by lovemaking." Her colour was high now, and she rose, making a gesture of dismissal. "I shall say no more about it, but remember, Janet you can catch more flies with sugar than you can with vinegar. Do I make myself clear?"

She waited until Janet bowed her head, and then she said, "I shall leave you to think about what I have said, and I shall expect a great deal more warmth from you in your next meeting with your fiancé. Of course, he will not seek you out if you remain so stiff and cold, but a soft smile, a pressure of your hand, a maidenly blush . . . and we shall see! I expect your obedience, Janet."

With this, Lady Lambert swept from the room, and Janet shuddered. She had never thought to hear such sentiments from her reserved mother, who throughout her life had behaved as if what went on between a man and a woman was too disgusting to talk about. Her daughters had always known that a dignified submission was all that was required of a Lambert wife—that and plenty of children. That her mother insist that she make love to a man she disliked was unprecedented. She went to bed with a feeling of revulsion for the task set before her, having no idea how to begin, and most reluctant to do so in any case.

❧ 11 ❧

Meanwhile, the Countess of Grant was quick to see that Tony, far from being a gracious guest, pleased by the presence of his particular cronies, and agreeable to all the amusements that his aunt and uncle had arranged for them, was more apt to withdraw from the rest of the company, and when he finally did appear, wore a frown more often then a smile. Nothing could have been more encouraging, she thought, although she had to reassure the earl that his nephew was not sickening and tell Lord Fitch and Lord Wells several white lies as well. Triumphantly she sent out invitations to a Christmas ball, including in the note to Rundell Court a letter to Agatha saying how she was looking forward to meeting Miss Janet Lambert's sister at last, and how much she anticipated seeing her young friend and her fiancé as well. Agatha was begged to bring any other guests who might be staying at the Court with her, but Agatha had no intention of going. It was fifteen long miles to Stearings, the earl's estate, and she did not want to take the chance that the jolting of the carriage might bring on a premature labor, besides being most reluctant to appear among strangers while she was so very large with child. Lord Farquhar, while agreeing with her reservations, nonetheless insisted that the rest of the family attend.

"Kn-kn-knew m'father, the earl did! M-m-must not be discourteous! Old family fr-fr-friends! Insist!"

So, on the evening of the ball, a reluctant party of Lamberts, accompanied by the even more reluctant Sanderses, shared a carriage and drove to the ball. In the interim, Lady Ralston had been busy. As soon as she received the note of pleased acceptance from the Court, she summoned her nephew to her sitting room and smiled warmly at him as he came in, with his usual air of distraction.

"My dear Tony! I have a special treat for you, but before I tell you about it, I have a confession to make," she said. When the duke raised a cynical brow as he took a seat, she continued, "You remember that I told you I would be on the lookout for a suitable wife for you? Well, I have located the very girl, but I have not mentioned it before because I wanted to be sure of your feelings in the matter. Since it is obvious to anyone with an eye in his head that you are head over heels in love with Miss Lambert, I shall dare to confess."

"In love? With Miss Lambert?" Tony asked, sitting up abruptly. "Of course you are mistaken, aunt. The lady is engaged to another; I have come to see that I must only have felt sorry for her."

"And who would not be sorry for her, tied to Ernest Sanders?" Lady Ralston interrupted. "But do not try to fool *me*, Tony. You have been behaving like a bear with a sore head ever since the gel left town; moody, preoccupied, impatient. Any fool can see you are in love, and I am not a fool, nor am I two and ten." When the duke would have spoken again, she raised a protesting hand. "Do not, I pray you, waste our time denying it. I have something to tell you, and I insist on speaking. Oh, Tony, I have been so clever you will stare."

It was so typical of his aunt to ride roughshod over everyone's objections that Tony grinned at her in spite of himself, and, encouraged by this sign, the lady began to explain.

"The evening of the Jersey reception, I had occasion to speak to Lady Sanders. I was very naughty, Tony, for I

193

deliberately let slip that Janet had been at my salon. I mentioned all the guests she would find most disreputable—such a silly woman, I have always thought, so provincial—and what is more, I told her that Janet had gone alone to play for Roccani." She paused and saw an expression of intent interest on Tony's face, so she continued. "Well, it did not work. You see, my dear, I meant to separate Janet from her fiancé and his loathsome mother, and free her for *you*. Instead, Lord Sanders whisked her away to the country and has now decided that their wedding will take place in February instead of May."

Tony got to his feet. "As soon as that!" he exclaimed, and the countess nodded.

"You will be interested to know, my dear nephew, that Janet is visiting her sister Lady Farquhar of Rundell Court at the present time. The Court is only fifteen miles from Stearings, and since the Sanders estate is also in the neighbourhood, I have invited them all to my Christmas ball."

"Janet is coming here?" the duke asked, his voice wondering.

"I wish you will not repeat everything I say," the countess snapped. "You sound dim-witted. Yes, she will be here, and if you do not know how to go about getting her to break her engagement, you are not the man I thought you were. Do not be thinking she loves Sanders, or ever did; I am sure from her behaviour toward him that the marriage was arranged against her wishes."

The duke got up and began to pace the room. "Yes, I have just remembered that when I was visiting the Grange, she told me that her parents chose their daughters' husbands for them, without even consulting their wishes in the matter. I had forgotten. . . ." He frowned and then said, "And now I have a confession to make . . ."

The countess listened, fascinated, as he told her of his trip to Roccani's studio to escort Janet home, and what had happened between them. When he finished with his account of trying to put Janet at her ease by treating their kiss so lightly, the countess clapped her hands in dismay.

"*Men!*" she said forcibly. "So that was why she behaved as she did at Lady Jersey's. Of course she would cut you dead. Treating it so casually, as if she were of no more account than a dairy maid. How could you be so stupid?"

Before her nephew could defend himself, she rushed on. "I hope the situation has not become impossible! Of course, it is hard to believe that any girl would settle for Sanders when *you* are waiting in the wings, so very handsome, witty, and elegant, with your august title and really indecent fortune; in short, everything a girl might dream of in a husband."

"Why, thank you, aunt. I never knew you to flatter me with so many encomiums. So unlike you," Tony murmured, not even trying to hide the grin his aunt nobly decided to ignore.

He went away then without telling her his plans for Miss Lambert, but the countess was much encouraged when she saw him laughing with his friends over a game of billiards that evening.

Although Stearings was not the earl's principal seat and was nowhere near as elegant as she might have wished, the countess was well pleased when she looked about her the evening of her Christmas ball. The trappings of the season hid the old-fashioned air of the furnishings very well, she thought, and the crimson velvet hangings at the long windows and the gold brocade of the chairs and sofas were complimented by the many swags of evergreens that decorated the hall. Every chandelier had been polished till the prisms glittered in the light of the tall red tapers that filled them, and footmen dressed in the earl's livery stood in attention around the gleaming parquet floor with its intricate diamond pattern. A massive Yule log burned in the fireplace over which was hung the earl's coat of arms, decorated for the ball with a large wreath of holly trimmed with crimson bows. It all looked gay and festive, and the countess was satisfied with the setting she had provided for the play that was about to begin.

She smiled as she moved forward with her husband to greet the first arrivals, and when the butler announced the Lambert party, she was gracious to them all, although she thought Janet very subdued and pale, and wondered at it. Janet kissed the cheek the countess offered, but she had very little to say for herself. Lord Sanders was cool and aloof, and his mother was sporting her most disapproving sniff in honor of the occasion. It did not take the countess long to sum up the elder Lamberts, and she shuddered to herself. Janet was to be pitied even more than she had imagined. Lord Lambert she dismissed as an insensitive clod, puffed up with his own importance, after she had heard him speak only a few words; it was his wife who ruled that roost, and the look in her eyes was chilling, in spite of her smiles and gentle greeting. The party moved on into the ballroom, where the orchestra was already playing.

Janet was following her mother and the rest of the party to some chairs along the wall when she looked up to see the Duke of Stour bowing before her. There was no smile on his dark face; indeed, he looked almost somber as he stared at her and said, "Miss Lambert. How delightful to see you again, and of course, you as well, Sanders. I hope you will allow me some dances with your fiancée?" He paused until Lord Sanders was forced to say he would be delighted to oblige the duke with Janet's company. The duke turned away to renew his acquaintance with Lord Lambert and be introduced to his wife, and Janet sat down abruptly, her heart pounding. She had had no idea that the duke was to be a member of the house party, and his appearance had startled her. She hoped no one would notice how her hands were trembling as she tried to school her features into a mask of indifference, for she knew she was being watched very closely by Lady Sanders.

Although Janet danced first with her fiancé, the duke was there beside them almost as soon as the music stopped.

"My dance, I believe, Miss Lambert," he said formally, smiling a little now as he extended his hand and bowed slightly to her angry partner. Janet stole a glance at her fiancé and paled at his expression. She knew she should, on some pretext, deny the duke, but as Tony put his arms around her, Ernest Sanders, his mother, and her own parents as well, all disappeared from her mind. If this was all she was to have of Tony, she would not be such a coward as to refuse it, no matter what the consequences!

It was a waltz; she remembered that Ernest did not approve of waltzing, even as she put her hand in Tony's and tilted her chin in defiance.

Surprisingly, he spoke not a word, although he held her closer than she knew society could approve. As if in a dream, they turned around the floor, and Janet felt there was no one in the room but Tony and herself and the music. She felt the pressure of his hand on her waist, the warm clasp of his other hand holding hers so tightly, and she could even hear his heart beating and feel his warm breath stirring her hair as they danced.

How right it feels to be in his arms, she thought dreamily as he held her closer still. I never knew the waltz could be so wonderful! And how easy it is to follow him, even held so closely against his strong, lithe figure.

Although Janet and the duke were oblivious of the others, several people noticed them, and one old lady went so far as to wipe her eyes, remembering another ball so many years ago when she had been in love, just as they were. The Countess of Grant smiled and nodded her head. She had been right. Tony and Janet belonged together; anyone could see that by just watching them dance together so gracefully. They appeared to move as one, and for a moment the countess felt a lump in her throat as she saw Tony bend his head to whisper to the girl, and the trusting way Janet raised her face to his, her eyes half-closed.

Their love was so obvious that she stole a glance across the room to where the Lamberts and the Sanderses were seated together in a disapproving line against the wall, and she saw that the situation was more than plain to them. Ernest Sanders' pale face was white and furious, and as she watched, she saw his lips tighten and his hands clench into two fists. His mother, next to him, had her hand to her heart, but the countess thought she looked pleased, in spite of her expression of concerned horror.

Lady Lambert sat bolt upright and glared across the space that separated her from her daughter, as if the sheer weight of her will could force Janet to look her way and be reprimanded. Lord Lambert was the only one who seemed unconcerned, but since he was busy signalling a footman for another glass of champagne, perhaps he had not noticed what a display his daughter was making of herself. Lady Ralston was sure his wife would bring it to his attention very quickly.

For a moment she was a little frightened. She had set these wheels in motion, she had intended Tony to have Janet, but what might not come of all her meddling? The girl was still Ernest Sanders' fiancée; would Tony's behaviour provoke him into some wild exhibition of wrath? Lady Ralston said a little prayer and was almost relieved when the music stopped. But then she saw that although the other couples were beginning to leave the floor, the duke remained there, still holding Janet in his arms and staring down into her face. She wished she might clap her hands and break the enchantment they were under.

Janet looked up at Tony, wondering at his somber expression, but before she could speak, he shook his head a little and released her, and the spell was broken. Suddenly she was aware that they were alone on the dance floor, and she would have hurried back to her mother except Tony led her in quite the opposite direction. Why doesn't he say something? she wondered, but before she could ask what was troubling him, he signalled the musicians, who began to play another waltz.

"And this is my dance too!" he said, his voice harsh as he took her back into his arms.

"Your Grace!" Janet whispered, trying to free herself. "You must be mad! Let me go, for Ernest will be so angry with me."

Tony raised an eyebrow, but he did not release her, and short of making a scene in the middle of the ball, Janet did not see how she was to escape him. When the dance was over, there was no question of her remaining with the duke a moment longer, for Lord Sanders was there, bowing and offering his arm, the thin smile on his face not fooling her one little bit. Now she was for it!

He took her back to a seat next to her mother, telling her through clenched teeth exactly what he thought of her behaviour. "How dare you dance twice with that . . . that *rake*, and waltzes, too, when you know how I feel about their impropriety!" he hissed as they reached Lady Lambert's side. "I will not be taunted in this manner, do you understand?"

Janet nodded as she took her seat, wishing she might rub her arm where he had pinched it so tightly, for once glad to be safe beside her mother, where Ernest could not hurt her again.

She was glad when Lord Wells came to claim a dance and she could escape the cold air of disapproval that emanated from both the Lamberts and the Sanderses, and she was quick to accept Lord Fitch's invitation as well. Eventually, she danced with Ernest again, and he never ceased to lecture her in harsh whispers.

Sometime later, the duke came back to her side. Ernest had gone to fetch a glass of negus for his mother, but she knew from what he had said that he would be even more furious if she danced with Tony again. Two dances were permissible; three was a sign of such distinguished attention it could not fail to escape anyone's notice. But the duke was holding out his arm, his eyes daring her, and she rose. Then, to her dismay, the orchestra struck up another waltz, and she put out her hand to deny him.

"I am sorry, Your Grace. I am not allowed any longer . . . I mean, Ernest has forbidden me to waltz. I must ask to be excused."

Without a word, the duke tucked her hand through his arm and led her to the hall. "How very fortunate. There is something I must speak to you about, Miss Lambert, and it is so difficult to converse while I am holding you in my arms." When Janet looked up at him, he added, "You see, I cannot think of the words because you are so close to me. Come, let us find a place where we may be private."

"But . . . I cannot!" Janet exclaimed, her face now as

white as her silk gown, the one trimmed with green velvet ribbons she had worn so many times before. "Lord Sanders is sure to be very displeased, and his mother as well, and as for my parents . . . Oh, please, can we not talk here in the hall?"

The duke looked around. There were several others in the hall, talking and laughing, and he shook his head. "Definitely not. What I have to say is for your ears only. Come, I will explain to your fiancé and the others if they take exception."

Janet felt herself propelled down the hall and into a small conservatory. For a fleeting moment she remembered that it was in a conservatory that Lizzie had met her fate, and then, stealing a glance at the duke's handsome face and feeling such longing for him in her breast, she wondered if she were like her sister after all—wanton, wishing only for his kiss again as she had in the hackney.

The duke closed the French doors behind them and then came to where Janet was standing in the middle of the flagstone floor, her eyes dark and worried and a little afraid. He took both her hands in his.

"Do not be frightened, my dearest Bella," he said as he gazed down at her intently. Janet wondered if she were going to faint, her breath was coming so unevenly. "I have been so very unhappy since that day I met you at Maestro Roccani's, for even though I tried to make light of our embrace to spare you embarrassment, I could not make light of it in my heart. I knew I loved you then, knew I would always love you, knew that I had to have you with me forever."

Janet tried to pull away from those strong warm hands, but he tightened his grasp. "No, do not try to escape; you must let me finish. I did, in honor, try to draw back because you were engaged to another man, but now I know I will never be satisfied until I hear from your own lips that you wish to marry Sanders, that what passed between the two of us did not matter to you as it did to me, that you do not love me."

He paused and waited for her reply. Janet could not

know how much self-control it took for him not to pull her into his arms and kiss her until she admitted her love.

"I cannot . . ." she began in a trembling voice. "How can you ask it of me, Tony? To break an engagement, to ignore the wishes of my parents—why, every feeling must be offended! My parents would disown me, and we would be ostracized by society and never received again."

The duke released her to take a turn about the room, while she clasped her hands together tightly so he would not seem them tremble. "I never thought you were a coward, Bella," he said softly at last. "Are the mores of society so important to you that you would marry a man you do not love, and—if I do not sound unbearably conceited—give up the lifetime of love that we could share together? I would cherish you always, and what do we care what the rest of the world thinks if we have each other? Come, tell me you love me, Bella Rosa. Marry me!"

He held out his arms, but before Janet could run to him, the doors were thrown open and her mother and both the Sanderses rushed in.

"Janet!" Lady Lambert said in an awful voice, as Lord Sanders turned crimson and his mother smiled in triumph. "What are you doing here, alone with that . . . that man?"

The duke moved forward and raised his quizzing glass to survey these new arrivals. "Have you forgotten my name, Lady Lambert?" he asked, his voice bored and slightly incredulous. "Anthony Northbridge, Duke of Stour. Your daughter told me she was not allowed to waltz again, so I took the liberty of showing her my uncle's conservatory instead."

Everyone looked around. Outside of one dying palm in a corner, and a few dusty pots of ivy, there was nothing of interest to see. Lady Sanders sniffed; Lady Lambert stiffened.

"How very kind of you, Stour." Lord Sanders sneered. "But now, Janet, having seen all the wonders of the earl's exotic plants, you will return with me to the ballroom, from which I insist you do not venture again."

Janet was forced to allow him to lead her away. As she passed the duke, her eyes downcast, he said gently, "Remember what I have asked you, Miss Lambert; the offer still holds."

"And what was that all about?" Lord Sanders hissed, his hand so cruelly clutching her arm that Janet thought she might cry out with the pain.

"It was nothing, Ernest. The duke kindly offered to drive us both in his curricule to visit the cathedral," Janet invented swiftly.

"A likely story!" Lady Sanders exclaimed. "The man's a disgrace to his title, a rake, and a ne'er-do-well. Churches indeed! Another lie, no doubt. It is obvious not only to us but also to the entire party that he is the sort of man you enjoy consorting with, Janet, along with artists and musicians of the lowest class."

Lady Lambert interrupted, her colour heightened and her massive bosom heaving in indignation. "You are mistaken in my daughter, Lady Sanders. I am sure it was just that she did not feel she could be rude to the countess's nephew. One does not snub a duke, after all. Why doesn't Ernest take more care of her, help her to avoid these embarrassing situations, I ask you that?"

Janet was stunned at this unexpected support, but then she remembered her mother's face as she burst through the French doors of the conservatory. For one moment a calculating expression had crossed Lady Lambert's face, as if she were weighing the advantages of exchanging a viscount for a duke for her daughter, but then the stiff, cold frown of disapproval came back, and Janet realized with a sense of despair that rank was nowhere near as important to her mother as what society might say if her daughter broke her engagement to marry another man— and such a talked-about, rakish, dissolute man at that, even if he were a duke. No Lambert would ever do such a thing, for then the Lamberts would be gossiped and laughed about, and that was not to be borne! No, she would abide by her first choice. Janet, in spite of her resemblance to that bad man, Black Jack Lambert, would not be allowed to emulate him and disgrace the family.

She would marry Ernest Sanders, Viscount Broughten, after all.

When the little party reached the door to the ballroom, they found Lord Lambert standing there waiting for them, his eyes searching his wife's face. A confused expression came over his features at what he saw there.

Lord Sanders stopped Janet and turned to speak to the others. "I think it might be wise for us all to retire to some room where we can be private. I have put up with a great deal, but my patience is not inexhaustible."

"Dear son," Lady Sanders cooed, putting a comforting hand on his arm. "You have been truly noble to persist so long. You remember that I warned you, did I not?"

For once, Ernest seemed impatient with his mother. "Yes, yes, but we cannot discuss it here! Come, perhaps the earl's library will be empty."

He strode away, still holding Janet captive on his arm, and he was followed quickly by his mother, who threw a glance of pure triumph over her shoulder at her rival as she was taking her husband's arm to hurry him after the others.

"What's to do, Ada?" Lord Lambert whispered loudly.

"You shall soon find out, Horace," she replied in a tight, controlled voice that caused a shiver to run up her husband's spine.

Fortunately the earl's library was indeed empty. Lord Sanders told the butler that they did not wish to be disturbed, and that worthy nodded his head, his expression unmoved by this unusual request as he closed the doors behind them. Lord Sanders dropped Janet's arm and she went away from him in relief to stand before the fire and stare down into the flames. Tony loved her, he wanted to marry her! In spite of her fears of her family and Ernest Sanders, she could not help the tiny bubble of joy that was beginning to fill her heart.

Lady Lambert began to speak, perhaps feeling a good offense was her best defense. "My dear Ernest, you are distraught. I am sure it was very naughty of Janet to let the duke take her apart from the company, but after all, as I have pointed out, one cannot be rude to a duke.

Come, dear boy, be calm. I know my daughter and I can assure you there has been no impropriety between them; Janet has been too carefully reared for that, is that not so, Janet?"

She looked at her daughter, but before Janet could speak, Lady Sanders gave her most disapproving sniff. "So she has been 'naughty,' has she? As for her 'careful upbringing,' I am amazed you boast of it! If I had a daughter who encouraged writers and artists, herself performed in public, and who was even so bold as to visit a man's studio *alone*, I do not think I could hold my head up in company. *'Naughty'* is nowhere near a strong enough word to describe your daughter, my dear, *dear* Lady Lambert."

Lord Lambert bustled forward, rubbing his hands together as Lady Lambert drew herself up and prepared to make short work of the hated Lady Sanders.

"Now, now, ladies. Let us have no angry words which we might regret. I think, Janet, you owe your fiancé an apology; yes, and his mother as well. I know you, puss, and you did not mean to be bad, now, did you?"

Janet turned from the fireplace to see everyone's eyes on her. Ernest was glowering at her, his fists still clenched as if he could hardly wait to get his hands on her to punish her. His mother was smiling broadly, her joy in the scene that was sure to end in a broken engagement plain to see. Janet turned toward her own parents. Lady Lambert looked stern and forbidding, Lord Lambert uneasily jovial in his role as peacemaker. Janet could almost picture her mother sitting down to write to Mrs. Rustin about her odious son Charles if Janet did not apologize and make all well right now. She drew a deep breath, reluctant to do what she knew was expected, but just then there was a sharp rap on the door, and it opened to reveal the Duke of Stour.

"I gave orders that we were not to be disturbed, Your Grace," Ernest snarled. "This is a private matter that is none of your concern!"

"You gave orders? In my aunt's house? How very singular," the duke drawled, his eyes never leaving Janet's face. There was such a yearning expression on his face, so much naked love and the wish to compel her to admit that she returned that love, that she felt as if the air between them crackled with lightning.

"I must insist that you leave us at once!" Ernest continued, his voice a little shrill with his pent-up anger.

"I shall leave when Miss Lambert tells me that that is what she wishes," Tony replied, coming to lean casually against the heavy library table. Everyone's eyes swung around to Janet again as he added, "And do you want me to leave, *mia bella*?"

For a moment there was nothing but silence in the room, and then a log crackled in the grate and Janet put up her head and stared straight at her love. But before she could say that she never wanted him to leave her for the rest of her life, the door was thrown open once again to reveal the Countess of Grant.

She had seen Tony take Janet to the conservatory, had observed as well Lady Lambert and the Sanderses going in search of the couple, and what was worse, finding them. She had seen the procession as they returned to the ballroom, from Ernest Sanders' barely concealed fury to his mother's air of distressed delight. And then she had watched them suddenly pause, and instead of joining the other guests, make their way to the library. She had hesitated, thinking hard about what she might do to mend things, for she saw that in trying to help Janet and Tony, she had created a situation that was about to turn into a debacle. Before she could decide on her best course of action, Tony strolled into the hall and made his way to her butler's side. After a few words, he walked purposefully toward the library in pursuit.

Now Lady Ralston was all but wringing her hands, and without pausing another moment, resolved to join the group as well. As she swept in, she heard Lord Lambert mutter that a private room in this house was as bad as the village street on a busy market day.

"There you all are!" her blithe voice exclaimed from the doorway, as everyone turned. "But I cannot allow these lengthy family conferences, not on the evening of my ball. My dear Janet, the earl has been asking for you. I implore you to go to him at once before he becomes quite put out; you know his temper when he is cross."

As she spoke, the countess reached Janet's side, and taking her hand, led her in no seeming haste to the door, talking all the while. "My husband has such a fondness for your daughter, Lady Lambert, I do congratulate you, and you as well, Lord Sanders. She is such a distinguished, talented, and charming young lady."

As the pair reached the library door, she whispered to Janet, "Go at once to my rooms. I shall be with you presently."

When Janet looked at her, her dark blue eyes wide, the countess added, "Can't explain now . . . know all! . . . Tony and you . . . go!"

She saw Janet nod a little before she disappeared, and taking a deep breath, she turned again to the frozen tableau before her. "But you are all so solemn, and it is Christmastime, too. Come, let me order some champagne before we all return to the ball."

As she moved to ring the bell, she saw that at least Lord Lambert's face lit up at her gay words. Lord Sanders stood staring into the flames just as Janet had done a few moments ago, while his mother sat looking like a fat, disappointed baby whose treat has just been stolen away from her. Lady Lambert smiled gently at her hostess, which did not fool the countess at all, and the duke leaned once more against the library table, one polished evening pump swinging a little. His face was carefully expressionless, although a glint of laughter showed in his eyes, as if he wondered what on earth his madcap aunt was up to now.

"Tony, dear boy. I have completely forgotten to tell you and I fear I will be in the lady's bad graces now for being so remiss. Greta—Lady Greene, you know—sent me to remind you that you are promised to her for the next dance."

Smiling around at the others, she added, "Bad, bad Tony. He is such an accomplished flirt that I fear Lady Greene has definitely succumbed to his charms. Would that he could find such a lady to wed as you did, dear Lord Sanders."

Tony's eybrows rose, and for a moment she was afraid her ploy had failed, but then he came erect and bowed to the company.

"You must excuse me; my aunt is right. And of course, when Lady Greene beckons, I am sure to be quick to obey."

Lady Sanders sniffed and Lady Lambert looked most offended at such rakish behaviour as the duke blew a kiss to his aunt and quit the room.

In the bustle of the footmen bringing a tray of glasses and buckets of champagne, and Lady Ralston's determined cheerfulness and endless questioning of her guests, some time passed. She held them all there as long as she could, but eventually Lady Sanders asked to be excused, and taking her son's arm, begged him to escort her back to the ballroom.

"I cannot feel easy leaving Janet to her own devices this long," she said with a frown.

Lady Lambert stiffened, but before she could speak, the countess trilled an amused laugh. "My dear Lady Sanders. I will take your remark as a compliment, and my husband will be flattered to hear you say so, but I assure you he is nowhere near as dangerous as his nephew, besides being well past the age of dalliance, even with such a beautiful young lady as your son's fiancée."

Lady Sanders flushed, Lord Sanders looked annoyed at the countess's levity, and Lady Lambert took the opportunity to take her husband's arm and beg to be excused as well.

As they all left the library, Lady Ralston uttered a heartfelt "Whew!" before she went back to the hall and spoke to her butler once again, then hurried up the stairs to her room.

There was no one there, and for a moment she felt a pang of disappointment that her plan had not worked, until she saw the notes on a table, weighted down with Lord Sanders' engagement ring.

The first note was for her, and she picked it up eagerly. It was from Tony.

> Dear Aunt:
> While my beloved Bella is writing to her parents and her late unlamented fiancé, I shall take the opportunity to tell you that instead of going to Lady Greene alone, I decided to bring my Bella Rosa with me. How could you? My heart was in my mouth all the time you were speaking! "Lady Greta Greene" indeed! If they had had one ounce of wit between them, they would have guessed the truth. I did not intend to wed my Bella this way, but perhaps it is for the best and will alleviate the need for earnest Ernest calling me out, and other unpleasantness as well.
> We shall return here shortly, when I shall have the pleasure of introducing you to the new Duchess of Stour. Dear aunt, a kindness if you will! Procure some clothes for her on our return. I was forced to borrow one of your fur capes and a small portmanteau of necessities, but I cannot take the Duchess of Stour on her wedding journey in a ball gown. We both send you our love and thanks for all you have done, and only worry about how you will fare when the devil is out. Knowing you, I am sure you will sweep all before you.
>
> Stour
> P.S. You were right, you know—she will be the making of me!

Lady Ralston smiled, and then she could not help reading the other notes, since they were not sealed. The first was to Lord Sanders.

> I must break our engagement, and I beg your pardon for promising to be your wife in the first place. My mother made me accept your offer, even though I did not love you, and that was very wrong of me. I hope someday you will find a lady who loves you in return, and that you will both be happy.

The last letter was to her parents, and Janet had begun with no salutation.

> I can no longer endure the cruelty and indifference that you have always shown toward me—no, not even to preserve the sacred name of Lambert. I cannot waste my life bowing down to the great god of propriety that you worship so much, and the thought of marrying Lord Sanders has become impossible for me to contemplate. I have never loved him; you know, Mama, that you forced me into my engagement, so I can feel so qualms in breaking it.
>
> I have gone with the Duke of Stour—I love him as he loves me. Good-bye.

The note was signed "Janet Rose Lambert," and Lady Ralston was glad she would use that name no more.

The countess summoned her butler and gave him the letters and the ring, which she had wrapped in a handkerchief, to be delivered belowstairs.

"Ask them to step into the library again, all of them, Woodson, before you give them these notes. I shall be down presently."

She did not hurry. First she summoned her maid and had her straighten her gown and redo her coiffure as well as fetching her another, larger handkerchief. When she was ready, she went slowly down the stairs. Not that she really thought that Ernest Sanders would rush off into the night after his errant bride, not after he read her note to him, but it was just as well not to take any chances. Picturing Tony and Janet racing through the dark on their way to the border, she smiled. It had all worked out just as she had planned, and now there was only this tiresome bit of bother to get through.

The scene that met her eyes as she flung open the library door would have made a lesser lady consider it a great deal more than a "bit of bother." Ernest Sanders was pacing up and down muttering oaths, his note from Janet clutched in his fist, while his mother followed him patting his arm and imploring him to be calm.

"I knew she was not worthy of you, dear Ernest, and what a lucky escape you have had. How fortunate it is that her true nature has been discovered at last."

Nearby, Lord Lambert was waving his handkerchief before his wife's face as she lay half on and half off a leather soft, her colour unusually high for someone who was supposedly in a dead faint. Every so often he paused to mop his own face, looking most distressed.

"Well!" Lady Ralston said, coming in and shutting the door firmly behind her. *"Well!* I see I have harboured a nest of vipers this evening, and never did I think to see the infamous day that such terrible behaviour would occur under *my* roof. I swear I am overcome."

She came forward, wiping her eyes with her handkerchief as Lady Lambert recovered enough to sit up straight and her husband dropped down beside her as if his legs could hold him up no longer. Over by the fireplace, Lady Sanders clutched her son, her mouth open in shock.

"I do not mean you, m'lord and Lady Sanders. You have my complete sympathy! To think that that brazen girl would steal the Duke of Stour right out from under everyone's nose, and she an engaged young lady, too. My butler just informed me that they left in the duke's carriage not ten minutes ago. But of course, you are not surprised, are you, Lord and Lady Lambert, for you must have planned the whole thing. A viscount is not to be compared to a duke, as we are all aware. You may be sure I shall air your part in this treachery the width and breadth of town."

Lady Lambert moaned, and her husband turned a shocking shade of puce.

"We had no idea, Countess . . ." Lady Lambert began, while Lord Lambert muttered something about Black Jack and his dissolute ways, which Lady Ralston did not understand and decided to ignore.

"Indeed?" she inquired in hauteur.

"No, no!" Lady Lambert said. "We did not know anything about it and are as distressed as you are, my dear countess."

As Lady Ralston flinched at the familiarity and looked

disbelieving at her words, she hastened to add, "Such behaviour is repugnant to the Lamberts. The name of the Duchess of Stour will never be mentioned or acknowledged in our family again—we disown our daughter."

"Indeed?" the countess inquired again. "I pray you will not be too disapointed that *you* will be unable to snub the Duchess of Stour. Tony is no green lad to be trapped into marriage, you know, and I am sure that the young lady understood her position in his life completely. These modern misses—so shameful and abandoned."

Lady Lambert turned pale with shock, as Lady Sanders sent her a glance of triumph and said, "I, for one, am not in the least surprised. Come, Ernest, let us take our leave. I have no desire to remain in the same room with *that woman* another minute." Drawing a silent and ashen son beside her, she added, "You must excuse us, Lady Ralston. This has been a tremendous shock to my trusting Ernest, although when he has had time for reflection, he will see how very fortunate he was to escape the coils of that *Jezebel*. She never fooled me, not for a moment. I had her true worth, and that of her pushy, provincial parents right from the moment of our first meeting, but—"

"Really?" the countess broke in, sure that Lord Lambert was about to explode, and his wife to do murder, if their expressions were anything to go on. "I am sure I understand completely why you *all* must leave. I shall have your carriages brought round at once."

"But . . . but . . ." Lord Lambert stammered, "we *shared* a carriage coming to Stearings, m'lady."

For a moment Lady Ralston had the unholy urge to shrug and leave them to a fate of fifteen miles of frozen silence or screaming invective, but then she realized that that would never do, for surely no one would arrive at Rundell Court in one piece.

"In that case, I shall of course order my own carriage for the Sanderses," she said grandly, going toward the door. "I bid you good evening."

After giving her orders to her patient butler, she went

back to the ballroom, her heart lighter than it had been for some time. It had all been so very satisfying, although she wondered if at heart she was a *very* wicked woman, for she had taken such pleasure in besting the horrid Lamberts and prosy Sanderses. The earl glanced at her as she came and took his arm and gave him a brilliant smile, and under cover of the music he asked, "Now, what have you been up to, m'dear? I know that look."

The countess kissed him. "You will soon find out and applaud me, love. I have been so clever that we have come out of the adventure with a whole skin, and all is well."

"What adventure? I know of no adventure. You've been up to your tricks again, haven't you?"

The countess laughed, her eyes brimming with mischief as she shook her head and refused to enlighten him.

"But where is Tony?" the earl asked next. "I particularly wanted to speak to him, and he has been engaged elsewhere for hours."

His wife chuckled. "Yes, he is 'engaged,' but not for very long, my dear."

❧ 12 ❧

Two months later, on the shores of an island in the Aegean Sea, the Duke of Stour leaned against the parapet of the whitewashed terrace of his villa and stared down at the wine-dark sea, so far below him. There was some faint moonlight, and he could see the gentle ripples as they washed softly on the sand. The slight breeze was scented with flowers, and the evening was warm. He sighed, and taking another puff of his cigar, decided that life could hold nothing more perfect than this moment. Behind him, the strains of a sonata came clearly through the open doors of the salon, and he was content to listen to his love play, and to revel in their happiness.

If you had asked him, Tony Northbridge could not have told you what he and his duchess had had for dinner, nor exactly what they had done that day, he was so lost in the magic of their love. Suddenly he smiled to himself, his grin white against his newly tanned face, as he remembered waking with the dawn to find Bella held close in his arms. He had raised his head to watch her sleeping, those thick dark lashes hiding her magnificent blue eyes, and the rise and fall of her breasts stirring the transparent lawn of the nightgown he himself had chosen for her.

Suddenly, as if she felt his gaze, her eyes opened and

widened. No, not blue, he corrected himself, nothing so common as blue. He knew from the past how they could darken with anger, and now he knew how deep and velvety they could become when he was making love to her.

His arms tightened around her and he heard her delighted intake of breath as he began to caress her, bringing her even closer to him, and watching her eyes as they began to burn with passion. His dark head bent over hers and mingled with the black hair that was streaming behind her on the pillow, and he kissed her softly until she stirred and sighed with contentment. Suddenly he lifted his head and put one strong hand gently over her lips.

"Tell me, my love," he whispered. "Do you regret our hasty wedding at Gretna? Just a simple service over the anvil instead of the pomp and circumstance that was your right when you married a duke?"

Bella shook her head violently, her eyes sparkling, and he lowered his hand, his own eyes questioning.

"Indeed, Your Grace, I cannot regret it!" she said formally, and then added, "However, I must tell you that the best part of being married to you—well, no, perhaps not the *best* but certainly *one* of the best—Tony, stop that! How can I explain when you are doing that? As I was saying, one of the best parts is that I have been excommunicated from the Lambert family. To never have to see them again more than makes up for our hasty dash to Scotland. I wonder what they are doing right now?"

The duke appeared to give her question serious thought. "Well, dearest, I imagine your father is petting Princess Patty; we can be sure he is not petting your mother." As Bella laughed, that long, lilting trill he loved so much, he bent and kissed the white column of her throat before he continued. "No doubt that lady is deep in domestic chores, or perhaps she has taken your Meccleston cousins under her wing and is busy bullying them into suitable marriages. Your eldest brother is riding around his fields; not dreaming of any bride-to-be, to be sure, but wondering whether to plant this particular field to oats or barley. Wilbert we will not try to fathom. If he is not on duty, he is probably engaged in something extremely un-

Lambert-like and therefore not worthy of our consideration. Elizabeth—poor girl—is undoubtedly fending off her oafish husband or waiting on his mother, and Henry is trying to escape his lessons. Agatha is admiring the Farquhar heir. Surely she is a true Lambert from top to bottom; worthy, serious, and ever bearing in her mind her consequence and duty. If you should begin to emulate her, my love, I shall beat you. Your ex-fiancé is no doubt listening to his mother tell him that this lady or that is the image of you and therefore not to be trusted . . . but why are we wasting our time discussing such uninteresting people when we have . . . hmm . . . more important things to do?"

He reached out for his laughing bride, but she held him off and said, suddenly serious, "You know we have put ourselves outside the bounds of society by our actions, Tony. Will you mind being snubbed?"

He drew back from her, and a haughty sneer came over his face as he asked, "But who would dare? What the Duke and Duchess of Stour do is beyond censure. Besides, the people who matter to us will not snub us, and as for the rest, who cares about them? But come, tell me the truth. How do you feel about being considered as dissolute as your husband?"

There was a worried look in his eyes now, and Bella reached up to brush a lock of hair from his forehead and to smooth away the lines of his concern.

"I shall love it. Does that make me a rakess as well as a duchess?" she asked innocently.

"Imp!" the duke said, his eyes bright with laughter now as he buried his face in her hair. His hands moved impatiently, but his wife added, "Shall we never go home again to England and take up our lives there, Tony?"

"Who knows? Perhaps, someday—when we get tired of doing this . . ."

"Heavens! Exiled forever!" she whispered, holding him closer. "I shall never get tired of *that!*"

"Or this . . . or this, *mia bella*?" he asked softly. She sighed, and instead of answering, turned and moved slowly and provocatively against the length of his lean hard

215

body, holding him to her with suddenly urgent hands. The duke kissed her more passionately, still caressing her, and when he raised his mouth from hers, she caught her breath and nodded to him, never taking her eyes from his face as he made them one. The duke moved more impatiently now, but always with care, for he had discovered that in making love to his wife, her desires became more important than his own. And yet, in satisfying her so completely, he himself was more fulfilled than he had ever been before.

Only when at last he heard her glad cries and felt her convulsive shudders did he allow himself a respite from that iron self-control, and quickened his thrusts, his arching body driving hard into those velvet depths. Bella matched his passion with her own, and together they climaxed in an explosion of feelings stronger than they had ever shared before.

They clung together like children for a long moment, their breath mingling in hard gasps after their glorious exertion, utterly forgetful of the world in their triumph.

"My dearest Bella," Tony murmured at last, awed by the response she was always able to stir in him.

"You are like the most beautiful music I have ever heard, my love," Bella told him, her shining eyes rivalling the magnificence of the sapphires and diamonds he had given her for her wedding band, as she looked up at him.

" 'If music be the food of love, play on . . .' " the duke quoted from the Shakespeare he had been reading aloud to her in the quiet evenings, his voice gently teasing her for her compliment. "Oh, yes, my darling wife, play on!"

Bella Northbridge, Duchess of Stour, drew her husband back down into her arms. The golden sunshine and gentle breeze touched their entwined bodies like a benediction, and slowly the world came back. Outside the open window of their room she could hear the bells of the village goats as they made their way up the hill from the village to the upland pastures, and the cheerful whistle of the goatherd and the barking of his dog, as well as the muted sounds of crockery and pots and pans as their breakfast was being prepared on the other side of the villa. We really should get up, she thought dreamily, running her fingers through her husband's dark hair as it lay against her breast.

But not yet. Oh, no, not for a while yet.

About the Author

Barbara Hazard was born, raised, and educated in New England, and although she has lived in New York for the past twenty years, she still considers herself a Yankee. She has studied music for many years, in addition to her formal training in art. Recently, she has had two one-man shows and exhibited in many group shows. She added the writing of Regencies to her many talents in 1978, but her other hobbies include listening to classical music, reading, quilting, cross-country skiing, and paddle tennis.